This Side of Married

RACHEL PASTAN

*This Side
of Married*

VIKING

VIKING
Published by the Penguin Group
Penguin Group (USA) Inc., 375 Hudson Street,
New York, New York 10014, U.S.A.
Penguin Books Ltd, 80 Strand, London WC2R 0RL, England
Penguin Books Australia Ltd, 250 Camberwell Road, Camberwell,
Victoria 3124, Australia
Penguin Books Canada Ltd, 10 Alcorn Avenue,
Toronto, Ontario, Canada M4V 3B2
Penguin Books India (P) Ltd, 11 Community Centre, Panchsheel Park,
New Delhi – 110 017, India
Penguin Books (N.Z.) Ltd, Cnr Rosedale and Airborne Roads, Albany,
Auckland, New Zealand
Penguin Books (South Africa) (Pty) Ltd, 24 Sturdee Avenue,
Rosebank, Johannesburg 2196, South Africa

Penguin Books Ltd, Registered Offices: 80 Strand, London WC2R 0RL, England

First published in 2004 by Viking Penguin, a member of Penguin Group (USA) Inc.

10 9 8 7 6 5 4 3 2 1

Publisher's Note: This book is a work of fiction. Names, characters, places, and incidents either
are the product of the author's imagination or are used fictitiously, and any resemblance to actual
persons, living or dead, business establishments, events, or locales is entirely coincidental.

LIBRARY OF CONGRESS CATALOGING-IN-PUBLICATION DATA
Pastan, Rachel.
This side of married : a novel / Rachel Pastan.
p.   cm.
ISBN 0-670-03306-5
1. Philadelphia (Pa.)—Fiction.   2. Single women—Fiction.   3. Sisters—Fiction.   I. Title.
PS3616.3.A865T48   2004
813'.6—dc22   2003066576

This book is printed on acid-free paper. ∞

Printed in the United States of America
Set in Simoncini Garamond   Designed by Francesca Belanger

For my mother and father

"If I can but see one of my daughters happily settled at Netherfield," said Mrs. Bennet to her husband, "and all the others equally well married, I shall have nothing to wish for."

—Jane Austen, *Pride and Prejudice*

Acknowledgments

I would like to thank all the fine and knowledgeable readers who took the time to help me with this book: Kathy Flann, Andra Gordon, John Galligan, Carl Grossman and Julie Harkness, Oliver Bond, Mary Tonkinson, Julianna Baggott and David Scott, Lisa Cohen, Hilma Wolitzer, and, of course, Linda Pastan and David Cohen, who pondered every aspect of every question with me at all hours of the day and night. Special thanks to Rolph Blythe for liking the book at a critical moment, and to Henry Dunow and Pamela Dorman for their hard work, encouragement, good judgment, and clear-sighted suggestions.

This Side of Married

CHAPTER ONE

"I don't know if I mentioned that we have a new doctor at the medical group," Evelyn Rubin said at brunch one Sunday, a meal for which she regularly assembled her three grown daughters. She gazed down the table and addressed her words to her husband, who was methodically spreading cream cheese on a bagel.

He paused, sunlight glinting off the knife as he smiled his thin, skeptical smile. "The one you think would be just right for Alice? You mentioned it once or twice."

"Oh, William, nonsense!" said Dr. Rubin, but a flush spread across her cheeks. She was an imposing, broadly built woman of sixty-one with a handsome face carefully made up to emphasize the fine dark eyes she had long considered to be her best feature. Her hair, too, had once been fine and dark and still was thick, if more gray now than black.

Alice, slicing strawberries onto her plate, blushed and concentrated on dividing each berry exactly in half and then in half again with her thin, steady fingers. At thirty-eight, the oldest child, she had passed through periods of shame as well as despair at failing to get herself married. Turning thirty single had been mildly painful, thirty-five more so. Lately, however, she had emerged into something like acceptance. She enjoyed her work, her apartment, her friends. She read Latin American literature in the original and Chinese literature in translation. And although she held out some hope that the right man might come along, she no longer went on blind dates or examined the personals column of the *City Paper*. She had put herself beyond the reach of such humiliations, and her current, mild embarrassment was as much for her mother as for herself. Looking across the table, she exchanged a glance with her sister Isabel. They had long been used to their mother's plots, well-meaning, certainly, but irritating, especially as they never came to anything.

"He's a very brilliant man," Dr. Rubin went on. "A cardiologist, trained at Harvard and Columbia. He's from New Jersey, but he's been out on the West Coast for years. He moved back recently for personal reasons. I think his father's ill."

"The dutiful son," Judge Rubin said, picking up the newspaper and turning to the editorial page.

"I think it's very nice," Dr. Rubin said. "Only it's hard starting over in a new place when everyone else is settled. I invited him to the party, and Alice, I did hope you would be nice to him and make sure he doesn't just wander around with nobody to talk to."

"What about me?" Tina asked. "Why are the brilliant men always for Alice?" She was the youngest of the sisters, with a body kept in shape by StairMasters and Lifecycles and revealed through tight silk sweaters, Lycra tank tops, and form-fitting designer jeans. Tina was usually in the middle of a passionate romance with a young Aetna executive, or a handsome MBNA trainee, or the membership director of the Riverside Health Club, but none of these men ever turned out to be the Right Man. At twenty-nine, Tina had slept with as many men, more or less, as she had lived years on a vexing planet that hid its prizes—where? In the boardrooms of regional banks or the free-form office spaces of new-media start-ups? Tina was still looking. She was still waiting for destiny to open its arms.

"Oh, he's far too old for you, Tina," Dr. Rubin said.

Alice bent her head again over her strawberries so that her expression could not be seen. Tina nibbled half a bagel, held carefully in her strong, square hands with their fingernails painted the same deep mauve as her dress. The last man their mother had wanted Alice to "take care of" at a party had been a handsome, silver-haired radiologist who had asked almost immediately to be introduced to a woman across the room, who had happened to be Tina.

"Of course," Dr. Rubin amended, "people said the same thing about your father and me when we started dating."

"That's why you should always listen to your elders, Tina," Judge Rubin said without looking up from his newspaper.

Dr. Rubin smiled the tolerant smile that so nearly resembled a frown, meant to express long-suffering affection. She stirred her coffee and picked at a spot on the linen tablecloth. The silver and the tablecloth had belonged to her grandmother back in Germany, and she liked to use them when the family was together. One day all the things would belong to her daughters. Isabel already had the Royal Copenhagen dinner service for twelve. Dr. Rubin had given it to her when she got married. Isabel, watching her mother, knew what she was thinking as clearly as if she had said the words out loud. Sixty-one, and only one of her three daughters married! Sixty-one, and not a single grandchild to buy presents for, or to dandle on her knee, or to show pictures of to the other doctors. What had gone wrong?

"Are you done with the business section?" Isabel's husband, Theo, asked Judge Rubin.

"Nice blouse," Tina said to Alice. "Is it new?"

Alice looked down to see what she was wearing. "I got it last week at this little store, Larissa. They were having a sale."

"Oh, Larissa, I love that store!" Tina said. "What were you doing all the way over on Twenty-second? You should have called me. We could have had lunch."

"I'm sorry," Alice said, knowing very well that she should have called her sister, which was doubtless why she had mentioned the name of the store when there had been no need to. Otherwise she would have felt she was concealing it deliberately to protect herself. She had been in a hurry, and Tina was always late, and she talked incessantly about the latest man in her life. Or sometimes, as if suddenly remembering the injunction not to talk too much about oneself, she offered Alice advice about meeting men.

When they were children, Tina had followed her older sisters everywhere. She would scream with rage if Alice shut the door to her room, tears springing from her eyes, her clenched fists looking like two curls escaped from her head. With the curls and her fat cheeks and her chubby, dimpled legs, Tina had been the kind of child adults fussed over. She had also been jealous and stubborn, trying to run as fast as Alice and Isabel, to read when they could read, to carry what they could carry. She was so frustrated by being the youngest that it was hard not to feel sorry for her, but Isabel's sympathy was tempered with wariness. Once she had shown Tina a snakeskin she had found in the woods, and Tina had ripped the head off. She had let Tina play with her rock collection, and Tina had slipped the shiny ones into her underwear when she'd thought Isabel wasn't looking. Tina never seemed to do things like this to Alice. Perhaps she sensed that her scrupulous oldest sister would simply turn her back to her and keep it turned. Isabel found Tina's desire to be included harder to resist.

"That child will push you over the cliff if you let her," said Cicily, their babysitter, and Isabel had wondered, What cliff?

"They have this great dress at Larissa," Tina said. "Indigo silk with spaghetti straps and slit halfway up the thigh! But all the stuff there is so expensive. I'm the one who can't afford to shop there except when there's a sale."

"Alice has always been thrifty," Dr. Rubin said approvingly. "She always saved her allowance."

"And gave it away to homeless people on the street," Isabel said, smiling. "When Cicily took us into the city."

"I'm sure Cicily never let her do that," Dr. Rubin said firmly. "Alice dear, I'd be happy to take you shopping if you need clothes for work." Alice was a lawyer who worked with Central American immigrants at a small nonprofit.

"I'm fine, Doc," Alice replied equally firmly. "My closet is full."

"Alice's clients don't care what she wears," Tina said. "Not like those rich guys Theo represents." Her gaze rested on lean, heavy-browed Theo, frowning over an article about interest rates.

Judge Rubin, registering the snobbish remark, gave Tina a look over the top of his paper.

That was how it was at brunch. The men read *The New York Times* (although they lived in Philadelphia), and the sisters talked about clothes and squabbled.

"His name is Anthony Wolf," Dr. Rubin announced, going back to the previous subject. "What's the guest list up to now, Isabel? About a hundred?"

"One hundred and twenty," Isabel said. Not currently employed, she had been drafted as her mother's assistant for the Rubins' fortieth-anniversary party. Dr. Rubin felt it would give Isabel something to do. She herself had worked nearly constantly

for thirty-five years, and she worried that her middle daughter was languishing.

"Isabel," she said, "I thought we could take some of the photographs from the wedding, get enlargements made, and hang them up for the party."

"All right," Isabel said. She looked up at Theo, and he smiled at her. It was the same warm, bright, sly smile that had once made Isabel feel chosen, golden, bathed in light. Now it seemed to her to be a reflex, like turning your head when someone called your name.

"We can go through the album Tuesday," Dr. Rubin said. Tuesday was her day off. She loved throwing parties—giving orders and organizing people. A sentimental and tactless woman, she was also bold and determined enough not only to have gone to medical school in the 1950s, but to have pursued a surgical subspecialty. "There are some wonderful pictures," she said. "Oh, the stephanotis!"

"I would have roses," Tina said dreamily, her face expressing the same mixture of innocence and carnality it had at thirteen, contemplating the same subject. She had been planning her wedding all her life.

"The cake was from Zeidman's," Dr. Rubin went on. "Everyone loved it, but I couldn't eat a bite. I was so nervous! Imagine, girls—just twenty-one, and not knowing all the things you know today. What innocents we were! We had only known each other six months. It was love at first sight, wasn't it, William?"

Her husband put down his newspaper, folded it neatly, and set it on the edge of the table, creating a pause that gave weight to his words even here among the cluttered plates and spoons, the way his robes and gavel did in his courtroom. "We were a new breed," he said, looking at his wife thoughtfully, as though she were a tricky piece of evidence. "My parents had had an arranged marriage, complete with a yenta and a dowry."

Dr. Rubin's smile attenuated. She deferred to him out of long habit, but in the rest of her life she seldom deferred to anyone.

"Our generation rejected all that," Judge Rubin went on, turning his gaze on his children as though they were jurors, the two sides of the table the two rows of seats in the jury box. "We said: We are free, we were born in a free country, we will make our own choices! And they allowed us to do this. They thought we might know better than they did; that our ways were the right ways for a new country." He shook his head slowly, smiling his thin smile, his wire-rimmed glasses catching the light and reflecting it back in brilliant shards.

"Your New York grandparents wanted your father to marry a woman who would stay home and iron shirts, girls," Dr. Rubin said. "And my parents wanted me to marry a German Jew. A mixed marriage, they called it, because the Rubins came from Odessa! We had to defy them."

And yet, Isabel thought, how upset Doc became if one of her own children defied her.

Judge Rubin nodded. "What chance did their advice have in the face of a bombshell in a canary yellow bathing suit? Girls, from the moment I saw your mother I couldn't get her image out of my mind. I was wild about her—absolutely off my head! I wasn't going to rest until I got my hands on her. And in those days, that meant marriage."

"My mother told me that bathing suit would get me into trouble," Dr. Rubin said.

Judge Rubin smiled and said nothing, but Dr. Rubin was moving confidently back to familiar ground.

"Your father was the handsomest man on the beach," she said, as she had said many times before. "I saw him, and he saw me, and that was it! It was all over."

Her older daughters looked away, knowing what was coming.

"Sometimes you just know," Dr. Rubin said, her warm eyes glowing, in the same tone in which she had said, "It was love at first sight."

When they were young girls, that phrase had the power to make Alice and Isabel melt. They had yearned toward a time when a glance exchanged with a boy would ignite a whole future. But by now they had heard the words too often, and experience had long since called them into question.

"Forty years," their mother said, and Isabel, who had been married for twelve, felt a little ill. She didn't dare think the faint nausea might be the sign she had been waiting for. She had taken the latest pregnancy test only the day before, and it had come out the same as the rest of them. Blue, the color of the great empty bowl of sky under which she was compelled to live and to try to be as happy as she could. The color of the pattern on her great-grandmother's Royal Copenhagen dishes, which, she sometimes thought, would never be passed on to anyone. What unnatural silence underlay the talk at these family meals! Would there never again be children in this stark white room with its jade green vase of pussy willows? Children to cry, and spill their juice, and tease the dog as she and her sisters once had. To inherit ancient expectations and newer, but still venerable, dishes.

CHAPTER TWO

*A*fter brunch they wandered out to the backyard and sat on the swept slate patio in the mild air. The teak chairs and chaises of cushioned ironwork, usually grimy and festooned with spiderwebs, gleamed in the sun. Dr. Rubin's little white dog chased a squirrel to the border of the double lot, where it disappeared into the yew hedge.

In previous years, the hedges had all been ragged and bushy with spindly, pale green arms, but today they were neatly trimmed. On the other side of the property, the split-rail fence had long been overgrown with a mass of English ivy, Japanese honeysuckle, and Virginia creeper into which, every year, more glossy, triplet leaves of poison ivy insinuated themselves. Now, however, the fence had been cleared and a rosebush planted, its stems trained neatly around the rails.

"The yard looks great," Isabel said. "Marco's working out? The azaleas have never bloomed like this." A gardener herself, she had regarded the dull, weedy expanse of her parents' yard with a sense of waste for years until, quite recently, she had persuaded her mother to hire someone to take care of it. Now she looked around in satisfaction at the rich suburban ground, no longer fallow.

"Oh, yes," Dr. Rubin said. "He's a nice young man. And his English is so good, too. The Stanleys have someone working for

them now, and he tries, but you can't understand a word he says."
Her eyes were on the little dog crouching and growling by the
hedge. "Prince!" she called, snapping her fingers for the dog,
who turned and looked at her, his fluffy stub of a tail waving.

"If he's a gardener, I'll bet he has great muscles," Tina said.

"Don't tease me, Tina," Dr. Rubin said. "You're as bad as
your father. Come, Prince!"

The dog bounded across the grass and leapt into his mis-
tress's lap.

"Dirty paws," Dr. Rubin scolded affectionately, kissing him
on the nose. "You showed that squirrel, didn't you, you noble
beast."

"He's getting dog hair all over you," Tina said.

"Oh, Prince doesn't shed," Dr. Rubin said complacently. She
was never happier than when sitting with the dog in her lap or lying on her bed with her shoes off and Prince stretched out at her
feet.

"I think Izzy should get another dog," Theo said, leaning
back in his chair and folding his arms comfortably behind his
head.

"I don't want another dog," said Isabel, whose beloved Daisy
had died the year before.

"She says she doesn't want another dog," Theo said. "But I
think she could be persuaded. Alice? Doc? A wolfhound, maybe.
Or a malamute. Something big to guard the house and sleep in
front of the fire."

"Oh, yes!" Dr. Rubin said. "It's just what she needs to keep
her company. I wasn't going to say anything, but now that Theo
has brought it up—"

"A malamute wouldn't sleep in front of the fire," Isabel interrupted. "It would be too hot."

"What about me?" Tina asked her brother-in-law. "Don't you want my opinion?"

"You're not much of a dog person," Theo said.

"Of course I am!" Tina said. "I'm warmhearted."

"I don't want a dog," Isabel repeated. "Maybe someday, but not yet." She had had Daisy even before she met Theo, had walked with her by the river nearly every day, been comforted by the soft muzzle on her knee. The joke about pets looking like their owners had been true of them. The Portuguese water dog was slender and lanky, with messy brown curls, a long snout, and bright brown, lively eyes. Isabel missed her more than she wanted to admit.

"Obviously, it's Theo who wants a dog," Alice said. "Have you checked with Hollis and Stoltz? Maybe they'll let you bring it to work with you if you get it a tie instead of a collar."

"It's just that they don't allow pets in my apartment building," Tina said.

"I suggest a snake," Judge Rubin said. "A boa constrictor. Or an iguana. Isabel *is* a herpetologist."

"No, I'm not," Isabel said affectionately. She had completed a master's in herpetology before going to vet school but had not pursued the Ph.D. her father had hoped she would earn. "We used to have those water dragons. But Theo didn't like them."

"They smelled," Theo said. "And they were so—cold-blooded."

Isabel laughed. "We don't say 'cold-blooded,'" she said. "We say 'exothermic.'"

"Just so no one can understand you," Theo said.

"*I'm* thinking about going back to school," Tina said.

"Really, Tina, what a good idea!" Dr. Rubin said.

"There's a program at Manalapan in massage therapy. What

do you think of that, Theo? You can be my first client. You could
stand to relax a little."

Theo smiled but said nothing.

"Did you say a program at Hahnemann?" Judge Rubin said,
referring to the prestigious medical school.

"Oh, look!" Isabel cried, her eyes wandering down the fence.
"Marco's planted hellebores."

"And he cuts the grass every week," her mother said. "He
doesn't let it grow up into a meadow."

"I never let it get that bad," Judge Rubin said.

"You did. Prince positively disappeared under there."

"You're a short little guy, aren't you, Prince?" Isabel said,
scratching the terrier behind the ears. He was a one-woman dog,
but he tolerated Isabel's attentions politely.

"I liked cutting the grass," Judge Rubin said. "A man should
cut his own grass."

"Well, darling," Dr. Rubin said, "in that case just ask Marco
to leave it. But really, at our age, I think we've earned the right to
have someone else do some of the work."

"Of course you have," Alice said soothingly, adjusting her
straw hat to shield her face from the sun. With pale reddish hair,
she was the fairest of the sisters, her skin dusted with freckles.

"Like they never had anyone to help them before!" Isabel
said. "Only Cicily to take care of us while they were working, and
Gladys to clean. And before her, Betty."

"And what would I have done without them?" her mother
demanded. "It wasn't easy raising the three of you, you know,
and working full-time, and your father busy fighting injustice
every minute of the day and night. At least I had a day off every
now and then! Remember how I used to take you horseback riding on Saturday mornings? Alice was a natural, of course. And

Tina looked so cute on her own little pony! And Isabel was always whispering in the horses' ears. You swore they understood everything you said, Isabel."

"I used to tell them to take me away to live in the land of the horses," Isabel said. "But they never would."

"I remember how impatient we were on those Saturdays," Alice said. "Waiting for you to get home from the hospital. Cicily would give us breakfast and you'd come in and tell us how many babies you'd delivered that night."

"Oh, so many babies!" their mother cried. "It must be thousands by now. Tens of thousands. And thousands of abortions, too. You're always swamped in this business. You'd think it really worked the way my mother used to say, that a man could get you pregnant just by looking at you. Oh, Isabel, honey, I'm sorry. I didn't mean—"

"I know you didn't," Isabel said.

But Dr. Rubin would not be reassured. "I *am* an OB/GYN, and even if infertility isn't my specialty, you'd think I'd be able to do something!"

"Dr. Abramowitz says nothing's wrong," Isabel said, as she had said a dozen times before.

"Ed Abramowitz is a good doctor, of course," Dr. Rubin said. "He's very smart, and he knows everything. He's helped hundreds of women, but sometimes I think he could do a better job of sitting down and talking to his patients. Explaining things to them, going over what they should be doing."

She would have continued, but Isabel, who couldn't bear having her most intimate failures discussed out loud, interrupted, "Doc, Theo and I are perfectly clear on the proper procedure."

Across the table, Theo's face had closed up tight. He had

mostly learned to let his mother-in-law's effusions roll over him like waves and break harmlessly elsewhere, but he liked having his personal affairs discussed in public even less than Isabel.

Dr. Rubin flushed. "I don't know why you have to turn every innocent comment inside out, Isabel," she said. "I just want you to be happy. *I* don't care whether you have children or not!"

Isabel wondered whether Dr. Rubin believed this. Maybe she did. She had always tried to be a good mother in her own slapdash, tireless way.

CHAPTER THREE

*W*hen she got home, Isabel changed her clothes and went out into her small garden. Dandelions stuck their heads through the cracks in the pavement, and tendrils of creeping Charlie colonized the ground under the azalea. Once Isabel would have pulled them out, but now she let them stay, a touch of wildness among the nursery plants.

She loved the resilience of the garden. Green and red shoots appeared in the ground after the icy winter. She didn't know how the tender plant tissue pierced the hard surface of the Philadelphia clay, but she didn't wonder about it very much anymore. She loved the natural world, but she no longer cared how it worked. In graduate school, working on her master's thesis ("Microhabitats of the Terrestrial Amphibian *Bufo americanus*"), it had occurred to her that she had lost interest in the size of convex polygon areas fitted to toad locations. Her college zoology professor had encouraged her to get a Ph.D., but it wasn't the right life for her.

That was when she decided to become a veterinarian: not a dog-and-cat vet, but a specialist in exotic animals—a profession even harder to get a job in than academic zoology. But she was young and confident, and for a while her luck had held. After vet school she got an internship at Baltimore's National Aquarium, commuting two hours each way, and after that a coveted three-year residency at the Philadelphia Zoo.

At first she had loved the zoo work: the daily rounds of the animals, the consultations on parasites and nutrition, the pathology lab, the wonderful animal smell of the place. She loved working outside in big rubber boots while lions roared in the carnivore house and peacocks wandered down the paths, gobbling up spilled popcorn. It wasn't much money, but Theo was at Hollis and Stoltz by then, their West Philadelphia student days behind them. The permanent veterinary staff at the zoo was set to expand in a couple of years. Why shouldn't she be the one they hired?

The screen door slid open. Theo stepped out onto the bricks and sat down, squinting in the light. He seemed to take up an inordinate amount of space on the terrace, his long legs reaching almost into the peonies.

"It looks great out here, Izzy," Theo said. "You've done amazing things. Probably increased the property value ten grand."

"But we can't sell it now," she said, smiling. "I've put too much work into it."

"You're out of room. Don't you want something bigger?"

"Bigger's not always better," Isabel said.

There was a pause.

"What's up with the rosebush?" Theo asked. Its leaves were yellow, and its flowers, once red, had shriveled to a washed-out beige.

"Something's eating it. Aphids, I think."

"Can't you spray it?"

Isabel shrugged. Watching the rosebush die was oddly interesting. She liked seeing the way the leaves turned slowly to lace. "The Victorians thought death had a place in the garden," she said. "They grew black flowers and left trunks of dead trees standing."

"That's pretty morbid."

Isabel laughed. "Maybe. I think it's just realistic."

"Listen," Theo said. His voice went slack, like fishing line drifting down through water. "I want to talk to you about something."

She looked up at him, at his green eyes and his firm jaw, at his cropped hair, black as a panther's coat. "What?"

"I think it's time to consider the possibility that we're not going to have children."

She stared and could not speak at first. "I don't agree," she said at last in the small, flat voice that was all she could manage. There suddenly seemed to be very little air.

"How long has it been?" Theo said. "Theoretically nothing's wrong, but obviously something is. We've tried Clomid. We've tried Pergonal. You hated them. We agreed we didn't want to do in vitro. We've waited, but waiting hardly seems to have helped."

"I saw Dahlia the other day," Isabel said. "You know they adopted a baby from Korea. A beautiful little boy, they got him when he was four months old! Samuel. He's three now. I saw him riding his tricycle in the park—"

"We're not going to adopt a child!" Theo interrupted. "We've been through this. There are all kinds of health risks. Things they don't tell you. Things they cover up."

Isabel noticed Theo didn't even blink. He didn't consider the possibility that he might not be in the right. "But if we're careful," she said. "If we do our homework and choose a reliable agency—"

Again he cut her off. "Do you think it's that simple? Did I tell you that Victor is suing an adoption agency right now for concealing evidence of maternal drug use? I know about these things!"

It seemed to Isabel that when she was working, Theo never would have spoken to her in that tone of voice.

"Are you listening?" Theo said. He got up from his chair and sat beside her on the bricks. "Don't just disappear inside your head. Talk to me!"

Under the lime fragrance of his shaving cream Isabel could just smell the Theo she had first known, a faint, musty, human odor. She didn't know what to do. Talk to me, he said, but she didn't know how to begin to talk about all the things that were wrong between them. That what they cared about in life was increasingly divergent. That they lived in the same house side by side, but not together. That they could not conceive a child. She was afraid to say any of this out loud; to be responsible—or held responsible—for the destruction of the walled city that was their marriage. "Theo," she said softly, "I know it's hard. But I want to have a baby."

He waited. After a minute he said, "That's all you can say?"

"I can't give up on it yet."

Theo sighed and got up, brushing off his pants. "Fine," he said, and went back into the house. Isabel put her face in her hands, feeling the cool garden dirt against her skin. She could hear Theo moving around inside the house, hear the rush of water in the sink and the clatter of the kettle on the stove. He would make tea and bring it up to his office and work. Next to his office was the room that would be the baby's room, if there was a baby. It was painted pale green with yellow trim and currently held nothing but a couple of chairs, an extra bookcase, and the ironing board. Isabel, whose clothes were mostly wash-and-wear, did some ironing in there from time to time, just to make it feel as though the room had a reason for existing.

CHAPTER FOUR

*W*hen Isabel had met Theo, at a house party on 43rd Street the summer after college, his hair had been shaggy and his ragged jeans had hung low on his hips. He wore a dull silver stud in his ear and sat at the kitchen table drinking beer and talking about the intrigues at City Council (he had been a junior staffer for a councilman at the time).

Isabel had gone to the party with a couple of friends, young women who, like her, were just out of school, floating in and out of jobs in coffee shops and clothing boutiques while they waited for their lives to begin. When she walked into the kitchen and Theo turned his appraising green gaze toward her, it felt as though hers just had. All through her teens she had rolled her eyes whenever her mother said "love at first sight," but on that hot summer night in the dim room with the stereo blasting and the smell of burned rice hanging in the air, all her worldly-wise sophistication seemed to melt away.

Their first apartment had been a tiny place on West Spruce, a bedroom and a kitchen in an old, partitioned house. The grout in the shower was crumbling, and none of the windows closed properly. The place was freezing in winter and the roof leaked, but the bedroom had a big bay window with a window seat, and Isabel painted the walls hyacinth blue. They ate pizza or Ethiopian food, and their friends came over and they listened to music and stayed up late, as though they were still in college. They were married and earning a little money and working on their graduate school and law school applications. Their friends all slept on futons, but Theo insisted they buy a queen-size bed. "Why shouldn't we be comfortable?" he said, and spent the money his uncle from Cleveland had sent as a wedding gift.

Alice was in law school by then, and she used to drop by sometimes with her friends. Alice always had lots of friends, a gang that traveled together and didn't pair off much. This law school group was just the latest incarnation, practically indistinguishable, Isabel thought, from the senior choir or the Spanish club from high school: smart, boisterous girls and quiet, serious-looking boys.

"You really should get the locks fixed on these windows," Alice had said the first time she saw the apartment. "Anyone could break in here. This is not exactly the best neighborhood."

"The landlady must have lied to us," Theo said with a sigh.

"She seemed so nice," Isabel said. "I liked her skull-and-crossbones tattoo."

"And you shouldn't plug so many things into one extension cord," Alice went on. "The wiring in these old houses is appalling." Her braid had swung back and forth severely as she looked around, inventorying hazards.

"My brother used to live on the next block," said Anne, a plump, cheerful law school friend of Alice's who was sitting cross-legged on the bed. "He said he would hear gunshots at two o'clock in the morning."

"Not here," Theo said firmly, putting his arm around Isabel and slipping his fingers up the sleeve of her T-shirt. "No gunshots after midnight. That's the rule."

"Isabel," Alice said, ignoring Theo, "you should take these things seriously. I don't want to have to worry about you!"

res of steel and concrete and naturalistic plantings squeezed between the Schuylkill River and the railroad tracks. It wasn't that she stopped loving the place, more that in and around her love, a web of doubt, skepticism, and ambiguity grew up. It was one thing to treat a Massasauga rattlesnake for worms, another to dart a terrified female gorilla in order to take blood to try to figure out why she wasn't eating. And then to dart her again to get her to surgery, four of them carrying the enormous body on a canvas sheet to the truck to cut her open and find the tumor in her stomach the size of a fist, smaller tumors growing on her intestines and her liver, so much cancer that they just sewed her up again without doing anything. Isabel herself gave the gorilla the euthanizing shot in the vein (as she had injected Daisy when the old dog could no longer move her hind legs, could no longer eat, could barely lift her head to look at Isabel when she came into the room).

Isabel knew as well as anyone that if the gorilla had been "at home" in the mountains of Rwanda, chances were she would have been shot and killed by poachers or her habitat destroyed. But that knowledge didn't make her feel better about her own role: inflicting suffering on animals in the name of curing them when most of them were, in fact, beyond saving. She had darted cheetahs with ketamine to disinfect wounds the animals would rub raw against a wall as soon as they were alert again, had rehydrated lemurs dying of toxoplasmosis spread by stray cats. The zoo supported conservation work around the world, but still, here in Philadelphia, it kept animals in cages, and as the years passed, Isabel had to work harder not to think about this. Once or twice she had let her feelings show when she shouldn't have—at a curatorial staff meeting, for instance. She still wondered whether this was the reason she hadn't landed the job on the permanent veterinary team after her residency, the job she had as-

Isabel had felt so happy, her feet bar⟨ floor, her side pressed against Theo, whose sh⟨ mination were a match for her family any day. "⟨ Doc said when she saw the place?" Isabel asked her said, 'And I thought Alice lived in a slum!'"

It was almost impossible to see the Theo of the Spruce apartment in the man she was married to now. His hair was ways neatly trimmed, and his jeans, when he wore them, were cleaner and fit him better. Only something in his expression was the same—a certain alertness, like a wild animal looking for a meal. Once he had looked at Isabel in a way that made her believe that she herself—her own lean, hungry body—could be enough to satisfy him. But that had been a long time ago.

Sometimes she thought a baby was the answer, that a baby would make all the difference. Other times she thought she stayed in the marriage *because* she wanted a baby or because she dreaded her family's disappointment. Or because leaving would mean admitting to herself how big a mistake she had made. Sometimes she thought she stayed because she still loved Theo, if only she could chip down through the layers of the years and find that love.

Nonspecific infertility, Dr. Abramowitz said. Probably a combination of her age and Theo's, of the morphology of her reproductive system and his. No obvious problems to solve—just the big, thus far unsolvable problem.

The same kind of thing happened at the zoo. Part of her job there had been trying to breed animals who seemed determined not to reproduce (and at the same time trying to keep hoof stock like sheep and buffalo from overpopulating). The vets used many of the same techniques as human fertility doctors: hormone monitoring, in vitro fertilization. But sometimes Isabel thought the animals knew best. She looked around at the zoo—forty-two sumed would be hers. She hadn't even bothered applying for any others—not that there were any within two hundred miles of Philadelphia. And she was not prepared to leave the city where Theo had just made partner at Hollis and Stoltz, where her sister Alice and most of her friends still lived. Though the truth was that she didn't see those friends very often anymore. They were busy with careers of their own, as vets or graphic designers or violinists. Or they had joined the sorority of young mothers whose gatherings, though she was always welcome at them, Isabel couldn't bear to attend. She still went to the park sometimes with her college friend Sarah and her two boys, but since Sarah had moved up to Mt. Airy, it often seemed more trouble than it was worth.

Still, when the zoo had hired someone else, she had told herself it was all for the best. Dr. Abramowitz had said it was possible the stress of her job was making it more difficult for her to conceive, and conceiving was what she cared about the most now. It wouldn't be so bad, anyway, she'd thought, to have some time to herself. To go to galleries and coffee shops. To paint the house and cook real dinners and read books.

But after a few months, Isabel was restless. She thought about looking for work. Possibly a small-animal practice would hire her, but she didn't want to spend all day in an office treating ear mites and being friendly to a lot of pet owners. Anyway, she wanted to give her body a little longer. She started leaving the house every morning and just walking—to Penn's Landing or Fairmount Park or the Italian Market, places she had walked with Daisy. Or she crossed the Schuylkill into West Philadelphia, past the place she and Theo had lived (looking up into the windows and seeing only torn, yellowed shades, always drawn), down the sprawling streets of tumbled houses and abandoned cars and beautiful, locked limestone churches.

One day, out past 50th Street, she came across an old woman working in a vacant lot, a kerchief on her head, hoeing neat rows in the dirt. A bucket of water reflected the morning clouds as they swept across the sky. Isabel stopped.

Most of the lot was packed hard and overgrown with burdock, goutweed, and dandelions, littered with trash and old tires. The woman worked steadily in the thin spring sunshine, her jacket zipped against the wind, faded pink gardening gloves on her hands. After a while she turned and looked at Isabel. "How long you plan on standing there, child?" she said.

And although, except for her skin color, this woman didn't look anything like Cicily, the rhythm of her speech and the authority in her voice went through Isabel like a knife. "Sorry," she said, blushing, but still she stood where she was.

"Pass me that bucket, why don't you," the woman said. "This dirt is as dry as the Sahara desert."

Isabel picked up the bucket, but instead of passing it over, she splashed water carefully along the rows herself, while the woman came behind her, doling out seeds from a plastic bag and tamping the dirt down over them.

When they were finished, the woman looked down with satisfaction. "That'll do nicely," she said.

"What are you growing?" Isabel asked.

"Tomatoes, sweet potatoes, wax beans."

"No flowers?"

"I got no time to be fussing over flowers," the woman said, and Isabel remembered suddenly the sunlit kitchen of her parents' house and Alice asking, "Cicily, how come you never got married?"

"I got no time to be fussing over men," Cicily had said.

But she must have found the time, because a few years later she had gotten married and left them.

CHAPTER FIVE

*A*ll three girls arrived early on the morning of the anniversary party, a bright, warm Saturday in the middle of May. The caterers had taken over the kitchen. They carved fillets and picked over lettuce, arranged crab balls and mushrooms stuffed with garlic on silver trays, while the exhaust fan roared. Out in the yard, men set up tables and chairs on the cropped grass, pursued by Dr. Rubin giving directions in a fuchsia silk bathrobe and plastic clogs. "No, no—a little farther to the left! A little more. Just a touch back the other way—that's perfect. But this one's still too close to those tree roots. Now let's see—" Until at last her daughters persuaded her to come inside and let the men finish their job in peace.

Two of the men wore black pants and tuxedo shirts, the uniform of the caterers. The third was dressed in grass-stained jeans and a worn checked cotton shirt, his workboots covered with grass clippings. While the first two moved slowly and awkwardly, lurching the heavy round tables across the grass, the third had a quiet efficiency of motion. He worked quickly, finding the most level bits of lawn and the proper distance between the tables without difficulty, so that except for the struggles of the other two, the sisters (watching from an upstairs window) would have thought it was the easiest thing in the world.

"That's Marco," Isabel said. "I'm glad Doc likes him. He got

fired from the place he was working in Wayne. Some money disappeared and the owner accused him of taking it."

"You didn't tell Doc that!" Tina said.

"Of course not. And don't you tell her, either."

"I won't," Tina said. "But how do you know he didn't take
the money?" She adjusted the straps of her midnight blue silk
sheath.

"Because I know him," Isabel said.

They stood, watching the men work.

"He's what, Salvadoran?" asked Alice.

"I think he grew up in Wisconsin or Nebraska or somewhere," Isabel said.

"He does have nice muscles," Tina said. "He's pretty killer-
looking, actually." She paused. "On the other hand, so are the
other two."

Her sisters laughed.

Tina shrugged. "I like men. Women always talk behind each
other's backs."

"Women pay attention," Isabel said. "They see what's going on."

"Men pay attention," Tina replied. "Just to different things."

Alice, changing the subject, said, "How are you ever going to
choose between them all, Tina?"

"I'm not worried about it," Tina said. "You know what Doc
says, you just *know*." She laughed, but she was partly serious. She
was too much her mother's daughter not to be.

"Oh, please," Isabel said. "It takes a long time to get to know
someone. To figure out whether you're compatible. Whether
you're even interested in the same things. Whether you mean the
same thing when you talk about love, or about having a family!"

Her sisters exchanged a look. "I'm sure Theo's thrilled when
you say stuff like that," Tina said.

"It was so long ago for you, you don't remember," Alice teased.

Downstairs the doorbell rang. Their mother called out, "Girls! Somebody get that!"

"I'll go," Alice said.

Tina lingered for a last look at the men out the window. Watching her, Isabel tried to make herself remember that her sister was twenty-nine, an age at which Isabel had considered herself entirely grown up. Tina, however, despite having her own apartment and a respectable job, looked to Isabel exactly as she had in sequined, satiny, dress-up clothes and makeup stolen from Doc's dresser drawer.

"Coming?" Tina asked. She smoothed her dress over her hips and went out of the room, heels ticking against the polished wooden steps like a time bomb.

Isabel got downstairs just as the front door was opening. A tall, olive-skinned man she had never seen before stepped into the hall. He had thick, dark, curly hair just starting to gray at the edges and dark brown, deeply shadowed eyes that made him look as though he didn't get enough sleep.

"Come in, come in!" Dr. Rubin said, dressed now in a gold silk suit and gold sandals. "I'm so glad you could make it. William is around somewhere, and I did especially want you to meet— Oh, here she is. Alice, come say hello to Anthony Wolf. Anthony, this is my daughter Alice."

She stood back, flushed with hope. She couldn't bear the thought of Alice living alone in that horrible apartment forever, subsisting on ramen noodles and cottage cheese. She was too thin, and she didn't make enough money to live decently. Having a job that helped the poor was very nice—Dr. Rubin was all for it—but if you didn't earn enough to move out of South Philly yourself—well, it was all right *now,* but what would happen when Alice got older? Dr. Rubin had always been a proponent (and an example) of women's liberation, but nonetheless, Alice needed someone to take care of her.

"Glad to meet you," Anthony Wolf said.

Alice smiled. Her small white freckled hand disappeared inside his big dark square one. She flushed pink, and her red gold hair glowed and sparkled in the light falling through the open door. She looked youthful and particularly slender in the pale yellow sundress—like a wood nymph who found herself accidentally indoors—and something seemed to pass between them as they gazed at each other there in the hall: pale, clear, expectant blue eyes into brown. Dr. Rubin beamed.

A second man came in. He too was tall, but less well proportioned, so that he seemed, if not gawkier, exactly, more angular, as though his shoulders and elbows took up more room than they should. He had black hair, thinning across the top, and a trimmed black beard—not quite a goatee—and he was dressed in a brown wool suit jacket, slightly rumpled and too heavy for the season, over a rumpled shirt. He cleared his throat as he came in and looked around with casual confidence. "Hello," he said with a laconic smile, showing small, uneven teeth. "I'm Simon Goldenstern. Tony said it would be all right if I tagged along."

Anthony, apparently with some effort, disengaged his hand from Alice's. "I hope you don't mind," he said to Dr. Rubin with his own white, even smile. "Simon has been staying with me."

"Of course not," Dr. Rubin said with just the slightest shade of annoyance. "Very glad to meet you. Alice, please show Anthony where to put his gift. You really didn't have to bring anything." She stepped deftly forward to detain the uninvited guest, who was casting an eye across the foyer, with its modern black steel table topped incongruously with pink azaleas in a crystal vase; its woven wall hangings from New Mexico; its faux elephant's-foot umbrella stand.

"So you're a friend of Anthony's," Dr. Rubin said inquiringly, and was suddenly overcome with fear that Anthony would turn out to be a homosexual. There always seemed to be difficulties and obstacles where Alice was concerned! Maybe she created them for herself, Dr. Rubin thought in her darker moments. Maybe it was her extremism. She seemed agreeable and mild mannered until you really knew her, and then you saw that under the surface she was actually dragonlike: immovable in her beliefs and opinions. Fire-breathing. Perhaps men sensed it. Although, of course, she reminded herself, if Anthony Wolf turned out to be a homosexual, it wouldn't be Alice's fault.

"Anthony's oldest friend," said Simon Goldenstern. "Maybe his only remaining friend." He laughed. He had an odd, exaggerated manner that made it hard to tell to what extent he was joking.

Dr. Rubin laughed, too, deciding to hope that she was wrong, that maybe things would work out for the best this time. What else was there to do, after all, but hope? "I'm sure Anthony has lots of friends," she said. "It's just so hard starting over in a new place at his age."

"Tony's very good at starting over," Simon said.

The doorbell rang again. "Excuse me," Dr. Rubin said. "Isabel, this is Simon Goldenstern. Please find him a drink. Simon, this is my daughter Isabel." The door opened and she turned toward her incoming guests with exclamations and embraces.

Isabel shook Simon Goldenstern's hand, more amused than annoyed at her mother's tactics. This man wasn't good enough for Alice or Tina, so he fell to her to look after.

"So you're one of the daughters," he said. "I saw one of the other ones when I came in."

"That was Alice. There are three of us."

"Like in a fairy tale. Which are you?"

"The middle one."

"Not destined for the prince, then," he said with an ironic smile.

Isabel could only assume he was trying to be funny. "You'll have to ask my husband what he thinks about that," she said lightly.

Simon seemed surprised. "You're married? Tony told me the daughters were all single."

"He told you wrong." Isabel looked over his shoulder for a reason to excuse herself but could not immediately find one.

"Well, good for you. Good luck with it! So few people seem to manage marriage for long anymore," he said. "Luckily it's not as necessary as it used to be. Men cook, and anyone can take the car to the garage to get the oil changed."

"If you think marriage is purely about the division of labor, I guess you're right. There isn't much point to it anymore," Isabel said carelessly.

"That just leaves love." Simon Goldenstern smiled his not altogether pleasant smile. "That old wild card."

"I don't know," Isabel said, irritated by his manner. "Plenty of people seem to manage love just fine outside of the confines of marriage."

"Confines of marriage," he repeated. "There's a phrase for you."

"It's just an expression," Isabel said.

He smiled and changed the subject. "I'm an only child," he said. "I don't know what it's like to have siblings. I never had to share anything."

"It must have been lonely," said Isabel, who couldn't imagine life without her sisters.

"I don't have anyone to blame but myself. My parents were going to have more kids, but after me they decided they didn't want more after all."

"Why not?"

"Oh, I was a limit tester." He laughed. "My mother used to say if she'd known what I was going to be like, she would have got a golden retriever."

"She actually said that?" Isabel was as shocked by his half-gleeful tone as by what he said.

"It bothered me when I was a little boy, but I developed a thick skin. I'm grateful, actually. It turned out to be very useful. In my line of work."

"Which is what?" Isabel asked automatically, and then wished she hadn't. She knew what would be coming in another minute but, slightly panicked, couldn't think of any way to forestall it.

"I'm a journalist. It's my job to ask a lot of uncomfortable questions. Sometimes people don't like it, but it never bothers me. And you?"

"Me?" Isabel said, and to her annoyance she felt herself blush.

"What do you do?"

"Oh—I'm not working right now." She didn't feel she could say she was a vet. She didn't think it was likely she'd ever work as a vet again. Anyhow, it was none of his business.

Simon smiled, condescendingly, it seemed to Isabel. "You're doing the mom thing, then?"

Isabel's face went from red to white. "I don't have any children," she said, holding her gaze defiantly to his. She could see he thought she was a parasite with some harmless hobby like tennis or pottery. She could hardly blame him. Many days she thought so herself.

CHAPTER SIX

*I*t had to be admitted that Dr. Rubin's idea of inviting Anthony Wolf to the party had been a good one. He was, as she had said to Simon Goldenstern, an agreeable man. He was bright, knowledgeable on a broad range of topics, quick to laugh and to pay a compliment. He was full of praise for the house and the food, for the champagne and the company. Alice took him on a tour of the garden, and Isabel, who had watched her sister freeze up and seem cold and haughty in the presence of self-assured, attractive men before, was pleased to see her blossom, her eyes sparkling, her laughter quick and lively. It seemed too good to be true that their mother could finally have got it right. And yet it had to happen sometime, didn't it? A beginning. A first few heady hours.

Theo came over to the patio and stood with her. "Do they know everyone's watching them?"

"They seem oblivious," Isabel said. "But stop staring." She was staring, too. Anthony spoke and Alice laughed, her head tilted back as if to drink in the afternoon sunlight, her silver earrings sparkling.

"This is a little different from the party you and I met at," Theo said.

"The quality of the alcohol is better, for one thing," Isabel said.

"Also the furniture didn't come out of Dumpsters."

"Do you remember that armchair I used to have? The beige one with the peacocks on it and the holes in the arms?"

"God, it was ugly," Theo said.

"I loved it," Isabel said.

"Sometimes it's hard to believe how we used to live."

Isabel didn't reply. They could go on agreeably or they could fall into an argument, it was hard to say which would happen. She steered the conversation back to Alice and Anthony. "They seem to like each other so far. If he asks her for a date, Doc will be unbearable."

Theo smiled, as if to say Isabel's mother was always unbearable. "You disappointed her by finding your own husband."

"That's the least of the ways I disappointed her. But you're right. I should have let her do it. Maybe I would have ended up with an obliging, good-natured kind of guy."

"You would have been bored. Anyhow, lots of people think I'm obliging and good-natured."

"Sure," Isabel teased. "Debbie." Debbie was his secretary.

"Not just her."

"And not the least bit conceited, either."

Theo smiled and appealed—good-naturedly, Isabel had to admit—to her father, who was passing by. "Your daughter's calling me names," he said. "Did you bring her up to insult her husband?"

"I tried to bring all my girls up to be deferential creatures," Judge Rubin said. "But what chance did I have?"

He went on past them, slightly stooped in his suit and tie, his eyes gleaming through his glasses like two steel ball bearings. Isabel could never tell if he enjoyed his wife's parties or merely tolerated them, as he tolerated her emotionalism, her interfering nature, and her constant chatter. He was a quiet man who valued

intellect over feeling and who had found useful work that engaged his mind and filled most of the hours of the week. If his
family life was not all that it might have been, he had his conso-
lations. He loved his daughters and was proud of their successes.
He had, however, left their upbringing mostly to his wife, who
had strong, vociferous opinions about these things.

Isabel saw Alice leave Anthony and go into the house. "Let's
talk to him," she said to Theo.

"You go," Theo said. "I need another drink."

Isabel and Anthony talked about sea turtles. He had spent his
junior year abroad in a remote Costa Rican village whose inhabi-
tants' principal source of income derived from the collection and
sale of sea turtle eggs.

"They weren't the endangered kind, of course," he said.
"There were hundreds of them! Maybe thousands." His eyes
grew dreamy as he spoke, as though he were seeing the creatures
in his mind, paddling toward the beach. "They came in at night,
and the whole village would go down to the shore. It was extraordinary. The ocean was black and the whole sky was lit up
with stars, and these enormous turtles would be lumbering up
out of the water. Pushing through the sand. They laid their eggs,
and in the morning they were gone."

Isabel liked his enthusiasm so much that she didn't tell him
the leatherbacks probably would have been threatened, if not actually endangered.

"I understand you used to study reptiles," he said. "What attracted you to that subject?"

Isabel looked at him, at his thoughtful, attentive expression,
his warm eyes focused on her as though nothing mattered in the
world except her answer, and she found herself searching for a
response to match his interest. "Maybe because they're so in-
scrutable. They never give anything away," she said, smiling and

turning the conversation back to him. "What were you doing in Costa Rica?"

"Teaching English. Ostensibly." He laughed. "Going to the beach. Eating mangoes."

Isabel laughed, too. He had an expansive way of being pleased that made you feel that pleasure lay all around you, waiting to be picked up. "Why did you come back?"

"For a girl," he said. "Girls were my weakness."

"You got over that?"

"Oh yes. Growing up took care of it. Now my weakness is women." He laughed again and laid his hand on her arm, saying more seriously, "I'm nearly forty now, though. It's time to concentrate. Time to stop getting lost in the garden and find the perfect rose."

Alice came out of the house and walked toward them over the lawn. She was holding a tray of hors d'oeuvres. "Alice, stop it!" Isabel called. "That's the caterers' job."

Alice came over and offered them little quiches. "I'm just helping out," she said.

"Helping out," Isabel said to Anthony. "That's Alice's weakness." She took the tray from her sister and moved away, leaving the two of them alone. When she glanced back over her shoulder, Anthony had Alice by the hand and was leading her off in the direction of the bar, while she, laughing, protested that she didn't want anything to drink.

"But you have to," Isabel heard Anthony say. "You need to lose yourself in the spirit of celebration."

"I don't want to lose myself," Alice said. "I've spent too many years looking for myself."

"How brave," Anthony said. "Personally, I hide from myself as much as I can."

Isabel circulated with the tray of quiches, chatting with the Enrights and the Lowensteins, the Hochmans and Mrs. Schwartz. These were older men and women, her parents' friends, their hair silver or sparse or dyed, dressed in clothes they filled out more completely than they would have a decade or two before. People who had known Isabel all her life.

"Now, dear," Mrs. Lowenstein said, drawing Isabel close to her soft, pouchy, powdered skin, to her big teeth framed in orange lipstick. "When are you going to start a family? I wouldn't leave it for too long if I were you. And it would make your mother so happy."

"Oh, my mother is happy enough," Isabel said.

"Nonsense! You young people think life is all about careers and cars and vacation houses. Wait until you get to be old, darling. You'll see what's important then."

Isabel did her best to smile.

There were no men under thirty-five at the party, so Tina was talking to Theo. They sat together under an umbrella. Isabel offered them the last quiche.

Tina waved the tray away. "Those are eighty percent fat. And all afternoon all anyone has said to me is how exactly I look like Doc!"

Isabel looked at their mother, who was talking to frail, stooped Sylvia Wirth. "She looks pretty good compared with some of them," she said.

"Maybe if she lost twenty pounds," Tina said. "Your figure never recovers after you have children, no matter what they say about situps and vitamin E cream." She recrossed her legs, showing another inch of brown, slim, muscular thigh.

Alice, Isabel noticed, was drinking champagne with Anthony Wolf by the fence. But as she watched, Simon Goldenstern joined them. He put his arm cozily around Alice and walked her a few steps away. His brow was furrowed as though he were talking seriously, but he carried his long limbs so casually, with such insouciance, that he seemed not to care very much about anything. She heard him say, "Don't believe anything he says to you. He's dangerous. I've known him since we were twelve years old."

Alice laughed helplessly and stumbled on the grass. Simon caught her arm and held her until she got her balance back. He smiled his half-amused smile. "He's plied you with drink, hasn't he?"

"No, no," Alice said.

Anthony came back toward them now, just as Isabel, too, approached. All four of them converged on the trampled lawn. "What's Simon saying?" Anthony said. "He's always been jealous of me."

Alice looked at the tray Isabel was still carrying. "You got rid of all the quiches!" she said. "Good work! The catering people are just standing around in the kitchen."

Isabel looked at her sister with concern. Her cheeks were flushed, and she really did seem to have had too much to drink.

"Alice," Anthony said, "let's go sit down." He laid his hand on her arm and tried to lead her toward a table.

"Don't go with him, Alice," Simon said.

"Let her go," Isabel said to Simon, watching in alarm as the two men seemed about to have a tug-of-war over her sister.

"Yes, let me go," Alice said. "I need to sit down."

Simon Goldenstern released his hold, shrugging. Alice stumbled off with Anthony to a table. Simon looked at Isabel and said, "He's really not to be trusted, you know."

"Men, as a rule, are not," Isabel said.

The party lurched on into the cool of the evening. The buffet tables filled with food and then emptied again, and the cake was produced, round and white and decorated with flowers.

There were toasts. Isabel, elected by her sisters, gave one for the family, a two-minute tribute she had sweated over and that, she hoped, was reasonably honest. She said, among other things, "My parents' married life may not have been without its moments of contentiousness"—at this she smiled, hoping people would laugh, which they did—"but here they still are after forty years! Still committed to each other, and as well matched as they ever were." To her surprise, tears came into her eyes as she spoke.

After her speech, and the showy embrace by her mother that followed it (her father kissed her on the cheek and gave her a dry little smile), Isabel felt she had to get out of the crowd. She crept slowly toward the back until she was able to slip around the side of the house. There she found Marco, sitting on the steps, smoking a cigarette.

She was pleased to see him. He seemed young and vibrant after her parents' friends—probably twenty-four or twenty-five. "Did you get anything to eat?" she asked.

"I'm not hungry. Is it a good party?"

"I don't know. I hate parties." She had meant to throw this off casually, but the words seemed to take shape and acquire weight as she said them, like the fairy tale where the princess's words turn into toads.

"Your mother's been very excited about it."

"My mother's a very excitable person."

"Well, forty years. That's a big deal."

"How long have your parents been married?" Isabel asked, trying to change the subject.

"My father's dead," Marco said. "But they were married about twenty-five years, I think. Now my mom's worried he's up in heaven ruining his health the way he did down here, without her around to look after him."

"What did he used to do?"

"He worked too hard. Not that she could stop him. He had a

factory job, but he was also a labor organizer. He'd come home, have dinner, and go out again to meetings."

"My dad's like that," Isabel said.

"And he never exercised. He never walked anywhere. You know that motorcycle of mine? It was his. When I got home from college after he died, my mom had had it all tuned up and everything. She said he'd want to look down and see me riding it."

"Where did you go to college?" Isabel asked, surprised.

"Georgia Tech. I played baseball, but I hurt my rotator cuff and I couldn't pitch anymore. So I went home." Marco lit another cigarette. A bird trilled in the holly behind them.

"Is that a wren?" Isabel strained her ears to listen. She was happy to have been able to get Marco the job with her mother, but she wasn't sure she wanted to know the story of his life. "When I was a kid, my babysitter could identify all the birds by their songs."

"I went over to Rudner's today," Marco said.

"I'd think you'd want to stay away from there." Rudner's was the nursery from which Marco had been fired.

"It's because of the Kawasaki. Rudner has it locked up in his office. He says I can have it when I give him back the money."

"But you didn't take the money," Isabel said.

"He thinks I did."

She stared at him. His matter-of-factness shocked her. She could see that something had to be done and that he was in no position to do it. She stood up. "I'm going to get my sister," she said. "Wait here. I'll be back in a minute."

"Your sister?" Marco said, mystified.

As Isabel went back around the house, she heard doors opening and shutting, footsteps crunching gravel. A car started up. Something had shifted in the party. An invisible message seemed to have gone out like a scent, announcing that it was time to go.

People gathered up purses and sighed, wishing one another good night. The caterers had already cleared away most of the dishes, and now they waited like vultures for the tablecloths.

"Good-bye!" voices called out of the dusk.

"A wonderful party. And you were so lucky with the weather!"

"Do you have to go already? Good night! Good night!"

Isabel slipped through the guests like a fish, looking for Alice. She was all the way down at the bottom of the garden, where it was quite dark, when she heard a familiar voice say, "So, Prince Charming has made his choice."

Someone laughed. "She does look like a princess, doesn't she? It's that hair, that pale, red gold hair. You had your eye on her, too, didn't you?"

"I've got to give you credit. I guessed you'd go for the younger one."

"No. Those days are over."

"You've said that before."

"Well, this time it's true."

In the pause, Isabel was sure Simon Goldenstern was smiling his ironic smile. "It's funny," he said. "The three of them don't seem like sisters. They're so different. There's the . . . let's see. The princess, the sex kitten, and, what would you call the third one?"

"Oh God, Simon. Don't start."

"The little missus," Simon finished with satisfaction, and Isabel fled silently back up the dark lawn, bursting with fury and hilarity.

CHAPTER SEVEN

*T*he doorbell always sounded distinct when Alice rang it—Isabel couldn't explain this—as though it communicated itself directly to her body. She was expecting both Alice and Marco, but when the doorbell rang, Isabel knew it was her sister. Theo, as he often did, had gone back to the office after dinner.

Alice stood on the stoop with her hands over her head, fending off the rain. Isabel pulled her inside. Alice's hair dripped and sparkled in the hall.

"Where's your umbrella?" Isabel said, leading her sister into the kitchen and finding a dish towel.

"I left it somewhere," Alice said vaguely. She dried herself off, combed her hair, and put on fresh lipstick. She should have looked like her usual, decorous, professional self, but she didn't quite.

The house was brick, with green and ocher walls inside and dark yellow silk drapes by the street windows. It wasn't a big house, but it was elegant. Isabel liked the sense that everything was not immediately exposed, that you had to look carefully into the corners to see what was there. You had to sit still and let your eyes adjust. She and Alice sat in the two armchairs facing the fireplace with the old wooden clock ticking on the mantel beside the glass bowls, the soapstone turtle, the amber egg. Natural history prints hung on the walls: a frilled lizard, a legless glass lizard, a wood frog, a spring peeper.

"Thanks for doing this," Isabel said.

Alice said, "I was glad to have something I had to do tonight."

"An excuse?" Isabel asked, smiling.

Alice laughed. "Yes," she said. "To slow things down a little."

Was it that she looked tired? Isabel wondered. Alice did look tired, but at the same time she seemed to glow with a pearly light. Even the shadows under her eyes glowed, blue black, like mussel shells. "Do you really want things to slow down?" Isabel asked.

"Oh," Alice said, "I don't know."

The doorbell rang again, and Isabel went to let Marco in. He stood on the step under his black umbrella, holding a dish covered in foil.

"You didn't have to bring anything," Isabel said.

"It's nothing." Marco smiled as he came into the hall and stamped water from his shoes, trying to conceal his discomfort. Isabel had said her sister wouldn't take money for helping him, which was good, because he didn't have any money. Still, he felt awkward. At the last minute he had grabbed the dish of sweet Salvadoran quesadillas Marielena had left in his fridge so he wouldn't arrive empty-handed. He was getting tired of Mari, her tears and demands and her cheap perfume, but she reminded him of home in a way he sometimes felt a need for, although other times he felt he could not get far enough away.

Isabel took the dish and he followed her into the living room, where Alice rose from a chair to shake his hand. She was older than her sister, with fine lines around her eyes and across her forehead, but there was something about her—a kind of brilliance—that made him look again. She had fine bones and fine, reddish hair, and her plain black skirt and gray silk blouse and light makeup were completely different from the red dresses and crimson lipstick Mari liked to wear, as though she were trying to attract the attention of a bull. "Are you really a lawyer?" he said, smiling, as he shook her hand. "You're far too beautiful."

Isabel narrowed her eyes, but Alice just laughed and accepted the compliment. Isabel lifted a corner of the aluminum foil. "What are these?"

"Oh, quesadillas!" Alice said. "I love them." She smiled warmly at Marco. She was so happy lately, she smiled at everyone.

"A man who cooks," Isabel said. "You'll make some lucky girl a good husband."

"Actually, my upstairs neighbor made them," Marco said. "She knows I like them. My mother is a terrific cook, but I was a bad student. She tried to teach me how to make rice when I was ten, but I let the pot boil over. Maybe accidentally on purpose!" He laughed, and they laughed with him.

Isabel went into the kitchen and came back with a tray. She had put the quesadillas on plates beside the teapot and cups. Alice and Marco were talking about neighborhoods. It turned out they lived not far from each other, south of Washington Avenue near the Vietnamese fish markets.

"I wouldn't have guessed you lived there," Marco said. He'd pictured her in a better part of town, like this one.

"One day," Alice said, "if I marry a rich man, I can live in a nice neighborhood, like Isabel." She said it jokingly, but she couldn't help flushing as she spoke, and in an effort to turn her mind from her train of thought, she put her hands together and said, "Tell me about the motorcycle."

"It belonged to my father," Marco said. "Oscar Alberto Peña."

Just saying the name brought his father back to him, as though the big man had fluttered invisibly into the room, angel's wings straining over his bulk. *See,* he seemed to say—*I told you to get an education!* He had been a big man with a big, square face scarred from smallpox, a face that could look stern when Marco had disobeyed his mother or joyful when Marco brought home an A on a history paper. He had been a secondary school science teacher in El Salvador before he got in trouble and had to flee, an educated man who had given his son the complete set of junior biographies of American heroes for his eighth birthday. Marco read them, although he preferred books about Babe Ruth and Joe DiMaggio and Roberto Clemente. Baseball was all he cared about. School was all right, he was quick enough. He could do very little work and get by. But he knew what he wanted, and what he wanted was to pitch. Anyone could see how good he was, even at ten or eleven. In high school, the cheerleaders with their red-and-white uniforms and their bare white legs and their silky blond hair made up a cheer just for him:

> He has an *ñ* in his name
> And Marco P will win the game!

He had never had any problems because of being Salvadoran. Anglo people might say things behind his back about his father who stirred up trouble down at the pork parts plant, but Marco was a star who had led the Warriors to the state championship three years in a row. If he wanted to take their daughters to the movies, or hang around in their basement rec rooms playing video games with their sons, that was all right with them. He used to date high school seniors when he was only a sophomore, and by the time he was seventeen he was involved with girls from Marshalltown Community College. He never got any grief from anyone except his father, who thought he was wasting his talents. Marco used to laugh at that. "Wasting my talents?" he would re-peat in English to his father's Spanish admonition—or warning, or curse, or whatever it was. "I'm out there on the mound honing them!"

"And what about your *mind*?" his father asked. "And what about your *heart*? What *good* are you doing in the world?" That was the way his father talked.

At sixteen, Marco thought the answer was self-evident. You only had to look around the bleachers when he was pitching. You only had to look in the trophy case in the lobby of Neil Kinnick Senior High School. It infuriated Marco's father that the high school was named for an athlete and war hero. "It used to be called Benjamin Franklin High School," he said. "A bunch of idiots changed it in 1955." Benjamin Franklin was one of Oscar Peña's personal heroes. Marco had liked him, too, when he was little, the exciting story of the kite and the key and the thunderstorm, although his father was more interested in the invention of the volunteer fire department. "Before Benjamin Franklin," he told Marco, "if your house caught fire, you were on your own, an ant struggling against an inferno. For centuries no one had the simple, civic-minded genius to see that if you got a lot of people together and made a social compact—"

Marco could see his father's thick finger raised in emphasis, his broad face frowning with seriousness. Marco used to make his sisters laugh by imitating that frown, that wagging finger with half the top joint missing because of an accident at Connolly Pork. His father was dogmatic and moralistic, a Salvadoran Don Quixote tilting at the establishment of American capitalism. And Marco was the shining son, quick and silvery as a fish, slipping through the ragged net of his father's discourse out into the hot Iowa July, swinging his arms to loosen up his pitching shoulder.

He looked up into the women's faces now, the pale solemn one framed in light hair and the frowning thoughtful one with the bumpy nose. He had forgotten where he was.

"The motorcycle?" Alice prompted, her pencil poised over a yellow pad.

Her arms were so thin and white, they reminded him of bird's bones. She moved the sweet cornmeal cake around on her plate without actually eating it. Probably she was just being polite when she said she liked them. It was unbearable, women being polite to him when once they had competed for his attention. He felt his charm, his confidence, his sense of life as a plush carpet into which he could bury his feet, draining from him in the way that had become so familiar since his father's death. His voice was flat as he said, "My father died five years ago. I rode the bike here last summer. It broke down outside of Toledo, and it took me almost a week to get it fixed. Once I got to Philadelphia and started working at Rudner's, I used to ride it there and park it in the lot behind the office. But the day Rudner accused me of taking the money, it wasn't there when I went to go home. Rudner had locked it up. He said it was to make up for the money he said I had taken."

Alice took notes. "How much money was missing?"

"I'm not sure. At first he said two hundred dollars, but when the police came he told them three hundred. They didn't seem to think they could do anything. Rudner didn't like that."

"Mr. Rudner told the police he thought you had stolen the money?"

"Yes. They wanted to see my wallet, and I showed it to them." He looked at the rug.

"Why did he think you had taken it?"

"I don't know," Marco said. He really didn't. There was always race, but he was reluctant to point his finger at it. For one thing, he didn't know if it was true. For another, he didn't like to admit to himself that the rules of that game applied to him now.

"Rudner was jealous," Isabel said. "He's a businessman who thinks he knows about horticulture, but he doesn't, and Marco knows everything. People would come into the nursery, and if they had questions, they wanted to talk to Marco. One time I was there and Rudner was talking to a customer about camellias and she kept saying, 'I wish Marco were here, he'd know.' He got so mad, he yelled at her! He said he was the owner of the place and she should listen to him."

Marco looked at the picture on the wall behind Isabel as she talked. It was a watercolor of cows grazing on yellow hills, and it made him nostalgic for Iowa, although the hills on the farms around Marshalltown were green. He wanted a cigarette. He never should have moved here. He should have stayed at home with his mother and taken care of her. There she was, all alone in the rattling house, shoveling her driveway in the winter in his father's wool overcoat and big leather gloves, drinking instant coffee all day long, and driving his sisters crazy on the telephone. He had felt as if he were suffocating there those four years in his old room with his mother and without his father and without baseball, hiring himself out to a local farmer in the summer, working at Jergen's Greenhouse in the winter, resisting his mother's hints that he enroll in classes at MCC. People had stopped him on the street at first to say how sorry they were about his dad, about his arm. But after a while no one said much of anything to him anymore.

It was better here in Philadelphia, the city he had chosen to honor his father's devotion to Benjamin Franklin. A foolish reason, no doubt, but there it was. He had thought he could start over. No one would know him—know about his pretensions to greatness. No one would know he had meant to be a star and failed.

How his father would have hated to see him working with his hands in the dirt! The thing was, though, he liked the nursery work. He liked transplanting seedlings, popping them out of the trays and burying them in fresh potting mix. He understood

what the plants needed. The percentages of nutrients stuck in his
head, potash and nitrogen, how much water, what kind of light.
In the back room at Jergen's in Marshalltown, he had read books
about plants—perennials, vegetables, vines, shrubs—and the information stuck. He could tell you Willie Mays's batting average
in every season of his career or recite league leaders in all the
important categories. This wasn't any different. He soaked up
botanical names, soil requirements, and hardiness zones as though
they were slugging percentages. He got to work before the sun
rose and walked through the artificial daylight of the greenhouse
gladly, touching the leaves around him, absorbing their different
textures and temperatures, able for the hours he was there to forget the past.

Growing plants was all about finesse. No need for over-
whelming strength, for flash, the currency he was used to dealing
in. Those were a young man's tools anyway, and Marco, at
twenty-five, no longer felt like a young man. It would have been
different if he were an Anglo. It would have been okay that he
liked working with plants. But as it was, he was just another
Latino nurseryman, and he didn't like that. He didn't like the
way people looked at him—white people—their eyes sliding off
his brown face and his dirty hands and not seeing the person who
had taken Laura Jansen to the senior prom, the person who had
had Neil Kinnick Stadium on its feet. He didn't like dating girls
like Mari and Vivi, the girls he met in the neighborhood bars he
went to with the men he worked with at Rudner's. He found himself, as he had done with Isabel, dropping into conversation the
fact that he had gone to Georgia Tech, that he had had a scholar-
ship. That he had been somebody: somebody else.

Tonight, sitting in this room with these two privileged, affluent women who looked at him not as though he were a star, but
at least as though he were a person, he felt relieved and com-

forted. At the same time, the fact that he drew comfort from their attitude toward him made him uneasy. It was wrong to judge himself by this standard, but he couldn't help it. It was the standard he had.

Isabel said to Alice, "Do you think you can do anything?"

"I don't see why not," said Alice, to whom the possibilities of life right now seemed boundless. She smiled at Marco, a smile like the sun coming up, and Marco felt the tight, sealed bud of his heart begin to open.

CHAPTER EIGHT

*A*fter Marco left, Alice wandered around the house, picking up her things and putting them down again, trying, not very convincingly, to get ready to go home. At last she gave up the pretense and sat on the sofa with her open handbag on one side, her legal pad on the other. Rain beat steadily on the window behind her. "When will Theo be home?" she asked.

"God knows," Isabel said. "It's not even ten."

"It seems like he's always at work."

"There's a lot going on right now. He's working on this one particular deal. An office building, or a series of office buildings."

"Too bad," Alice said.

"Well, corporate lawyers work a lot. Do you want to borrow an umbrella?" She did not talk with Alice about how things were with Theo. How could she tell Alice that as she and Theo sat at the dinner table and talked (or didn't talk, or watched the news), the air around them seemed to coalesce, holding them fast like two insects caught in solidifying amber? How could she complain to her sister about her marriage while Alice cheerfully, but with the growing awareness that it might never happen, kept her eyes open for someone to share her life with? When she looked at her parents' marriage, or at her own, she felt only cynical about the idea of romantic love. But when she looked at Alice's face, and when she thought about Alice and Anthony Wolf, she felt hopeful, as though anything were possible after all.

Alice accepted the offer of the umbrella, but still she sat on the sofa with her things around her.

"Okay," Isabel said, relenting. "Tell me about Anthony."

Alice leaned back and sank voluptuously into the cushions. "He's called me every day this week. I've seen him three times! He has tickets to things, he thinks of things I might like to do. It's very nice. It's lovely." She sighed and looked wrung out and at the same time alert, as though a part of her were expecting him every moment to walk in the door.

"But you like him. You're happy," Isabel said, a little impatient with Alice for second-guessing the first potentially good relationship in years.

"Yes! I do—it's just, what if I think I like him, but really I don't? What if I've unconsciously lowered my standards because I'm so grateful that somebody half possible likes me so much?"

"Oh, sure," Isabel said. "No doubt this is all about gratitude."

"Please be helpful. It's terrible to be thirty-eight, and the minute you meet someone you're wondering if you could spend the rest of your life with him! I don't know what to think. I can't eat. I barely sleep. My mind keeps circling around and around."

"That's what they call love," Isabel teased.

"He's so sweet," Alice said. "And he's so good-looking! I never thought I'd end up with someone handsome."

"Let's count his looks against him, then."

"He sent me roses. Roses! He says I'm the woman he's been looking for all his life. But how does he *know*?"

"You're right," Isabel said. "Probably he's making a mistake."

"Isabel," Alice begged. "I'm trying to be rational." She paused. "Did I tell you he's divorced?"

Isabel sat, swallowing this information. Did it make a difference? Her mind whirred, unable to decide. "No," she said. "But so what? Lots of people get divorced. They make mistakes, recognize them, try to rectify them."

"Yes," Alice said doubtfully. "But you don't think maybe it's a sign of something? Someone who makes a mistake once—don't you think maybe they're more likely to make a mistake again?"

"Maybe less likely," Isabel said. "Maybe it should make you feel better about him. He's not someone who's afraid of commitment, he's just someone who made a mistake."

"Maybe," Alice said.

"Does Doc know?" Isabel said.

"I told her."

"What did she say?"

"Pretty much what you said."

This didn't make Isabel feel any better. She shifted the conversation to firmer ground. "Anyway, I don't see what you're worried about. It's not as though you have to decide tomorrow whether you want to marry him. Enjoy yourself and see what happens in a couple of months!"

Alice said, "You know how they say if something seems too good to be true, it probably is?"

But Isabel just laughed at this. "Anthony Wolf is not a stock tip. He's an attractive, intelligent man who's old enough to know what he wants. And your impulse, when he tells you you're the woman of his dreams, is to cross-examine him!"

"So you think it's my problem," Alice said.

"I didn't say that. I'm your biggest fan. And I'm a very critical person."

"Yes," Alice said. "But you have blind spots." She was half persuaded by her sister, but, on the other hand, she had come tonight intending to let Isabel persuade her. So it was hard to know.

CHAPTER NINE

*W*hen she answered the phone, it took Isabel a moment to understand that it was Alice on the line, her voice was so faint and groggy. "I'm at Anthony's," Alice croaked. "I'm sick. Anthony had to go to work."

"Where does he live?" Isabel said.

Anthony's apartment was in an anonymous ten-story building on 15th Street and would have had a spectacular view of City Hall if it had faced the other direction. Alice, looking haggard, her dress mussed and wrinkled, let Isabel in.

"He couldn't lend you a shirt!" Isabel cried.

"I wanted to wear my own clothes." Alice sank miserably into the big leather couch that was virtually the only piece of furniture in the room. Her hair was pulled back in a thin ponytail, and her face and legs were the color of ash against the black cushions. "I feel ridiculous," she said weakly, shutting her eyes. "All I want is to go home and get into my own bed. I can't drive! I couldn't stand the thought of a taxi."

"Of course not!" Isabel sat beside her sister on the sofa and felt her hot forehead. She drew the thin hands into her lap and stroked them. "What happened?"

"We went out to dinner," Alice said, holding her body very still. "We had a nice time. He asked me to come back here for coffee, and I said I would. But almost as soon as we got here I got sick. It was so awful! I felt so terrible, I almost didn't care how humiliating it was. I spent the whole night in the bathroom."

"He poisoned you."

"Don't," Alice said. "He was so nice. And then he had to go to work after being up most of the night. He made me promise to call someone."

Isabel, gratified that she was the one Alice had called, looked around at the boxy living room, the small dining alcove, and the tiny kitchen. Three doors led, presumably, to two bedrooms and a bathroom. "Isn't that friend of his staying here?"

"He's away. Did you park close by?"

Isabel looked doubtfully at her sister. "I don't know if you're in any shape to go anywhere."

"Oh, I am!" Alice cried. "I feel so much better!" But even as she spoke, a fresh wave of nausea overtook her, and she heaved herself off the sofa and into the bathroom.

For the next hour Isabel nursed her sister as well as she could, giving her tepid water to drink and sponging her forehead with a washcloth. She coaxed Alice to take off the ruined dress and put on a T-shirt she found in Anthony's dresser. She got her to lie down on, if not actually in, Anthony's bed, with a blanket wrapped around her. She was shivering and feverish, too restless to fall asleep right away.

"Do you remember what it was like to be sick when we were little?" Isabel said. "Cicily would sit with you and read one of her magazines."

"And she made jelly omelets," Alice said dreamily, her eyes shut. "Cinnamon toast on a tray. I used to wonder why everything tasted different on a tray. Do you think it was being sick?"

"I don't know," Isabel said. "Do you remember that rhyme she used to recite?"

Matthew, Mark, Luke, and John,
Bless the bed that you lie on.
Angels sing your glorious song:
Sickness come, sickness gone.

Just saying the words brought back the soft, lilting way Cicily would speak sometimes, though other times her diction was as crisp and clean as a knife. Her hands were rough and wrinkled, toughened from years of washing and of working in the dirt. Her father had had a small chicken and truck farm, and she had told the girls about her garden at home in the country, where she grew collard greens, kale, and tomatoes.

Her clothes were almost like uniforms in their interchangeable sameness. Slacks and long-sleeved blouses in colors like brown and navy blue, the only bit of brightness the scarves she sometimes wore over her hair, flowers and patterns and swirls of red and yellow, turquoise and violet. She had a little room in their house, an extra bedroom under the stairs with a bed and a TV and a dresser, where she slept four nights a week and sometimes more, to save the long trip by city bus and Greyhound bus all the way down into Kent County, Delaware, where she lived in a house the girls had never seen. She was often stern, but they loved her—differently from the way they loved their mother, who indulged them with kisses and effusions and treats, exclaiming over them with distracted, often misdirected pride.

"Oh, Isabel, you're so creative!" Doc would say, looking at a paper plate jack-o'-lantern Isabel had made along with the rest of the third-grade class, and kiss her on both cheeks, big wet kisses Isabel ducked when she could. Sometimes it felt as though their mother were trying to make up in physical affection for what she lacked in time, touching the girls whenever she was near them, smoothing their hair, burying her nose in their necks. When she was home she whirled through the house, asking questions, giving advice, making shopping lists, checking homework, boiling water for endless cups of instant coffee, talking on the phone. "I'm so glad to be home with you girls," she would announce, while their father sat in his armchair in the living room reading the paper or made a circuit of the house in his bedroom slippers, emptying the trash.

Cicily was not demonstrative. The girls never jumped up to see her when she came into the house, yet her arrival early on a Monday morning was like the appearance of the sun after a restless night. They loved her, and they thought she loved them, too, although she never said so. Didn't she have to love them, she who bathed and fed and sang to them, and cooked tidbits of chicken liver for them, and gave them presents on their birthdays?

Did they ever give her presents? No, they did not. They didn't even know when her birthday was. They didn't even know how old she was, although once Alice had asked her.

"Not quite as old as Methuselah, *yet*," Cicily had replied. And then, when they had pressed her, "Little bees that mind their own business don't get stung!"

Would she have stung them, then? Or was this awkward maxim merely meant as a warning about the outer world, of which she was suspicious? *Did* she love them? Or was she merely paid to simulate love, that tall, lean, proud woman who was very good at her job?

Dr. Rubin used to say, "I don't know how I would manage without Cicily. I would trust that woman to the ends of the earth. Of course, she is extremely well paid, especially when you consider that we take care of all the Social Security. Still, I wouldn't want to have to replace her. She has a natural gift with the children!"

Alice was asleep. Her thin face glowed like a pale moon. If

Anthony could see her, Isabel thought, he would awaken her with a kiss as though she were Sleeping Beauty and marry her on the spot. Quietly, so as not to disturb her sister, Isabel got up and looked around the apartment for something to read.

Anthony had evidently not lived here very long. The rooms were sparsely furnished. No pictures hung on the walls, and except for the stereo equipment and a few CDs, the shelves in the living room were empty. The kitchen cabinets held only a few dishes, and probably only the microwave got much use. Isabel found a stack of moving boxes still taped shut in the coat closet, and at last, boredom and curiosity overtaking any remaining scruples, she turned the knob of the door to the second bedroom, the one where Simon Goldenstern was staying.

Like the rest of the apartment, this room had little furniture—only a bed and a straight-backed chair and a small table—but in every other way it was completely different. The bed was a single, tucked under the window and neatly made with a striped Hudson Bay blanket. The table held a computer and a milk crate jammed with file folders, a jar with pens and pencils, a few notebooks, and some round stones the size of plums. The printer was on the floor under the table, and all around the room—against the walls, arranged carefully in stacks as there were no shelves—were books. Paperbacks and hardcovers, novels, books about politics, religion, China, the Middle East, classics and new volumes with shiny covers, and a complete set of the *Encyclopedia Britannica* bound in blue. Over the bed, three photographs were tacked on the wall, each showing two boys, aged about six and eight, making faces at the camera. Both had brown hair falling in their faces, sun-browned skin, missing teeth. While Isabel was taking all this in, she heard a key scrabbling at the front door lock, and she went quickly back into the living room to greet Anthony.

But it wasn't Anthony. Instead, Simon Goldenstern came into the hall. His face looked red, as though he had just climbed a lot of stairs (Isabel had taken the elevator up), and his black hair was disheveled in a way that made his bald spot seem more prominent. He looked blankly at Isabel for a moment, and then he said, "You're the wrong sister!"

It was so exactly what she might have expected him to say that Isabel would have laughed if she hadn't been so flustered. As it was, she found herself blushing as she explained what she was doing there, which didn't make her like him any more than she had before.

"I'm sorry Alice is sick," Simon Goldenstern said blandly, stepping into the living room. He yawned, stretching his arms over his head and opening his mouth wide, showing his uneven teeth. "What a day, what a day." He threw himself down on the leather couch. "Where's Tony?"

"At work."

"Of course! Whereas you merely took the day off from, what? Grocery shopping? Washing windows? Does anyone wash windows anymore? My mother used to do it on the first Monday of the month."

Isabel said nothing.

"Was that rude? I can't help asking personal questions. It comes from being a reporter."

"Or maybe," Isabel said, "you became a reporter to justify your habit of asking personal questions."

Simon smiled. "I didn't think I was so transparent."

"Oh, sure," Isabel said. "You just need to know one or two circumstances of a person's life, after all, and you can infer everything important about them. Don't you think?"

"That depends on how astute the observer is. What else do you infer about me, besides why I chose my career?"

It was a relief to dislike someone so straightforwardly, to express hostility without guilt. "Oh, I think that you and I are a lot the same, temperamentally," she said airily, almost enjoying herself. "We're both moody and judgmental and consider ourselves superior to everyone."

Simon laughed, a loud, ringing laugh that gave his face a warmth she hadn't seen in it before. "That's an excellent description of me! Whether it applies to you equally well, I don't know yet."

"You're reserving judgment, then?" Isabel said. "I don't think I'm worth the effort."

But he was looking at her now with new interest, thinking that in fact, despite a certain superficial resemblance (the same brown curly hair, the same sharp brown eyes), she wasn't anything like his ex-wife, with whom he had just had an extremely acrimonious lunch. "Do you want a drink?" he asked. "I'm going to have one."

"Why not?" Isabel said. It was turning out to be such an odd day.

Simon got up and went into the kitchen, returning with a half-empty bottle. "Do you know anything about Scotch?" he said, setting the bottle on the glass coffee table where she could look at its label.

"Nothing."

"This is very, very good Scotch." His eyes narrowed, and Isabel understood suddenly that he was drunk already. "I'm celebrating," he said. "I bought a house. Tony will have to take care of himself now. If he can."

"He's a grown man," Isabel said, but Simon smirked at her.

"Drink it slowly," he instructed, pouring two glasses. "It's expensive." Even when he was sitting there was something restless about him, as though his mind were always whirring away a little too fast and his long limbs could never quite find a comfortable position.

"Anthony won't mind?"

"It's not his. Tony only drinks blends."

"To your house, then," Isabel said, raising her glass. She was glad he was moving out.

He watched her as she tasted the Lagavulin. It burned her tongue and slid hotly down her throat. "Well? Do you like it?"

"It's very nice," she said politely.

"My wife prefers Drambuie."

"Your wife?" Isabel asked in surprise. "Are you married?"

"Ex-wife, I should have said. Well, I'm thirty-seven. By the time you get to be thirty-seven, everybody's married. Or has been."

"My sister isn't," Isabel said.

Simon was silent for a moment. "Your sister seems like a very nice person."

Isabel looked at him, trying to gauge the tone of his comment. She remembered the way he'd put his arm around Alice when she had been talking to Anthony at the party, the way he'd looked at her and said, *Don't go with him.* "Alice is an extremely nice person," she agreed.

"And she's very pretty, too."

"Yes."

"Then why *isn't* she married?" he said. "Did something happen? Did someone break her heart? Did she dedicate herself to Diana?"

Isabel put her glass down. She had thought this question over so many times that she could barely think about it anymore. It was like a high, slippery wall that her mind balked at. The fact was, not only had Alice not gotten married, she had never even come close. She had never dated anyone for much more than a year (Wally, the litigator). Mostly it was just a matter of a few dates or a few months' worth of dates. A lot of men had been smitten with Alice. They pursued her with phone calls and flowers, but somehow these were never the ones Alice liked. She had glowed over a few of the others: Wally; Jim, who did publicity for the Academy of Music; Carlo, the urban planner. She had looked forward to their phone calls, had hinted to Isabel that there was a kind of natural understanding between them, that they looked at the world the same way she did.

But each time, something happened. The man got a job in Japan and moved away (Wally), or he announced he needed time to get over a previous relationship (Jim), or he just stopped calling (Carlo). Why was that? Was she too quick and devoted in her behavior once she decided she liked someone? Did she frighten them off? Or was she, on the contrary, too old-fashionedly demure and reserved? Or did it have nothing to do with her behavior at all, but with something else? Her judgment, perhaps? Did she only want precisely the kind of men who couldn't appreciate her? Was she unlucky, or did she unconsciously sabotage herself?

Did she, against all protestations, not really want to be married?

"She's never found anyone good enough for her," Isabel said at last, and Simon Goldenstern grinned.

"Of course not!" he exclaimed. "But you know, Tony isn't good enough for her, either."

Isabel laughed out loud. "There's a friend for you."

Simon laughed, too, companionably, as though they were on the same side. "I like your sister. I know you wouldn't want her to make a mistake. I've known Tony a long time, and he always looks like the golden boy. I've known him since we were twelve years old."

"You said that the other day."

"We were in Little League together. Did I tell you that? He was the pitcher and I was the catcher."

"No," Isabel said. "You didn't go into it." She tried to imply that she had no interest in him doing so now, either, but he clearly wanted to tell her about it.

"We developed an—alliance," he said. He took a slow drink from his refilled glass and looked at Isabel thoughtfully, as though deciding how much to say. "I had to keep a secret for Tony. A secret I knew because I was his catcher."

"Why did you have to?" Isabel asked, interested in spite of herself.

"He asked me to. And I promised. Maybe I shouldn't have, but I did. And then, after that, I felt responsible for him."

"I don't think a promise like that is binding," Isabel said. "Not if it's something serious. Something that affects other people, for instance."

"Don't you? I think if it affects other people, it makes the promise that much more compelling. If nothing's at stake, your good faith doesn't matter much to anyone, does it?"

He looked so serious that Isabel's curiosity got the better of her. "What kind of secret was it?"

"Should I tell you?" he asked almost slyly.

"It's so long ago. It can't still be important, can it?"

"Can't it? You'll have to decide." He took another drink. "He used to cheat. The truth is, Tony wasn't a very good pitcher. But he was a good cheater. He used to scuff the ball. He kept a piece of nail file hidden in his pocket. No one ever found out. Probably it didn't even make any difference, not at the speeds he was throwing. But he felt like it did. That was the point, I guess. How it made him feel."

Isabel laughed, but it was a forced laugh. A pall had settled over the room, and she couldn't help feeling that it did indeed still matter and that she wished she didn't know.

In the late afternoon, Alice woke up and felt well enough to eat some soup. Luckily Anthony had a few cans, or maybe they were Simon's. Simon had gone to work.

Isabel would have liked to arrange everything on a tray the way Cicily used to, but she couldn't find one. She had to carry each item in separately: the bowl, the cup of tea, the plate of crackers. She helped Alice sit up, fluffing the pillows for her and smoothing the covers the way she had imagined doing for a child.

Alice ate a few bites of soup. "I feel so much better," she said. But she seemed to have let go of her determination to go home. "I've ruined your day, haven't I," she said.

"No," Isabel said. "I was glad to come."

"You're taking such good care of me. You're going to be great when you have kids."

She knew Alice said this not to hurt her, but just the oppo-site—to insist on the reasonableness of the idea that Isabel would have children. She forced herself to smile. "You're easier to take care of than a child. You don't whine."

"I can if you want me to," Alice said.

The apartment door opened and Anthony's voice called out from the hallway. "Alice? Alice!" He came into the room in his striped shirt and his pressed slacks and his paisley tie, finding the two sisters looking up expectantly from his bed. The one on the edge was robust and pink cheeked, with her wild brown curls pulled back carelessly in a clip, while the other, under a blanket, was pale and elegant, her fine hair falling loosely over her shoul-ders. It was a sight, Anthony thought, any man would be pleased to come home to after a day's work.

"Hello!" he said. "I'm so pleased to find the patient awake and smiling. And look who I found at the hospital."

It was Dr. Rubin, her broad face furrowed with concern. "Poor Alice, let me look at you!" she said, stepping toward her daughter and lifting her chin to inspect her. "Poor thing, you're so thin. How do you feel, sweetheart? Have you been able to keep anything down? Some soup? Good, good, that's the best thing, you'll be yourself again in no time." Then turning to Anthony, she said, "Usually she's as healthy as a horse."

"I never know why people say healthy as a horse," Isabel said. "When I was on my large animal rotation we saw the sickest horses. Contagious equine metritis. Equine infectious anemia. Glanders."

Dr. Rubin laid her hand against Alice's cheek. "Where's the thermometer?" she said.

After the examination, the two doctors agreed the patient wasn't well enough to go home. Anthony seemed very pleased to look after her. When Isabel and Dr. Rubin left, he was sitting close beside her on the bed, coaxing her to drink a little more tea. He took her hand in his lap and held it there, counting her pulse.

"They look so natural together," Dr. Rubin said to Isabel as they went down together in the elevator. And even Isabel, who hated to agree with her mother, felt things were going reasonably well.

CHAPTER TEN

*I*t was June, the season of weddings, bar mitzvahs, and graduations. Dr. Rubin, although not without regret that she had no landmark events to celebrate, nonetheless called each of her daughters one rainy afternoon to summon them for Sunday brunch.

Isabel was in the kitchen with newspaper spread out across the floor, repotting the houseplants. "We're having a special visitor," Dr. Rubin said over the line. "A distant cousin. Do you remember I told you about some relatives of my grandmother's who spent the war in hiding in Sweden? One of them married a Swede, but later moved to New York City. We used to see them sometimes when I was a girl. He would have been a second cousin of mine, I think, twice removed. I knew his children a little, but I haven't heard from them in years. Decades! Since before I was married. We had a lot of cousins at the wedding, of course, but no one from that branch. And then at some point they got tired of New York and moved back to Sweden."

Isabel never tried to follow her mother's elaborate German-Jewish genealogies. It was all written down, anyway. Dr. Rubin kept the papers in a manila envelope in her dresser.

"Well, this morning," Dr. Rubin went on, "I got a phone call from one of *their* children! I've never met him. I didn't know any of his family was in the States, but he told me he's been out in Silicon Valley for years doing some kind of computer thing, and now—you'll never guess—he's living in Philadelphia."

"Wow," Isabel said, trying to sound enthusiastic. She balanced the phone against her shoulder and tamped down the dirt around the cyclamen. "What's his name?"

"Soren Zank. That's the Swedish influence, I guess. His parents are no longer living, but they had told him he had relatives here. We had a nice chat on the phone, and he's especially looking forward to meeting you girls."

"How old is he?" Isabel asked.

"Well, of course I didn't ask him," Dr. Rubin said. "Late thirties, I would imagine."

"That's kind of old for Tina," Isabel said. "And you wouldn't want anything to interfere with Alice and Anthony."

"You're so suspicious, Isabel!" Dr. Rubin said. "This is just a little family reunion! And thirty-eight, say—or thirty-five—is not so much older than twenty-nine."

Isabel gave up and offered, as she knew her mother expected her to, to pick up the bagels at Tannenbaum's. When she was younger she sometimes found ways not to go to her mother's brunches, but Doc made refusing so painful that it was scarcely worth the effort. She was like a steamroller and a puppy at once, a particularly irritating and formidable combination.

When Theo got home, Isabel dished pasta primavera onto two plates. Not her great-grandmother's Royal Copenhagen, but the plain white dishes Theo had given her once for her birthday. (Was that how he thought of her, plain, pure, solid?)

"What kind of a day did you have, Izzy?" he asked.

The blind in the bedroom wouldn't close properly; she had shopped for a new one. She had gone to the supermarket and run into Lucy Andrews, the wife of one of Theo's colleagues. "Lucy got her hair dyed," Isabel said. "Golden harvest. She told me where, in case I wanted to go." She smiled, and Theo smiled back. It was a joke, of course. Isabel, with her natural brown hair just lately streaked with gray, didn't even wear makeup.

"What do you think, though, really?" she asked him lightly, twirling pasta around her fork. "Should I dye my hair, now that I'm thirty-five? The gray makes me look a little washed out, don't you think?"

"You look great to me," Theo said. He always said that.

"Lucy also said you and Martin were finished with that Bartram deal. Congratulations. I thought that was what was taking up so much time."

Theo ate an olive. "No, not the Bartram thing," he said. "We've been done with that for a while. This new project is an outgrowth of that. Bartram wants to build a new office center near Pennsauken. Thirty thousand square feet. Only some of the land may have had some chemical contamination."

"So they have to clean it up first?"

"We'll have to see," Theo said. "It might actually be safer to cover the whole parcel with asphalt than to go digging and release all that material into the air."

"And cheaper, too, no doubt," Isabel said.

"That's not the point."

"Anyway," Isabel said, "I thought Bartram was retiring. I thought that deal was his swan song."

"Oh," Theo said. "Yes. But one of his kids is taking over the company."

Isabel told him about Soren Zank. "Alice says that Doc told her he made billions in computers and is using it for wetlands restoration. He has some big project down in Delaware he's working on."

"Alice took a moment out of her whirlwind romance to call you?" Theo said, unable to mention Alice and Anthony's relationship without irony.

"Alice is happy," Isabel said. "Things are going well."

"Things are going *fast,*" Theo said. "God knows Alice deserves to be happy if anyone does, but a month ago who had even heard of this guy? And he's divorced? Do we know the circumstances? Like, for instance, did his wife have some good reason to dump him?"

"It's just like you," Isabel said, "to assume the worst."

"And yesterday you tell me Alice is telling you that her friend's husband does beautiful wedding ceremonies. That's the kind of thing I expect to hear from your mother."

"You and I were talking about weddings when we hadn't known each other very long," Isabel said.

"So now you and I are a paragon?"

For a moment they looked at each other across the table, and it seemed possible that one of them might say something—might take an ice pick to the glacier that had become their life together. But the moment stretched out. Neither of them said anything. The food cooled on the white plates.

CHAPTER ELEVEN

*S*ometimes sex was the place Isabel and Theo could still reach each other. Tonight in bed, Isabel put her arms around him. With her eyes shut it was possible to feel they were still in that first bed in the apartment on West Spruce, with the glow of the streetlight slipping in around the edges of the shades.

In her head, Theo still looked the way he had at twenty-three, skinny and loose limbed, but really he was thick through the chest, solid, his biceps taut under his skin like a mouse inside a snake. He said working out at the gym relaxed him, but he was far less relaxed than he used to be. A twitch ticked in his jaw where there used to be a dimple. She could feel it, tonight, under her lips. She kissed him, and he kissed her back, briefly, and then turned onto his side, pulling her arms comfortably around him and holding them in place. She moved her hands across his chest. "Theo," she said softly, "don't go to sleep." She ran her tongue along his ear.

Theo pulled himself up out of her arms and sat, leaning back against the headboard.

"What?" Isabel kept her tone light. "If you don't want to have sex, fine!"

He didn't say anything for a moment, letting the silence work. Isabel lay where she was, the warmth she had felt for him the minute before shrinking and cooling inside her until it was like a stone.

"Izzy," he said at last, "I know your cycle as well as you do. I should, after all this time."

Now it was as though her heart itself were the stone, pummeling the inside of her chest. "I wasn't thinking about that," she said, but it was true that it was the fertile part of her cycle.

"I don't want to make love by the calendar anymore," Theo said. "I'm tired of being an insemination device."

"You're not an insemination device."

"I can't stand it," Theo said. "Hope and disappointment every month! I feel like making love has become so—intertwined with it that I don't even remember what it used to be like."

She could hear his words, but she couldn't take them in. "I remember," she said. She remembered the way his face used to go slack with sensation—opening up, becoming entirely legible.

Theo laughed now without softening. Then he looked solemn. "I'm sorry," he said. "But I can't do this anymore."

"What do you mean? What do you mean you can't?" Isabel felt panicked. She was on a raft and the horizon was slipping out of sight.

He raised his palms in a gesture of helplessness.

"You mean you won't!"

"I mean, Izzy, that the situation is impossible."

Now Isabel sat up, too. She pushed her hair back to see him better, but it immediately fell forward again, into her face. "Yes," she said. "If you refuse to have sex with me, I'd say having a baby is impossible!"

"Izzy," he said, as if she were the one being unreasonable.

"Have you decided you don't want children?" Her voice was so calm, she hardly recognized it. It was as if she had asked him whether he wanted the light on or not. Do you want to stay up and read? Do you want a child? Do you want our life together to continue?

Theo waited a long minute. "Not at this price," he said at last.

"Why do *you* get to decide that?" Isabel cried.

"I'm sorry," Theo said again. And he did sound sorry, but even more than that, Isabel thought, he sounded relieved.

It seemed to Isabel that she did not sleep all night. But when she opened her eyes at last, it was morning and Theo's side of the bed was empty. Sunlight lay in yellow stripes across the bed and the house felt still, like a great boat run aground. Outside she could hear traffic, birds, buses, footsteps, but it was as though those sounds reached her faintly, from very far away, the way the sounds of San Francisco's New Year celebrations were said to reach and torment the prisoners of Alcatraz. Ordinary life still went on outside the windows, while inside the house, up in the bedroom where the rays of light fell like gilded bars across the bed, everything seemed to have been battered to bits in a storm that had blown out to sea in the night.

And yet, Isabel reflected with a kind of despair, sitting up and looking around her at the maple dresser and the silver Mexican mirror above it, at the jewelry box and the books piled on the bedside table—everything was exactly the same. Even her body made its ordinary demands: to be voided and washed and fed, as though it were a dog.

Downstairs, in the bright, spotless kitchen, Isabel drank some coffee. She missed Daisy, who would have nudged her snout under Isabel's hand, looking for affection. Who would have jumped her front paws up onto Isabel's shoulders and licked her face, then pranced at the leash on its hook and wagged her tail until Isabel took it down. It would have been better to walk with Daisy, but Daisy wasn't here. Nonetheless, Isabel grabbed her purse and went out.

At the corner she remembered that she hadn't locked the
door and had to go back, struggling with the key while the black
shutters loomed above her and gawking crows gathered in the alleyway. She went up Quince Street, past the town houses with
their iron railings, and turned on Walnut. By the open glass doors
of a café, someone said, "Isabel!" She turned away instinctively,
but the voice called again, quite close now, "Isabel—Isabel Gordon!" (which was not her name, she had never changed her name
from Rubin) and a firm hand took hold of her sleeve.

"Oh, hello!" Isabel said, feeling her face arrange itself into a
semblance of a smile, amazed that it could still do that. It was Valerie Fullerton, a blond woman with lavender eyelids and smiling
scarlet lips, the wife of Theo's colleague, Charles Fullerton. Years
ago she had been a financial analyst, then quit her job, had three
children, and taken up horseback riding. Whenever Isabel saw
her she was dressed as though on her way to lunch at the Four
Seasons. Isabel had liked her ever since, at a Christmas party, she
had overheard somebody ask Valerie what she did and Valerie
had laughed and replied, "Whatever the hell I feel like doing."

"Isabel Gordon," Valerie Fullerton repeated now. "How are
you? I haven't seen you in ages."

"I'm all right," Isabel said. "How are you?"

"Come have coffee with me," Valerie commanded, and she
propelled Isabel by the elbow into the Xando café. It never
would have happened, Isabel thought with irritation, if Isabel
had had the dog.

"I've just left the kids with their grandparents," Valerie said
when they were seated. "We've been up at their place all weekend, fishing. Madeleine caught a little trout. She's just turned
four, it was her first fish! I took miles of video."

Isabel smiled at Valerie's pleasure and at the image of the lit-

tle girl, who had been a toddler sucking on a pacifier the last time
Isabel had seen her, proudly reeling in the trout, and then immediately she began to cry. Tears dripped onto the table even as she
turned away and let her hair fall across her face. To her relief, Valerie said nothing. When she had some control over herself, she
wiped her eyes and tried to smile, her face red with misery and
embarrassment.

Valerie watched her, her eyes soft under their bright lids.
"Why don't you tell me what's wrong," she said.

Isabel shook her head.

"Listen, honey," Valerie said. "Terrible things have happened
to me, too. Did you know I was married before? My first husband left me for another woman. Then I had cancer, when I was
thirty. I lost a breast." With her free hand she touched her left
breast through the cream silk sleeveless sweater. "This one's not
real." She smiled. "You're not going to tell me anything I haven't
heard before."

"I can't get pregnant," Isabel said, and her voice broke. After
a minute, when she felt that she could go on, she explained, looking up into Valerie's still, thoughtful face as she talked, although
her eyes kept straying down to the false breast. It looked exactly
like the other one, round and firm, lifted elegantly in its top-of-
the-line brassiere, like an emblem of the impossibility of ever
telling a falsehood from the truth.

"Oh, men," Valerie said impatiently. "They have to be in control of everything! If they can't be in control, they have to think
of a way to make it seem as though they are."

"But what should I do?" Isabel asked. She felt desperate. For
a moment she had looked upon Valerie as a kind of oracle, but
now she was making the jaded, clichéd comments of the kind of
woman Isabel was determined never to be.

Valerie laced her fingers together and settled them on the table with a clank of bracelets. "You'll have to use your feminine wiles," she said.

Isabel looked at her blankly.

Valerie laughed. "This is your call, isn't it? Theo goes out into the world, he does what he likes. Doesn't he? Who's going to carry the child, feed it, care for it nearly all the time?"

Still Isabel waited for Valerie's words to resolve themselves into something she could understand and do.

"When I wanted a new car and Charles thought it was too much money, I just told him the mechanic said that it looked like the transmission on the old one would go within a year. I knew he wouldn't check up on it. He hates talking to mechanics."

CHAPTER TWELVE

As Isabel stepped out of the café, a city bus pulled up to the corner. It was the same bus she used to take when she was working at the zoo. As the doors opened, Isabel could see a few women with children, young men in baggy pants, and one old lady weighed down with shopping bags. A black woman with two white children sat behind the driver. "I'll find it," the woman said wearily in a Caribbean accent, and began to rummage in a straw bag on her knee as the doors hissed shut.

Cicily used to take them into the city on the R-5 train, to Independence Hall or the Franklin Institute. Cicily approved of museums, but she had no use for paintings. "What are you going to learn in there?" she said scornfully as they passed the grand entrance to the Philadelphia Museum of Art. "Don't be wasting your time. You stick to science and that! You girls are going to be something, like your mother is." It was strange to Isabel how Cicily, so slim and tall and cool and beautiful, admired their mother. "She's not relying on anybody," Cicily said. Self-reliance was her doctrine, as the primacy of family was Dr. Rubin's. If Isabel told Cicily that a friend had sat with someone else at lunch, or promised to invite her to a party and then changed her mind, Cicily never had much sympathy. "People will do that to you," she'd say.

If she told her mother, Doc would call the other girl's parents, likely as not. Better to keep your mouth shut.

When the Rubin girls were growing up, it wasn't so common to see children with babysitters. Isabel felt that people stared at them: two (later three) small white girls with the tall black woman. It never seemed to bother Alice, but it made Isabel feel conspicuous and peculiar. Sometimes she hung back until Cicily scolded, "What's Dr. Rubin going to say if I lose you!"

The train didn't go to the zoo. When Cicily took them there, they had to transfer to the trolley or the bus, and it was a long trip. Still, they went. Cicily and Alice liked the elephants and the peacocks, also the seals swimming in the blue water. Neither of them liked the reptile house. Cicily would frown in the dim hall. "It's like being trapped underground," she said. "What do you want to look at these infernal creatures for, Isabel?"

Isabel didn't know. She just loved them, the cool, still elegance of the snakes draped across their branches, or curled and coiled up, doubled back on themselves, barely breathing. She liked the turtles, too, beak-nosed under their tiled shells as though they had been carved out of rock and the rock were still part of them. She liked the motionless alligators with their jaws wide open, cooling themselves in the summer heat.

"It smells like brimstone in here," Cicily complained. It was as close as she got to mentioning Satan (the Rubins didn't want her talking about religion with the girls), but Isabel knew what she meant. Sometimes Isabel thought the snakes held her attention because they bothered Cicily so much. Mostly nothing bothered her or impressed her. "I've seen worse," she'd say of a bee sting or a cut lip. Or, "Don't think you can impress me with your bad behavior!" She wasn't afraid of big dogs, or of thunderstorms, or of homeless people in the street, but the snakes unnerved her. They didn't even do anything. They just lay there in the dark behind a solid inch of glass.

What Cicily liked best was the bird house, the bright birds in their airy rooms hung with ferns and bromeliads. "Imagine where they've been," Cicily would say. "Up with the angels!" The air was warm and humid there even in the winter. Tiny humming-birds whirred by, and big, plump, showy pheasants sat in the paths. Cicily would whistle to the canaries, her head cocked on her long neck the same way the birds cocked their heads. "Pretty bird, pretty bird," she would say and stretch out her hand.

Back home at the Rubins', she put out seed and suet and watched through the kitchen window to see who came. In good weather she sat on the terrace while the girls played around her. Often she consulted a Peterson's guide she had found on the Ru-bins' shelf. "Ti-dee," she'd call to the goldfinch perched on the fence. "Ti-dee-di-di," and the finch—or cardinal, or chickadee—would seem to look at her with its beady eye as though wonder-ing what kind of strange, oversize bird she was. Sometimes they would even answer her—or seem to answer—calling, in any case, after she called, and then Cicily's face would light up with pleasure.

These were some of Isabel's best memories. Always it seemed to be springtime, the new green leaves on the trees and the air rinsed clean by winter. She and Alice would swing or play games with complicated rules that Alice would invent and strictly en-force: "No—it's Wednesday, so the mommy has to wear the hat." (Tina, in these memories, was in the house napping or so small she was just a bundle in Cicily's arms.) And always, on the wooden bench, Cicily sat with the sun on her face, tranquil; the still center of the world.

CHAPTER THIRTEEN

*I*sabel knew things were going well between her sister and Anthony, but she didn't expect him to show up for brunch at their parents' house. Neither, apparently, did Dr. Rubin. "Anthony!" she said as the two of them came, smiling, through the door into the front hall. "How nice! Nobody told me you were coming."

Anthony had the handsomely creased face of an aging television star. Beside him Alice glowed, as pale and lustrous as the string of pearls she wore around her neck.

"Alice didn't think you'd mind," Anthony said, one hand spread lightly on her back.

"Of course not! How could we mind? Come in, come in, we're delighted. Only it is generally polite, Alice," she went on when Anthony had gone through into the kitchen, "to let a person know how many guests to expect."

Alice smiled. Her mother's words floated through her as though she were a cloud. "I'll go set another place," she said.

Dr. Rubin turned to Isabel, who had got down on the floor to pat the dog. "It's a good thing I told you to get two dozen bagels. She might have given me a hint."

"What do you mean, a hint?" Isabel said, scratching Prince on the chest. "Someone's coming for brunch, his name has three syllables?"

"Of course it's a good sign," Dr. Rubin went on.

"What's a good sign?" Tina asked, slipping in through the front door and catching the end of her mother's remark.

"Alice brought Anthony to brunch, Tina, what do you think of that! For a while I thought you'd get yourself settled down before she did, but maybe not."

In the flurry of excitement over Anthony, the Rubins nearly forgot about Soren Zank. He pulled up half an hour late in a black Saab convertible and had to knock several times before anybody heard him.

Soren was a big, sturdy, broadly built man in his mid-forties with shaggy, reddish brown hair and a full, curly beard. He looked like a cross between a Viking and a Hassid and was dressed expensively in clothes that might have been designed for mountain climbing. Dr. Rubin greeted him warmly, but Soren ignored her extended hand and threw his arms around her. "Hello, hello! Cousin Evelyn, I feel like I know you already. There's nothing like family, is there? And these must be your daughters, one more beautiful than the next." With a happy smile he proceeded to embrace each of the sisters in turn, like a big, good-natured golden retriever that likes to put its paws up. Isabel found herself crushed against him before she could step back and was held, not longer than was appropriate, but very close. He shook Judge Rubin's hand, and Theo's, and that of Anthony Wolf, whom Dr. Rubin described, keeping her options open, as a friend of the family. She added that both men were, coincidentally, from the state of California: "And so I'm sure you'll have a lot to talk about!"

In the dining room Soren seated himself next to Alice, who was looking particularly radiant. "Did your mother ever happen to tell you," he said to her, "that your great-grandfather Hiram Zank was called Fiery Hiram because of his hair? You and I are clearly twigs from that tree." He had a slight accent that lent him an allure he would otherwise have lacked, reminding one continually that he was European.

"I always thought it was because of his temper," Dr. Rubin said.

"In that case, Alice can't have any of his genes," Anthony said, smiling.

"Are you talking about Alice?" Tina said. "My sister?"

"Soren," Dr. Rubin said, "did you know Tina does massage therapy? Does Swedish massage really come from Sweden, or is it one of those misnomers, like French fries?"

"I have no idea," he said, and, turning back to Alice, asked, "And what kind of work do you do?"

"I'm a lawyer," Alice said.

"Ah," Soren said. "Not just beautiful, but intelligent, too."

"Have some salmon," Dr. Rubin said. "Soren? It's Scandinavian. Well, Norwegian, to be specific. Do the Swedes smoke salmon? You never see it."

"Thank you very much," Soren said, "but actually I'm a vegetarian."

Dr. Rubin was upset. "I should have asked, but it never crossed my mind! It's not as though it were beef, obviously. Some vegetarians do eat fish, don't they? So many young people these days won't eat red meat at all, I always wonder how they get enough iron. I'm sorry, can I make you an egg?"

Soren assured her that he would be perfectly satisfied with bagels and cream cheese and grapefruit. "I love the bagels here in Philly!" he said. "In California they're like balloons. Except in L.A., but I never go there if I can help it. I like a slower pace of life. All anyone thinks about in Los Angeles is money."

"You've done quite well for yourself, though, I understand,"

said Judge Rubin, who was accustomed to being direct. "In computers, Evelyn says."

Soren helped himself to another bagel. "Who would have
guessed how the whole thing would turn out?" he said cheerfully.
"Those of us who fell in love with programming back in the
eighties, we weren't doing it for the money. We were just fooling
around, trying something new. Pushing the envelope. I was in the
right place at the right time, that's all."

Judge Rubin smiled skeptically, but Dr. Rubin's mind was still
on the previous subject. "The girls, of course, went through their
vegetarian stages when they were teenagers. Alice used to refuse
to sit at the table when meat was being served. I'm sure she only
did it to annoy me, and of course if Alice did it, Isabel and Tina
had to do it, too."

"I can't imagine why we would have wanted to annoy you,"
Isabel said.

"It was just the times," Alice said. "The seventies. It was a
cultural thing, like wearing those gunnysack dresses, remember
them?"

"And peasant blouses," Isabel said. "We were so disappointed that we had missed the sixties!"

"Ah, the sixties," Soren said nostalgically, but Dr. Rubin, who
was not interested in a discussion of that decade, which for her
had passed in a fog of pregnancies and forty-eight-hour hospital
shifts, interrupted him.

"Tell me about your plans," she said. "These waste sites
you're cleaning up."

Soren's face lit up. The topic of his foundation was dearer to
him even than his recollections of the sixties (also something of a
fog, although for different reasons). He talked at length about
the money he had donated, and the money he had raised, and the

money he had spent, and the projects he had taken on, and his vision of wetlands restoration. He talked about PCBs and DDT, about CO_2 and arsenic and leukemia rates, about herons and red-backed salamanders and invasive rushes. Despite his evident passion, it was difficult to put together any clear picture of his actual activities, aside from spending money as vigorously as possible. Judge Rubin asked him various clarifying questions, particularly with regard to the problem of a fertilizer factory that was continuing to dump waste water upstream from a marsh to which Soren was particularly committed. Whether he did this because he thought he might get a responsive answer, or because he hoped to influence Soren's plan of action, or simply from the long habit of interrogation, it was impossible to say.

"The thing about a project like this is that it makes you feel your life is worthwhile," Soren explained, his curls shaking with his enthusiasm and his cheeks glistening through his beard. "It isn't easy to make the leap from the drive to make money to the drive to give it away, but once you cross that chasm everything appears to you in a different light. Speaking for myself, I feel I've started my life all over again at ground zero."

"Isn't that a mixed metaphor?" Theo broke in.

"What?" Soren said.

"A mixed metaphor. Shouldn't it be 'starting all over again at square one'?"

"Theo," Tina said, "is uptight about how people talk."

"Of course, Soren isn't a native English speaker," Dr. Rubin put in quickly.

"Who wants another bagel?" Isabel said, passing the basket.

"I think what you're doing is great," Tina told Soren. "Most people get so tied to their jobs, their one little world, they can't make the jump to the next thing. I've been thinking of trying something new myself. Maybe in finance. I think I have the head for it."

"Money is very interesting as long as you don't get too hung up on it," Soren said. "Most people only think about getting more, not about what it can do."

"I think people think about what it can do," Anthony said. "They think about how it can buy them a bigger TV, or a nice vacation at the shore."

"Exactly! What it can do for *them*," Soren said. "Not what it can do for the world!"

"Most people don't have enough money to think about what it can do for the world," Anthony said.

"You're a doctor, aren't you?" Soren said. "You make a good living?"

"Everyone thinks doctors are so well-off," Dr. Rubin broke in as the conversation hit close to home. "And yet we're getting squeezed all the time. HMOs, malpractice insurance. Do you have any idea what I pay in premiums every year? It's terrible in obstetrics. People will sue you at the drop of a hat. Of course, you feel for the poor parents. They want someone to blame, and the lawyers descend on them like vultures."

"Still," Soren said cheerfully, bringing the conversation back to Anthony. "If you gave away ten percent of what you make, that would be something. I bet you could afford more—thirty percent! What would that be, fifty grand? What would you have to give up? A fancy car? A country club membership? But think what you would gain in exchange! A sense of peace and a feeling of self-respect."

"I have self-respect," Anthony replied. "I spend all day taking care of sick people."

"Of course! But you have to address the root causes. Why do you think people get sick? Because the planet itself is sick!"

"Are you saying," Theo broke in, "that you think people back in the stone age didn't get sick? That hunter-gatherers never fell ill?" Anthony's tone had been affable, but Theo didn't bother to keep the prosecutorial edge out of his voice.

"Of course they did!" Soren exclaimed. "But that was part of the cycle of nature!"

"It's natural for people to get sick," Anthony said. "We'd like to cure them anyway. That's what we call civilization."

Soren looked at him with dislike. He was predisposed to like most people, but this self-satisfied doctor epitomized a type he was fed up with—suave men who confidently told him that he didn't know what was he talking about. Soren had never finished college, but he had learned what he had needed to know. People told him he didn't understand ecology, but it wasn't as complicated as they wanted you to think, any more than computers were. Grasping the essentials was what mattered. A circuit was on or it was off. An ecosystem was clean or it was dirty. Of course, there were a thousand details to be worked out, but they were only that—details. "What some people call civilization," he said, "others call corruption."

"If everyone is done talking about money," Alice said before the argument could escalate further, "I have an announcement to make. Anthony and I are engaged!" Her words seemed to float and shimmer in the air above the table.

Dr. Rubin's voice rose above the general clamor of congratulations and chairs being pushed back and kisses and embraces. "Oh, Alice! I'm so happy for you!" she said.

Judge Rubin looked pleased as well. He kissed his daughter and shook hands with Anthony. "Every happiness," he said in a voice in which only someone who knew him well could have detected a tremor.

Only a little red-faced (he had always colored easily), Soren smiled as he kissed the bride—with a forgiving good grace, he felt. When he looked closer, he saw she was older than he'd thought, anyway. Whereas the sister with the bright, dark eyes was younger and also better dressed. He liked women, and he was not excessively picky. One type attracted him as much as another, and he prided himself on perceiving what was interesting even in less obviously alluring women. His cousin Isabel, for instance, had a very nice body under her unflattering clothes, and her thick, curly hair suggested sensuality. He shook hands politely with the groom-to-be. There was something familiar about the man, but he couldn't place it. The others were beaming and exclaiming, all except for Tina. She was looking at Soren's shirt, a short-sleeved button-down in guava plaid. "Is this organic cotton?" she asked, seizing the material in her fingers.

"Mostly," Soren said. "There's some kind of synthetic, too, to make it dry faster. It's a fly-fishing shirt."

"Do you fly-fish? It takes very sensitive hands, doesn't it?"

"Yes," Soren said. "Catch and release, of course."

For Isabel, the engagement was the best possible news. She couldn't help shedding a few tears as she embraced Alice. "Be good to my sister or I'll come after you," she found herself telling Anthony, although she hadn't meant to say anything like that. Everyone laughed except for Alice herself, who sat in her chair like a beatific queen while her subjects bowed down and paid court all around her.

CHAPTER FOURTEEN

*A*fter the excitement had died down a little, everybody went outside for a walk in the woods. "I want to show Soren our own little stream," Dr. Rubin said, leading the way through the backyard. Isabel lingered to look at the flowers Marco had planted along the fence and the herb garden he'd laid out near the driveway. Oregano, thyme, tarragon, and parsley sprouted around a potted rosemary shrub, but Isabel doubted that her mother, who was too busy to cook very often, would make much use of them. That was Marco, doing good work for people who didn't appreciate it. Dr. Rubin would have been just as happy with a bright clump of indestructible black-eyed Susans.

Now Doc's voice drifted up through the yard. "I-sa-bel! I-sa-bel!" she called, and for a moment Isabel was a child again. Or rather, she thought, going past the pink and white rhododen-drons, it was that she was a child still. All three of them were, de-spite their women's bodies, and they always would be as long as their mother was alive, whether they got married or not, or had children of their own, or moved away. They were her creatures—and their father's, too—as much as they were themselves. The trick was to learn to live fully within the constraints. To find free-dom within them, as had the great sonneteers.

"There you are," Dr. Rubin said as Isabel came onto the path, and then, turning back to Soren, added, "Isabel is wonderful at identifying wildlife. I can hardly tell a squirrel from a chipmunk myself, but Isabel has a knack for it. And of course, all her training is in wild animals."

Soren looked at Isabel inquiringly.

"I used to be a vet," she said.

"She worked at the Philadelphia Zoo," her mother added proudly.

"So in a way you followed in your mother's footsteps," Soren said, pleased to have made the connection. "I think it's so interesting how things run in families. You'll have to come do a program at my foundation. We have these little ecology talks. People bring their kids. It's very nice."

They were walking up the hill now, Dr. Rubin, holding her husband by the arm, leading the way. "Do you think they'll want a rabbi or a justice of the peace?" she wondered. "I hope Alice will wear my grandmother's veil, even though Isabel didn't want to."

"Animals deserve medical care as much as people," Soren said to Isabel. "We're all part of the same cycle of being." He used the term entirely unself-consciously.

"Are you a Buddhist?" she asked him.

"Not technically."

"Are you a vegetarian for health reasons or environmental ones? Or moral ones?"

"I don't separate those things. They're pieces of a whole. I don't believe in participating in the killing of nature's creatures." He raised his big hands as he spoke, as though to indicate the glory of the natural world all around them, here in the thin, suburban woods. His blue eyes glowed with feeling, and Isabel found she couldn't help liking him.

Nonetheless, she couldn't help teasing him a little, either. "A stalk of wheat is one of nature's creatures, isn't it?" she said, smiling.

"Yes." Soren seized the chance to explain his point of view. "And of course, you have to eat the fruit to spread the seed. Death is a part of the pattern. But I try to avoid the worst offenses. Slaughterhouses, for example, are an abomination."

Isabel, who had been inside a slaughterhouse, privately agreed, but she wanted to see what her cousin would say. "But weren't those cows only bred—only lived at all—because there are slaughterhouses? Without the beef industry, there wouldn't be so many cows."

"Maybe," Soren said. "But if people ate less beef, they would eat more cheese. We have some great local cheeses in California." He addressed this last remark to Tina, who was picking her way carefully just behind them, in her high-heeled sling-backs.

"I love California," Tina said. "I always thought I'd like to move there someday."

"I thought you wanted to move to Santa Fe," Isabel said.

"No. It's gotten so trendy."

Now they had reached the stream. Dr. Rubin said, "I have no idea what the water quality is, but it *looks* very clean."

"Probably it's full of fertilizer runoff," Judge Rubin said.

They stood in their good shoes in the dried mud and looked. The stream gurgled and splashed over the rocks. Sunlight filtered down through the trees. It was very peaceful.

Suddenly, Soren, who had been looking intently at Anthony, exclaimed, "I know you! Or rather, I know who you are. You probably don't remember, but we met in San Francisco two or three years ago. In John Cotter's office."

At the mention of the name, Anthony went very still, like a frog that had just become aware of a hawk.

"Amazing!" Dr. Rubin said. "What a coincidence! I always say if you're talking about German Jews, you're talking about no more than two degrees of separation. If everyone would like to go back to the house, I'll make some more coffee."

"Who's John Cotter?" Tina asked loudly.

Of course it had to be Tina, Isabel thought later. If she hadn't spoken, perhaps the conversation would have lurched forward, the frog would have leaped out of the way of the hawk. And would that have been better or worse, in the long run? Would it have made any difference at all?

"The lawyer who handled my divorce," Soren said. "Both my divorces, actually." Everyone's eyes were on him now. "Don't you remember? You and John were having dinner at the Blue Oyster on Russian Hill, and I came over to the table to say hello. He introduced us, and he was very talkative—I think you'd both had a lot to drink—and he said it was the second time for both of us, and we should make sure we came to him for number three!" Soren laughed.

"You must have made a mistake," Dr. Rubin said. "Anthony has only been divorced once. Isn't that right, Anthony?"

"Oh dear. Have I let a cat out of a bag?" Soren said.

Anthony's laugh was a gurgle in his throat. He opened his mouth and closed it again and looked at Alice. "I was going to tell you," he said. "I meant to tell you. But things happened so fast."

Alice was still regal—although cold now in her pallor, as though she had turned into a queen of ice. She looked at Anthony steadily with her pure blue eyes.

"The past is the past," he said with a sad smile. "As far as I'm concerned, I left all that behind when I left California!" He looked old suddenly, closer to the end of life than the beginning of it. Isabel almost felt sorry for him, wanting one more chance at the young man's game of love. She waited to see how Alice would dismiss him.

"And a child, I think, as well," Soren went on.

"Two, actually," Anthony said bravely. "A boy and a girl."

"Two children!" Dr. Rubin exclaimed. "Back in California!"

Judge Rubin put a hand on his wife's shoulder, which had begun to quiver, and turned to Soren. "Do you have children as well?" he asked with an air of getting all the facts on the table.

"Five," Soren answered with pride. "All boys." He stood in the middle of the knot of people whom he had reduced to anxious confusion, like a large dog that had shaken itself dry in the middle of a cocktail party.

Alice held her head high. "Yes, the past is the past, I agree completely!" She took Anthony's hand and held it in her own for everyone to see.

Isabel felt sick. She recognized Alice's expression of righteous stubbornness, as though any position became admirable because of the purity with which she clung to it. She had found a new cause, and she would fight for it as she always did, with unassailable, impassioned loyalty.

"But Alice, two marriages," Dr. Rubin said. "Two children!"

"Two, six, ten—what difference does it make?" Alice said, and, having made her choice, she turned and led the way back to the house.

CHAPTER FIFTEEN

*A*t Dr. Rubin's insistence—and nobody wanted to contradict her just then if they could help it—the men stayed outside on the patio while the women went in to clean up. Dr. Rubin trembled as she banged the china onto the counter and went back to the dining room for more.

"Alice," she said as she returned with the oily fish platter, "this is a very serious situation!"

Alice stood at the sink wearing yellow rubber gloves, loading the dishwasher. "The situation is none of your business," she said. She looked taller, the way she always did when she got angry, her shoulders squared.

"Alice!" Dr. Rubin repeated. "You're my daughter, and I love you. That makes it my business! I know you had your heart set on this man, but he's not who you thought he was. It's not your fault. You took him at his word. So did I—my God! I'm as much to blame as anybody."

"This is not about you," Alice said icily, rinsing each plate nearly clean before placing it in the rack. "It's my life, and I know what I'm doing."

"You think you know," Doc said. "But stepchildren, Alice! Two stepchildren you haven't even met—two strangers! Who will be a part of your life forever. Who knows how they'll feel about you, and part of Anthony's loyalty will have to be to them. It's only natural!"

"Anthony doesn't see his children much," Alice said. "They live with their mother in Santa Barbara."

"You knew about the children?" Dr. Rubin asked.

"Yes." Alice's face grew pink, and she lifted her chin a little higher. "And don't ask me why I didn't tell you. I think the answer is self-evident."

"What does it say about him that he doesn't see them much? I don't care where they live! Not to mention having been divorced twice." Prince was sniffing his way across the floor, looking for crumbs, and Dr. Rubin picked him up and held him in her arms.

"You make everything into such a big deal!" Tina exclaimed before Alice could answer. "I agree with Alice. The past doesn't matter." She had agreed with Alice about everything since she had been old enough to talk.

Isabel, who found herself in the novel situation of agreeing with her mother, wiped down the counters and kept her mouth shut.

"Children are not the past," Dr. Rubin said. "They are very much the present. And the future, too."

"Maybe," Tina said. "But three thousand miles is three thousand miles."

"He lied to you!" Dr. Rubin said to Alice.

"He didn't lie," Alice said. "He neglected to tell me something, and then he apologized for it."

"Being divorced twice is not a small omission."

"He told me he was divorced," Alice said. "You said yourself that a man who had a made a mistake would be more likely to know what he wanted!"

"One divorce is a mistake," Dr. Rubin said. "Two divorces is a pattern."

"One, two, who cares?" Alice cried. "Remarriage is legal in this country as far as I know!"

"Oh, don't start with your legalities! You sound like your father, attaching yourself to some abstract principle and not letting go for love or money. Surely you can see that a man who has been married twice and abandoned two children at the far end of the continent is not to be trusted? If he takes his prior commitments so lightly, why should the future be any different?"

"Because he loves me!" Alice said, and for a moment everyone was silent.

Dr. Rubin's face sagged as she stood in the middle of the kitchen floor in her neat blue shirtwaist dress, her strong hands with their short, blunt-cut nails clutching the dog. Hands that had delivered a thousand babies, that had wielded scalpels and suture needles, that had touched death. Hands that had braided her daughters' hair when they were little, sewn on buttons, unpicked shoelace knots—callused now and thickly veined. An old woman's hands. "Alice," she said, "you're a beautiful, smart, lovely woman, and yet you just can't seem to find someone who sticks! I ask myself if your father and I did anything wrong. We always had such a strong marriage. Did we set expectations too high?"

"Doc, are you listening?" Alice cried in exasperation. "I'm getting married!"

CHAPTER SIXTEEN

$\mathcal{F}$or a week Dr. Rubin went around in a state of agitation, trying her best not to pour out her anxiety to everyone she met. It was particularly difficult at work, where she avoided Anthony as much as possible. In exchange for a promise from Alice to consider, at least, the issues she had raised, Dr. Rubin had agreed not to confront Anthony about what she called his duplicity. She felt terrible for Alice, as well as angry at her for being so stubborn, but she also couldn't help feeling that she herself had been used and betrayed by Anthony almost as much as Alice had.

One evening she stopped at Quince Street on her way home from the hospital to beg Isabel to talk to her sister. She slumped on the sofa with her cardigan drooping from her shoulders and her voluminous handbag, so closely resembling a doctor's black bag, resting on the carpet by her shoes. "Of course it's hard for her," she said. "She's almost forty, and now another door is closing in her face! Maybe she'll listen to you."

Isabel had tried talking to her sister, but Alice had stopped listening the moment she understood Isabel wasn't taking her side. "Now *you're* going to tell me what to do?" she had said coldly.

"No, she won't," Isabel told her mother. "She's like an ice storm."

"She's like her father," Dr. Rubin said. "I thought my children would be warm like me, not a set of glaciers. I know Theo isn't perfect, but at least you don't have to worry about him running off and leaving you alone with a bunch of babies."

"That hardly seems to be a problem," Isabel said.

"I know you girls think I overreact to things like this. But I really don't think I am in this case."

"I never said you were," Isabel said. She looked at her mother's shoes, the same ugly, respectable, rubber-soled navy flats Doc had been wearing for years. It was impossible to find fault with them, yet the sight of them depressed Isabel. They made her feel as though nothing in the world could ever change.

"I know it's not easy to get through to her," Dr. Rubin said. "But if she'll listen to anyone, she'll listen to you, Isabel." She leaned forward and fixed her gaze on her daughter, who felt the intensity of her mother's will coming through it, powerful and electric. She had heard how, when women were struggling in the delivery room, Doc looked them straight in the eye and said, "You can do this."

"All right," Isabel said. "I'll go see her."

Dr. Rubin's eyes filled with a gratitude so palpable, Isabel had to look away.

Alice lived only a few minutes away by car but as they approached Washington Avenue, window boxes and freshly painted shutters gave way to sagging porches and sidewalks strewn with plastic bags. Sometimes there were needles, too, early in the mornings, but there were also families and dogs and the smells of cooking. "I don't know how Alice can stand to live here," Dr. Rubin said as they drove down 10th Street. "It's so dingy. And it's not safe."

"Alice has lived here for seven years and nothing has ever happened to her."

"Touch wood." Dr. Rubin pressed her fingers to the car's ve-

neer paneling and sighed. It was one thing for a young woman to
live in a one-bedroom apartment in a colorful part of town, but it
was another altogether once you had passed forty. Forty wasn't as
old as it had once been, but it wasn't as young as people pretended, either. "I'll just go up for a minute and say hello," she
said. "Then I'll head home. Your father will be waiting for me."

They buzzed in and climbed the narrow stairs to the second
floor, knocking on the battered door that Alice had painted
turquoise. Tina answered, wearing a black miniskirt, a black
V-neck T-shirt, tight and low cut, and black platform shoes. "Alice
is changing. We went shopping," she said, and smiled. "You'll
never guess what we bought!"

Dr. Rubin sat on the sagging sofa, trying not to look at the
cracks in the plaster, the cramped corner that served as a dining
room with its wobbly table decorated with candles, at the pass-
through to the awful kitchenette. "You girls certainly don't get
your interest in shopping from me," she said. "I don't think I've
bought a single item of clothing in two years."

"I don't think Isabel has, either," Tina said, looking at her sister's old jeans and faded blouse.

"There's nothing wrong with my clothes," Isabel said, eyeing
Tina's outfit. "At least I can move in them."

"I can move," Tina said. "This body is made for moving."

Alice came through the bedroom door. She was wearing a
wedding gown, and her eyes were bright with excitement.

"Oh!" Dr. Rubin cried. "Oh, Alice!"

The dress was an elaborate confection of lace and tulle and
satin, the low-cut bodice decorated with seed pearls, the sleeves
puffed like little clouds over Alice's thin shoulders. The fitted
skirt accentuated her slender waist, then fell away into a train as
flounced and gathered and trimmed as any piece of material could
dream of being. Diaphanous gloves began at the knuckle and

stretched to the elbow, revealing only an inch or two of freckled arm below the sleeve, and a white veil fell from a beaded circlet covering her hair. Alice glowed palely amid the billows of white, barely visible, like a moon in daytime.

"Oh," Dr. Rubin said again. "You look like a dream!" She blinked. She had waited so long to see a daughter of hers in a real wedding gown.

Tina beamed. "You belong on the cover of *American Bride.*"

"What do you think, Isabel?" Alice asked.

Isabel smiled uneasily from the sofa. She hardly recognized Alice under all the fabric. "It's very—frothy," she said.

"It's not frothy, it's elegant!" Tina said. "Not everyone would choose to be married in a—" For a moment Isabel thought Tina was going to say *"shmatte,"* but she came up with "sundress" instead, which was what Isabel had worn when she married Theo.

"It's beautiful," Isabel said. "Only I didn't think you were quite at the—dress-buying stage yet."

"We didn't start out shopping for wedding dresses," Alice said. "Only we passed this store and we thought we'd just peek inside. Didn't we, Tina?"

Dr. Rubin stared at her eldest daughter. If she lowered her eyes, she could begin to remember that Alice was rushing into a bad situation that was likely to bring her grief. But again and again her gaze was drawn up to the shining, pearly, luminous mass of bridal lace, and the sight dazzled her. And after all, Anthony seemed to love Alice. He would rescue her from these sordid rooms, the sirens at night. Roaches. She could not speak.

"The thing is, Alice," Isabel said, "everything has happened so fast. What's the big hurry?" She knew she needed to be more eloquent than this, but Alice intimidated her. It was as though she were still twelve and Alice fifteen, unimaginably smart and grown up.

"I'm thirty-eight years old," Alice said with a hint of exasperation. "I wouldn't say I've been in a particular hurry."

"You're too reasonable to do something just because other people are against it," Isabel said, wishing it were true. "And what kind of man is on his third marriage at his age?" Our age, she thought. She remembered Theo's doubts about Anthony. How clear-sighted they had turned out to be.

"I can't believe you're taking Doc's side," Alice said.

"Doc has a point," Isabel said.

"It's infuriating as well as humiliating," Alice said, "to have the whole family discussing something that isn't anyone's business! We all make mistakes. Even you, Isabel." She gave her sister a sharp look. "I wish you would trust me to decide what imperfections I'm willing to forgive in the man I love! I love Anthony, and he loves me, and it's the first time in my life I can say that."

Dr. Rubin couldn't stand it anymore. She broke in, "That's not what Isabel meant. Is it, Isabel?"

Isabel stared at her mother.

"I think we all need to accept things and do our best to enjoy Alice's happiness," Dr. Rubin said. "God knows she's waited long enough for it! And you know I *like* Anthony."

"Doc!" Isabel said.

"Oh, Isabel," Dr. Rubin said unhappily. "I never said I was absolutely against it."

$\mathcal{E}$arly in July, Isabel invited Alice and Anthony to dinner. "Be nice to him," she told Theo.

"Why wouldn't I be nice to him?" Theo said.

"I don't want Alice to think we don't like him."

"Alice always thinks exactly what she wants to think."

"I'm just saying. You can be abrasive. Or you can be charming. I'm asking you to be charming."

"I feel maligned," Theo said.

When their guests arrived, however, Theo greeted them warmly at the door. He made a show of embracing Alice, shook Anthony's hand heartily, then proceeded to congratulate them until Isabel sent him to the kitchen for drinks. "You should have bought champagne," he called to Isabel from the kitchen. "How can we toast an engagement without champagne? Or, since Anthony's from California, some sparkling California wine. You make some good sparkling wine out there, don't you, Anthony? Of course they're not allowed to call it 'champagne.' What do they call it? 'Sonoma'?"

Anthony laughed good-naturedly. "They have some good sparkling wines, but nothing like real French champagne. Of course, California cabernets are very good."

"I thought you might be a cabernet man," Theo said. "A man

who appreciates a good wine is the same man who appreciates a good woman, and you've chosen the best of them! After Izzy, of course, although I always said if Izzy hadn't been available, Alice would have been next on my list."

Alice laughed. "What makes you think I would have been interested?" she said, smiling.

"People used to marry a wife's sister if the wife died," Isabel said. "But I hope it won't come to that."

"Anyhow, Alice is taken now," Anthony said, enfolding her hand in both of his.

"I suppose you could still have Tina," Isabel said to Theo.

"To Alice and Anthony," Theo said, raising his glass. "I wish you all the happiness of marriage. May your passion never fade, and your true understanding never dim."

"A very nice toast," Anthony said before he began to drink. Isabel couldn't help thinking that Anthony was doubtless an expert. He must have been on the receiving end of many engagement toasts over the years.

Over Isabel's pork roast they had the usual conversations: travel, work, restaurants, current events. Anthony and Theo did most of the talking, comparing notes on Brussels and Montreal, Striped Bass and Le Bec Fin. Theo maintained his tone of exaggerated enthusiasm verging on irony, but only Isabel seemed to notice. Or maybe his tone was entirely right and it was she who watched the whole evening with weary, jaded eyes. She felt as though she were seeing with a kind of double vision. On the one hand here were two handsome, happy people, very much in love, but behind them lurked the ghostly images of two more desperate characters: an aging woman, frightened of loneliness, and a man who had failed (twice) at an endeavor at which he now asked them to have faith he would succeed.

The conversation moved on to opera, comparing Maria Callas and Renée Fleming. Theo said, "One shades the high notes with more finesse, but the other's vocal purity is so extraordinary." How did he know these things?

"I'm taking Alice to *Madama Butterfly* next month. I couldn't believe she'd never heard it sung."

"Anthony's a big opera fan," Alice said. "I promised to go to one opera a month, and he has to come hear one salsa band a month."

"Is Alice going to get you to take salsa lessons?" Isabel asked Anthony. "She's been pestering me to do it with her for years."

"I go to all these parties with people I work with," Alice explained. "Everyone dances. I've taken a few lessons, but I'd like to get better."

"I'd love to learn to salsa," Anthony said. "I'm pretty good at the tango."

Of course he is, Isabel thought.

"How do you like the wedding dress?" Theo asked Anthony. "I hear it's magnificent."

"I haven't seen it," Anthony said. "Alice is superstitious."

"I'm not superstitious," Alice protested. "I'm just enjoying all the trimmings of being engaged."

"Might as well," Theo said. "In a couple of months all the fun will be over, and you'll be settled into the grind of married life. Just kidding, of course."

There was a pause. The French doors to the patio stood open, and a breeze moved through the room, smelling of flowers and exhaust fumes.

Isabel turned to Anthony. "How's your father?" she asked. "Alice says you visit him every week."

Anthony's father, aged eighty-six, was confined by dementia

to a nursing home in Cherry Hill. "He's all right. Thanks for asking. Sometimes he knows me. Mostly, though, he treats me with
this terrible, blank politeness. He likes Alice, though."

"Not that he has any idea who I am," Alice said. "But he
kisses my hand."

"He was always chivalrous," Anthony said. "He just doesn't
know where he is."

"He keeps asking for Anthony's mother," Alice said. "We
don't know what to tell him. He divorced her twenty years ago!
Anthony's poor stepmother goes to see him nearly every day, and
he just looks at her and says, 'Where's Charlotte? When is Charlotte coming?' Anthony says he spent as little time as possible
with Charlotte when he was married to her. He worked all the
time, and when he wasn't working he was playing golf."

Isabel had a flash of Anthony in a nursing home in thirty years
saying to Alice, "Where's Martha?" Or Janet, or Louise. Isabel
didn't know the names of his former wives. She had just recently
learned the names of his children: Skye and Eugenie. Alice had
always said that when she had children she would name them
Paul and Ann.

"My friend Simon sends his regards to you," Anthony said to
Isabel. "I told him I was coming tonight and he made a special
point of it."

"Who's Simon?" Theo asked Isabel.

"He's the one Anthony brought to the anniversary party," Isabel said. She felt hemmed in on all sides by irony, first Theo's
and now, through Anthony, Simon's.

"He's a reporter for the *Inquirer*," Anthony told Theo. "He's
very good. He even had an offer once to write for *The New York
Times*, but he wasn't interested."

"Why not?" Isabel asked.

"They would have had to move to New York. Marla was dying to go, but Simon said he was a Philadelphian and he was going to stay in Philadelphia."

"That's how Isabel feels, too," Theo said. "She says she likes Philadelphia because everybody says what a terrible place it is."

"I never said that," Isabel protested. "I might have said that Philadelphia was pleasantly undiscovered."

"She's very strong-minded," Theo told Anthony. "All these Rubin women are, you should know that. They always win all the arguments."

"I *wish* I did," Isabel said.

"Just so you know where you stand," Theo said to Anthony.

"Of course, the whole point of marriage is two people making decisions together," Alice said.

"Yes," Anthony agreed. "If a person is very stubborn, it can be hard on a marriage. That's why Marla ended up leaving Simon."

Isabel was grateful to him for moving the conversation to less personal ground. The comment made her wonder what had ended his marriages, but she only said, "Because he wouldn't move to New York?"

"That was part of it. Another time he turned down a promotion. They were going to make him an editor, but he said no. He said he liked writing. Marla was furious."

"I don't see that it's one spouse's business what the other one chooses to do for a living," Isabel said, thinking about her own feelings when Theo entered the corporate world.

"They needed the money," Anthony said. "Marla stopped working when the children were born, of course. And Simon insists on living in the city. If he had taken the editor's job, they could have afforded private-school tuition and a house that wasn't falling down."

Theo said, "I hope you don't think Alice is going to quit her job to stay home with babies."

Anthony smiled. "I'm not worried about Alice," he said.

But Isabel was.

CHAPTER EIGHTEEN

*T*he next morning when Isabel got out of bed, her face in the bathroom mirror stared back at her with weary blankness. There were deep creases between her eyes and more gray in her hair than she had noticed before. Time was rushing on, it wouldn't wait for her to sort out her life. Alice would be forty a year from November, and then Isabel would be next. She knew how relieved her sister was not to face that threshold single. Isabel thought about how she would feel if she entered her forties without a child. She knew if she didn't have one by then, she probably never would. At the thought, panic fluttered through her like an illness. Panic could make you stupid. It could make you choose the wrong door. Was that what Alice was doing? Was there any way of knowing now—or could you never know until it was too late?

It wasn't that Isabel didn't like Anthony. She did like him, and anyone could see how happy Alice was. Isabel had spent years waiting for Alice's happiness, but now that it had arrived, nothing felt right. She went downstairs. Theo was already shaved and showered, dressed in his new beige suit. She said, "I don't know what to do about Alice."

Theo was looking through the papers in his briefcase. "There's nothing to do," he said.

"I keep looking at her and imagining how she'll look when he tells her he's leaving her."

"It seems to me they have as much of a chance at being happy as anyone," Theo said.

Isabel looked at Theo's slicked-back hair and his white shirt filled out by his broad chest. He reminded her of a Komodo dragon, slick and fast and dangerous. She formed the words inside her head: *We need to talk about how things are with us.* She needed to strike the right tone, to be calm, not to blame him. But how could she do that when she *did* blame him? When she was afraid of what would happen if she spoke to him? Theo had shut his briefcase and retied his shoe. I never used to be such a coward, she thought. She said, "I want to talk to you."

Theo was already at the door. "I don't think it'll make any difference," he said over his shoulder. Then the door shut behind him. Isabel didn't know whether he even knew what she was talking about. Maybe he thought she was still talking about Alice.

The phone rang.

"Cousin Isabella!" Soren Zank said. His voice burst across the telephone line. "I'm calling to follow up on your promise to give a talk at my nature center. We have an opening later in the month."

Cousin Isabella! It was so absurd, it was almost charming. "Oh," she said, pulling herself back with an effort to the sunny, slippery, everyday surface of life. "I don't know."

"I'd love to tell you about the Zank Center," Soren said. "Face-to-face. What a coincidence, but I happen to be in your neighborhood."

"I can meet you at the Xando on the corner of Walnut in half an hour," Isabel said, though it was obvious he had hoped to be invited to the house.

The Xando was the café where Isabel had discussed deceit

with Valerie Fullerton. Soren was already there when Isabel arrived, and he embraced her as he had the first time they met,
crushing her breasts against the waffle weave of his shirt.

"You look wonderful," he said when they had sat down at a
table in a quiet corner that was immediately far less quiet. Soren
seemed too big for his chair, partly because of the way he waved
his arms when he spoke, like a dog who can't stop wagging its
tail. "I like a woman who doesn't dye her hair. What's a little gray,
after all? Just a sign that we're human! We're mortal. I grow my
beard for the same reason. Why fight nature? What's the point?"

Isabel smiled. "Why wear clothes, either? Or take showers?
Or drive?"

"You're teasing me," he said, returning her smile. "But animals
wash. It prevents disease. As for driving a car, I always prefer to
walk when there's a choice, like your American Thoreau says in
Walden. And I'd be happy to do without clothes if I thought I
wouldn't get arrested."

"How about at home?" Isabel asked. "With the curtains shut."

"Oh, absolutely! And I spend a month at the Esalen Institute
every year, just to discharge my batteries. Most people go nude
there, it's very peaceful. Or, if you have your eye on someone, so
much the better! Desire announces itself, not to mention being
more quickly satisfied."

"Some people think overcoming obstacles is part of the fun,"
Isabel said.

"I won't argue with you. There are different methods for different seasons. Variety is spice, no?" He leaned across the table.
Isabel was glad for the approach of the waiter, who took Soren's
order for a soy milk latte and her own for a cup of tea.

"Tell me about the nature center," she said when the waiter
had gone.

Soren's pale Viking eyes lit up, and his strong-featured face became suffused with pleasure. "The Zank Center started with a donation of land from one of the old estates. Inheritance taxes are so high, many heirs can't afford to hold on to the properties. We've gobbled up almost two hundred acres by now."

"Gobbled?" She was amused to see that his eyes held the same gleam when he talked about his nature center as they did when he was talking about sex.

"Better us than the developers! Better us than the pharmaceutical companies! We've turned the main house into an education classroom. Conservation people come and talk to kids about what they can do to save the earth. We had one guy come and talk about organic farming. Someone else explained about the destruction of the rain forest. It was very nice. And then at the end the children could use their dollars and quarters to buy endangered land in Brazil."

"What if they didn't want to?" Isabel asked, half-appalled and half-amused.

"We have other little things. Stickers and coloring books. To raise money for the center."

"Well, I'm afraid I'm not a conservationist," Isabel said. "Or an idealist, either."

"I disagree. I think you are an idealist," Soren said. He leaned across the table again, and she could smell him, a strong smell of woodsmoke and laundry detergent and beard. "I think anyone looking at you could see that you're not willing to settle for second best."

Isabel leaned back in her chair, holding her cup of tea in front of her. "I guess I could talk about frogs."

"You have the most beautiful eyes," he said. "Like deep pools in a forest where nobody ever goes."

"Soren," Isabel said.

"Please," he said. "I can see you're unhappy! Anyone can see it. And I know why. I know you haven't been able to conceive."

Isabel, who had been only amused and slightly irritated, was now shocked and angry. "How do you know that?" she asked. But she knew how.

"I'm a member of the family, after all," Soren said. "Your mother knows I would never tell anyone. What she doesn't know is that I can help! I can help you, Cousin Isabella, if you'll let me."

"No," Isabel said. "No, you can't."

"Listen to me. I'm not bragging," Soren said. "I don't believe in flattery or self-promotion, but this is just a fact." He drew himself up in his chair, but Isabel was too astonished to make use of the brief silence to stop him, and he went on. "You were there when I said I was the father of five children. Well, the truth is, that's an understatement. I have five boys by my ex-wives, but there are at least two or three other children who belong to me. Possibly more! More important, each time it only took once." Here he looked solemn and paused to let the significance of his statement sink in. "I understand you've had tests. Your eggs are healthy."

Isabel, awash in rage and shame, could not speak.

"I am offering you my services," Soren said. "It would be, I assure you, no hardship on my part."

But now he absolutely could not be allowed to go on. "No!" Isabel said, and then, seeing his surprise, she continued, "Thank you. I mean, I can see you're trying to be nice. But it's absolutely out of the question!" Suddenly the situation made her want to laugh, but she was afraid if she started laughing, she would never stop. The look of puzzlement on Soren's face reminded her of Daisy when Isabel refused to throw the slimy tennis ball dropped at her feet.

"You don't need to worry about anyone finding out," Soren said. "I can be as quiet as a grave."

"Oh, I'm sure!" Isabel said, trying to match his solemnity. "I'm sure you can. But listen, I'm married!" It was ridiculous that she was saying it: that circumstances were forcing her to say it.

He sat back at last, looking annoyed. "I didn't think you were so small-minded," he said. "In this modern age, you know, certain attitudes have outlived their usefulness. Like stone axes!"

"Some of us are still attached to prehistoric weaponry," Isabel said.

CHAPTER NINETEEN

*I*sabel had an appointment to see her gynecologist for her annual exam. As she was leaving the house, it occurred to her to bring her old diaphragm along to see if it was still usable. It seemed to her that she had to do something. She had given in too easily when Theo said he didn't want to have a child. If she did nothing, things would go on as they were indefinitely. Theo seemed to think the life they were living was an acceptable life, but how could they pretend to have any kind of marriage if they didn't even sleep together? How could there be any possible future for them? If Theo's problem was really the entanglement of sex and the attempt to procreate, why not separate the strands by using birth control like everyone else? It was, at least, a place to start.

Isabel got her medical care at her mother's office. In college she had used the health service doctors, but afterward it had seemed easier to go back to the medical group than to find her own OB/GYN. Of course, it was not her mother she saw, but Dr. Ignazio, who had known her since she was a girl.

Connie, a tall woman with a cascade of wet-looking hair, was at the check-in desk today, as she had been for as long as Isabel could remember. "Hello, honey," she said. "How are you, doll? Here for your annual? We're all so excited about your sister and Dr. Wolf. I always knew Alice would walk off with the best of them."

"How are you, Connie? How's Zachary?" Zachary was Connie's grandson.

"Oh, you know how boys are," Connie said proudly. "Go and
have a seat, Dr. Ignazio will be with you in a minute. Oh, I remember when you three were in here crying about your booster shots."

"You must be thinking of Alice and Tina," Isabel said, smiling. "I never cried."

"You," Connie replied. "You had a set of lungs."

The nurse was a short woman with a sharp face, bright black
eyes like a bird, and a way of cocking her head when she looked
at you the way a bird would eye a worm. "Just slip your shoes off
and we'll get a weight on you," she chirped, leading Isabel down
the hall. "What I wouldn't give for your figure, honey. I hope
you're not on one of those crazy diets. Nothing but grapefruit.
Nothing but steak. Or that Slim-Fast business! It's not good for
your body to starve itself like that, especially for a woman wanting to start a family. Not that any of them work, I've tried them
all. But you were always a skinny little thing. Legs like sticks.
Your mother used to say you never ate anything she cooked. You
were a picky one!"

Dr. Ignazio was a pleasant, mild, soft-spoken man who filled
out his white coat nicely, like a sausage. He seemed well suited to
coaxing babies into the world with his patient manner and his
clean, pink, plump hands. He always tried to take Isabel's mind off
the brief exam by asking her questions that would take no effort to
answer. He inquired about the health of her relatives, one by one.

"How's Theo?" he asked, probing her abdomen carefully.

"He's fine. Busy at work."

"Ah-hah. And your father?"

"All right. Just fine."

"Ah-hah. And your mother seems well"—inserting the
speculum.

"Yes. Same as always."

It used to be that, because of the association between Dr. Ignazio and having babies, coming to the office filled Isabel with anticipation. As time passed, however, she approached the examining table with increasing anxiety. She hoped and feared Dr. Ignazio would find something Dr. Abramowitz had missed—a cyst, a blockage—which would explain why she hadn't conceived. Something treatable, of course. Though as the years went by and she began to believe it must be something more serious—something he had overlooked before but that would reveal itself in time in all its venomous glory—a part of her felt she would be grateful even for that. A bad diagnosis would be at least an answer. She felt like a person who begged God to strike her down just to prove that He existed.

"Ah-hah," Dr. Ignazio said. "And your sister Alice?"

"Alice is fine. She's getting married, you've probably heard, to the new cardiologist." She could feel the jaws of the speculum opening. What could he see? She felt afraid, as though her failures must be graffitied there on the walls of her vagina.

When he was done, he helped her up so that she was sitting again at the end of the table with the paper gown hanging around her.

"So," he said. He smiled at her, a smile that seemed full of regret or nostalgia. "You're still trying to get pregnant?"

She nodded.

He checked her chart. "It's been how long now? A year or two?"

"Three years."

"You've been seeing Dr. Abramowitz?"

"Yes."

"And you worked out a program with him?"

"We tried a couple of regimens," Isabel said.

"Good, good. You know what you're doing, then. And you're still taking the folic acid?"

It was time to take the diaphragm from her purse, but Isabel felt she couldn't do it. She saw now that she should have given a different answer when he asked if she was still trying to get pregnant, but it seemed too late to go back.

"The important thing," Dr. Ignazio said, "is to keep on living your life. People can get so worked up over not conceiving as quickly as they'd like that they stop doing the things they used to. Enjoying what they used to enjoy. You just need to relax. Trust to time." He gave a version of this speech every time he saw her. At first she had ignored it, knowing it was meant for other women but not for her. Now its syllables rang in her ears like a great bell. How could she talk to him about the diaphragm? How could she tell him that Theo refused to make love? How could she reveal to his clean pink ears, plainly visible beneath the strip of hair that circled his head like a silver crown, the brokenness of her life?

He left her to put her clothes on in privacy, as though dressing were a more intimate activity than probing a rectum. Life seemed to have shrunk to the size of this room. How could she have thought a birth-control device could be the first step toward a baby? The idea was ludicrous. She opened her purse, took out the smooth, beige, clam-shaped case, and threw it in the wastebasket. It clanked against the bottom.

But as she pulled on her clothes, an idea struck her. She didn't have to use the diaphragm the way she had intended. There was another way. The thought made the blood rush to her face, but it seemed to her—kneeling on the scrubbed floor to retrieve the clam shell—that the field of play had shifted and that actions that wouldn't have been acceptable a month before were no longer out of bounds.

CHAPTER TWENTY

*I*t was after eleven by the time Isabel was leaving the medical group, and she thought she would swing by Alice's office and see if her sister had time for lunch. She was retracing her steps through the waiting room when she saw a familiar figure standing in front of the directory, rocking back and forth on the balls of his scuffed sneakers. It was Simon Goldenstern, frowning up at the list of doctors and offices with his hands in his pockets. He was just looking around for somebody to accost when Isabel passed by.

"This directory is useless," he said, turning toward her with an irritable slouch. "Tony has been here for six months, and his name isn't even up there."

Isabel looked up at the black notice board with its white letters dusty even behind the glass. "You're not supposed to just go up and see your doctor anyway," she said. "You're supposed to check in at the front desk."

"Why have a directory, if you don't want people to use it?"

As before, Isabel found his manner so oddly exaggerated that it was hard to tell whether he was truly angry or just playing at anger for his own amusement. She was also struck, as she had been previously, by his inability to keep his body still. His foot tapped, his brow furrowed and smoothed, and he jingled his keys

in his pocket as though the conversation could not be expected
to be enough to hold his attention.

"Are you having trouble with your heart?" she asked him.

"Me? No!" He laughed. "I'm as healthy as a peasant. That's a
nice expression, don't you think? My great-grandparents wouldn't
have survived those winters in Poland or Belarus or wherever if
they hadn't been robust. All the sickly ones died in the fields." He
looked at her. "Where are your ancestors from?"

"Some from Odessa, and some from Heidelberg."

"Oh, German Jews. They had it easy, at least until 1933. Par-
lor maids, ice-skating parties on the Rhine. Tutors and Wiener
schnitzel! You're not in on the secret of where Tony's office is,
are you? I just stopped by to drop something off."

"Just because you tell secrets doesn't mean other people do,"
Isabel couldn't resist saying, thinking of his Little League revelation.

It took him a moment to figure out what she was talking
about, but when he did his fish-white cheeks flushed. "I'm sorry
about that," he said. "They weren't engaged then."

"Well, things have happened quickly," Isabel said.

"Tony is always lurching into things."

"Alice is very happy." It occurred to Isabel to wish that Anthony's oldest friend had something good to say about him once
in a while.

"Oh, Tony is, too. But I would have thought your sister was
the type to look before she threw herself over a cliff."

"I hardly think getting married is like throwing yourself off a
cliff," Isabel said.

"Don't you?"

Isabel pointed down the hall. "Anthony's office is down there
on the right, near the back door."

"Near the back door," Simon repeated. "Very convenient."

To get to the parking lot, Isabel had to go the same way she had sent Simon. She lingered a few moments to avoid walking with him, then hoped they wouldn't run into each other when he came out again. As she approached Anthony's door, she heard voices.

"But I already got the tickets." Simon's voice was clearly audible out in the hall. The door stood slightly ajar.

"I'm sorry," Anthony said. "I've changed my mind. I can't go now."

There was no one else in the hall. Isabel stopped outside the office and listened.

"Tony," Simon said, "this ticket cost me three hundred bucks."

"Isn't it refundable?"

"No! That's why I got a decent price."

"Well, I can give you a hundred now."

"You can't reset the odometer to zero, you know, just because you pick up a new passenger," Simon said.

Before Anthony could answer, Isabel heard footsteps behind her. One of the nurses was escorting a patient down the hall. "Hello!" she called cheerily as she approached. "Great news about your sister, isn't it?"

CHAPTER TWENTY-ONE

*A*rriving at Alice's office, Isabel was surprised to find Tina there, sitting in a chair by the desk while Alice talked on the phone. Alice smiled and waved. Tina said, "What are you doing here?"

"I came to see if Alice wanted to have lunch," Isabel said. "I didn't know you had plans."

Tina shrugged. "You can tag along if you want to." The two sisters eyed each other. They hadn't been particularly close as children, but as adults they had grown even further apart. They almost never spent any time together alone, although occasionally Isabel accepted an invitation to have coffee or dinner, if Tina called. She knew she should call Tina sometimes, but she never wanted to. Tina irritated her and, worse, bored her. Theo had said, "It's not that your sister is stupid. It's just that she doesn't have an interesting thought in her head."

"I guess it's lucky she has a nice body, then," Isabel had replied, and Theo had laughed.

"I don't want to intrude," Isabel said now.

"It's just lunch," Tina said. "If you don't mind vegetarian. We're going to the Purple Turnip."

Alice hung up the phone and held up a letter. "Look what came in the mail. It's from that nursery owner, Rudner, about your friend Marco."

Isabel took the letter Alice handed her. "It's addressed to Mr. Rubin," she said. "Did you pretend to be a man?"

"I guess he just assumed it."

"People are so stupid," Tina said.

Isabel read out loud, "'Dear Mr. Rubin, I am writing in response to your letter of June twenty-fifth. You say my former employee Marcos Pena says he didn't take the four hundred dollars that was missing from my cash register.'"

"See how the amount gets bigger?" Alice said.

"'It saddens me that Marcos still refuses to take responsibility for what he did. He had the freest access to the cash register of anyone on my staff, being as he had been so trustworthy in the past, so there's no question in my mind that it was him.'"

"That's my favorite part," Alice said. "He admits that other people had access and vouches for Marco's character, all at the same time."

"'Also, he needed money. It saddens me, as I have tried to help the young man as much as I could. I employ many workers of his kind and always pay them minimum wage, not like some people in the landscape business who try to take advantage of people. I am keeping the motorcycle as collateral until the four hundred dollars is repaid, with interest. I am confident this can be worked out at a minimum of everyone's convenience.' I suppose he means inconvenience!" Isabel finished, laughing.

"Alice," Tina said, "I've been thinking that scarf I gave you would look really nice with that suit."

"Do you think you can get the motorcycle back?" Isabel asked.

Alice looked down thoughtfully at her jacket. "I don't see why not," she said.

* * *

"Soren Zank would like this restaurant," Isabel said as she read the menu. "It says the cheese is made without rennet."

"He's the one who told me about it," Tina said. She sipped her iced green tea. "Everything here is certified organic, and pretty much all of it comes from California. They fly it in fresh."

"I wonder how much jet fuel it takes to get it here," Isabel said.

"Oh, Isabel," Tina said. "They're flying the planes anyhow, you know."

Isabel changed the subject. "Are you still dating that guy?" she asked Tina.

"Which guy?"

"The one with the car. Mick? Sean?"

"Patrick. I was never really dating him. He's barely twenty-eight. And he expected me to buy my own ticket when we went to see a movie or something. No, actually, there have been some new developments. In that part of my life." But before she could tell them what the new developments were, the food arrived. Alice and Tina had Asian salads with rice noodles and marinated tofu. Isabel had the roasted eggplant sandwich on flaxseed bread, which sounded safe but turned out to be a mistake.

"Remember when we were kids?" Tina said. "Alice and I always had cheeseburgers when we went to Chelsea's, and Isabel had spaghetti."

Alice laughed. "Or when we went to Armando's, Isabel had pepperoni pizza and you and I had plain."

"You could have had anchovy and Tina would have asked for the same thing," Isabel said to Alice.

"It always seemed to me," Tina said to Isabel, "that you didn't care what you had, as long as it was different."

"Anthony likes anchovies on his pizza," Alice said.

"You know what they say about men who like anchovies," Tina said.

"I don't talk about such things," Alice said, laughing.

"Why not?" Tina said. "The sex must be good or you wouldn't be marrying him, right? After all, you have lots of guys to compare him to. It's not like Mom, marrying at nineteen or whatever." (Tina was the only one of them who sometimes called their mother "Mom.") "You know what I think is weird," Tina went on, "is how she's always talking about how little they knew when they got married—meaning how little they knew about sex. Not that I want to think about it too much, but it makes you wonder. Is she telling us they made a mistake?"

"There's more to marriage than sex," Isabel said.

"Oh?" Tina said. "Really?"

Alice remarked casually, "Some people still decide not to sleep together until after they get married. Even if they've slept with other people before."

Silence fell. A new understanding of why the wedding was happening in such a rush broke over Isabel and Tina at the same time, and they stared at their sister, united, for once, in their disbelief. "Is that a good idea?" Isabel asked, while Tina exclaimed, "You've got to be out of your mind!"

Alice hardly seemed to hear them. A dreamy look had come over her face, and Isabel recognized the expression she used to have as a child when she talked about world peace. She said, "It's just remarkable! It adds a whole new dimension to things. It marks this relationship out as different from anything that came before. A lot of people are doing it. It's like stepping back to a more romantic era. I wasn't sure Anthony would agree, but he really seemed to like the idea."

"Alice," Tina said, "that's like marrying someone without ever having *talked* to them."

Isabel said cautiously, "Now that you're engaged, couldn't you just—go ahead with things?"

"It will all happen soon enough," Alice said. "We've settled on August twentieth for the wedding. If you have any other plans, change them now." She smiled radiantly, waiting for the exclamations of delight. If her sisters' responses were more muted than they would have been a few minutes before, Alice generously did not notice.

"Listen!" Tina said. "I have some news, too!" And to Isabel's amazement, Tina's face turned as crimson as her nail polish. "I'm pregnant."

Isabel felt as though a small explosion had taken place in her chest. "How do you know?" she said.

"Would you like to guess who the father is?" Tina beamed, basking in her sisters' astonishment. "You won't be able to, so I'll tell you. Soren! We're going to get married! I told him about the baby, and he got right down on his knees and proposed. It was like a movie. Oh, when I think about the wedding dress I'm going to have!"

"Oh, my God!" Alice said. "It's so sudden."

"You're one to talk," Tina said. "Anyway, doesn't love at first sight have to be sudden? By definition?"

Love at first sight, Isabel thought. The idea had never seemed more appalling. How could people rush into marriage as though it were a weekend at the shore? Why did everyone assume being married would make their lives better? How could they possibly know?

"So you knew?" Alice asked, leaning across the table toward Tina. "You knew that day when he came to brunch in Devon?"

"Maybe not that day."

"But you suspected? You felt something, but you didn't know if it was what you thought it might be?"

"I always planned to get married by the time I was thirty," Tina said.

How could Tina be pregnant? Isabel's ears buzzed and she couldn't hear what anyone was saying. She looked at her sister's face, then around the restaurant at the faces of the other diners, laughing and chattering soundlessly like faces in a dream. How long had Tina *known* Soren—a month? And Isabel had been trying to get pregnant for years. The buzzing in her ears crescendoed and then began to subside, leaving her feeling drained, dry as dust.

"Are you absolutely sure it's Soren's?" she asked, thinking of the profusion of men Tina dated. She wondered whether she should tell Tina what had happened at the Xando. Would it be in her sister's best interest or merely gratuitously cruel?

Tina looked at her blandly. "I believe I'm in possession of all the facts," she said.

"I'm so pleased for you, Tina!" Alice said. "I really am."

Isabel said, "I hope you'll be very happy."

Tina said, "I'm sure we'll be at least as happy as most married people. And happier than some."

CHAPTER TWENTY-TWO

*A*lice and Tina had to go back to work. Isabel envied them. She wished she had something she had to do that would distract her while she tried to digest what she had heard—as though her mind were a snake and the news a rat it had caught that was almost too big to go down.

She walked north along the river for a long time, and then she sat in the scrubby grass in Fairmount Park and watched the runners and the dogs. College students walked by hunched under backpacks or rowed by in sculls. How differently she had expected her life to turn out when she was a student—she who at twenty was always busy, taking extra classes, volunteering at the animal shelter, going out with friends, going to lectures, talking, never finding enough time to sleep. Now she had plenty of time. Time lay around her like dust.

That night, Theo had to stay late at work. He told Isabel not to wait up for him, but it was only a little before ten when she heard his key in the lock.

"Hello," she called down from the bedroom, but he didn't hear her. When he climbed the stairs and came into the room, he looked at her blankly. "You're still up."

"It's only ten."

He looked at his watch the same way he had looked at her, as though he weren't really seeing it.

"Everything all right?" Isabel asked.

"I just got done a little early."

"That's nice. For a change."

He puttered back and forth between the bedroom and the bathroom, perched at the foot of the bed and turned on the news, then switched it off again, put on his pajamas in the dark, and got into bed.

"I had lunch with my sisters," Isabel said. Once this had been her favorite part of the day, talking with Theo in the dark, their bodies pressed together or loosely linked by a hand on a stomach, a leg thrown over a leg. Now he lay beside her without touching her.

"Both of them?"

"Listen. Alice and Anthony have set a date. We'll have to find another weekend to go to Cape May."

Here they were in bed together and still there was a distance between them Isabel couldn't bridge. Was it the sex that was missing or something more fundamental even than sex? And if so, what was it? Respect, affection, kindness, acknowledgment?

"Alice Rubin is finally getting married," Theo said. "Just when one thought it was never going to happen."

"I never thought that," Isabel said.

"Another 'good' marriage, too. Doctor, lawyer. I guess Tina will have to marry an Indian chief." He laughed harshly.

"Tina," Isabel said, feeling the thrill of revealing an extraordinary bit of gossip, "is going to marry Soren Zank!" She waited for Theo's response.

"She's what?" he said.

"She's marrying Soren Zank! But it gets even crazier." She told him the whole thing, and when she had finished, Theo sat up and stared down at her.

"You're joking," he said. "She's pregnant?"

"Yes," Isabel said. "But so what? Let her go ahead and have the baby! Everyone should be childless because of us?"

"She's having the baby?"

"She says she is. I would have said Tina was totally predictable, but never again." She reached out and touched Theo's chest. His heart beat fast and noiselessly, like a thief running. "While we're sort of on the subject. I've thought about what you said, about making love getting too tangled up with trying to have a baby. I found my diaphragm. I thought—we could go back to how things used to be. Start again. Forget the baby part and just concentrate on us."

Under her hand his skin was cold. Gooseflesh stood out on his chest. When was the last time she had really paid attention to Theo's body? She had been remiss, and she regretted it. "I miss you," she said, and she found that it was true. Tears sprang to her eyes, and for a moment she was able to forget how she was betraying him. She kissed him gently. His lips were cold, too, but he surprised her by kissing her back, deeply, and then raising himself up and pressing her into the bed. He ran his hard, icy hand along her skin, and her whole body responded, arching toward him with a thrill that was partly relief. Theo had been right. They had lost this, and now it had come back to them. Love had come back to them, she thought as he lifted her nightgown over her head, as he squeezed her breasts in his cold hands with a kind of desperate passion she would have thought he was no longer capable of. Just as this bubble of thought lifted away and her mind was shutting down like a house going slowly dark at night, the fact plunged into her consciousness that what she was feeling was based on a lie. Her deception had precipitated it. Her body began to close itself against him. She tried to concentrate her way back to pleasure, but all she could think of was the pale circle of rubber in its case in the bathroom and that this new beginning must not be allowed to founder on subterfuge. She put a hand on his chest and pulled herself out from under him.

In the bathroom, she looked at the flimsy cup with its thick rim, wondering whether it still worked. She held it up to the light. It seemed sturdy. She filled it with water and it didn't leak. What more could she do? She rummaged in a drawer and found, miraculously, an ancient tube of spermicide. It didn't seem to have an expiration date. She unscrewed the cap and squeezed some out, then eased the slippery disk into her body, where it floated like a moon—like a charm, warding off sperm and evil spirits. She washed her hands and opened the bathroom door.

But something had happened. She could feel it as she lay down beside him—a kind of coldness burning through his skin. She kissed him, but when he kissed her back his desire seemed stoked by something beyond the bed, beyond the life they had together. Still they went on touching each other in all the familiar ways, just as their marriage went on through breakfasts and dinners and evenings out and exchanges of information about when the car needed servicing. She began to cry, but silently, so that Theo, who had his eyes closed, wouldn't notice. So that he would mistake her trembling for the shudders of pleasure.

CHAPTER TWENTY-THREE

*T*he next day Dr. Rubin called Isabel from the hospital. Isabel could hear bells chiming and pages coming in over the public address system. "I only have a minute," Dr. Rubin said, "but I wanted to tell you before you heard from anybody else. Isabel, are you sitting down?"

Isabel, who had been on her way out, was standing in the kitchen with her handbag on her shoulder. There wasn't any place to sit that the phone cord would reach.

"I know this is going to be hard for you," Dr. Rubin said. "Try to take it as well as you can. For your sister's sake."

Isabel's heart pounded. "What is it?" she said. "What's happened to Alice?"

"No, not Alice," Dr. Rubin said impatiently. "It's Tina. I hate to tell you this, honey, but your sister Tina is pregnant. She's going to have a baby, and what's more, she's going to marry Soren Zank!"

It was amazing, Isabel thought, how her mother managed to sound mournful and exultant at the same time. The thought helped ease her back from the rush of terror. She let out her breath. "I know," she said. "Alice is getting married, so Tina has to do something even more dramatic."

"You know." Doc was taken aback.

"I just found out," Isabel said, hoping Doc's feelings weren't hurt by not being the first person Tina had told.

"You're not upset, are you?" Doc said. "I know how long you've been waiting. But these things just happen sometimes."

"Believe me," Isabel said, "I would rather never have children than have them with Soren Zank."

"Please don't talk that way in front of Tina," Dr. Rubin said. "I remember the way she used to follow you around, gazing up at you with those big brown eyes, when she could barely walk!"

"Not me," Isabel said. "Alice."

"You were six and starting a new school, and you thought you were such a big girl. You used to shut the door to your room right in her face. Well, I always said it was your right to be alone, if that was what you wanted."

Isabel drove to the zoo to meet her former boss, Allan Jefferson, the senior vet on the team. She had hardly been back since she'd quit, but she had agreed to take a look at some treefrogs the reptile and amphibian curator had purchased. She'd heard that the man who had got the job she'd wanted had quit after six months, wooed by a better offer from San Diego, so she didn't have to worry about running into him. She remembered when he had come to interview—Ed Mulcahy—a big man, very confident, smiling at everyone under his big mustache as if to say he already knew they'd hire him. He knew; Allan Jefferson knew; the head of the zoo knew. Apparently only Isabel hadn't known.

It was a hot summer day, and the entrance courtyard was crowded with families and camp groups. During the years of working here, Isabel had come almost not to see the children as she threaded her way among them, but today they caught her attention as though they were the creatures on exhibit. They were

exotic, at least to her, and as out of reach as if they were on the
other side of the glass. A boy of four or five held tightly to a red
balloon. A fat toddler chased the pigeons. She watched two girls
in plaid dresses holding hands as they skipped toward the ticket
window. She thought she could remember holding hands like
that with Alice.

She passed Monkey Junction, the statue of impalas leaping,
the vending machines selling soda, candy, disposable cameras.
She breathed in the smells of hot asphalt and animals and sun-
screen, the familiar smells of the place she had sped around in a
golf cart with her vet's bag, unlocking doors and gates with her
master keys, most of the animals known to her by sight. The
place she had wandered through with Alice and Cicily, awed by
the strange animals, fascinated by the way they moved and the
sounds they made, Cicily having to speak to her sharply to move
her from one enclosure to the next. She never wanted to leave the
one where she was, she might miss something—a lion roaring, a
wolf cuffing its brother, an orangutan turning to look straight at
her with its big brown eyes. She had loved the zoo as a child as
nowhere else in the world. She had wanted to be a zookeeper the
way other girls wanted to be ballerinas.

She went into the Penrose building, stopping to chat with the
secretary and the lab technician, exclaiming over the orphaned
baby marmot and hearing who had left in the past year and
which animals had died. As she approached Allan's lab, she
could hear him talking. Not yelling, although that was the ef-
fect, but scolding in his dry, precise, scathing voice. "Didn't you
X-ray the leg? That's the first thing you should have done! It's
not as though we're talking about a rhinoceros, though we have
X-rayed those more than once when the occasion required it. Go
back and do it."

Isabel waited in the hall until the recipient of the reprimand emerged, a young man who seemed to be trying to pull his head back into his body like a turtle.

"Hello," she said.

"Hello," the young man said glumly.

Allan stuck his head out of the door. "Isabel! Come in." He smiled out from his gray, leathery face, looking the proper veterinarian in his white lab coat and heavy boots. "Did you meet the new resident? Sandy's been with us, what is it, Sandy, six months now?"

"Three months," Sandy said.

"Three months! It seems longer. Sandy's from Cornell. Top of his class, allegedly. Sandy, this is Isabel Rubin. She was the resident before you. Isabel could diagnose a sick gorilla by the smell of its wind."

Then why didn't you hire me for the team, Isabel thought.

"Nice to meet you," Sandy said, and skulked off down the hallway.

"That one's got about as much sense as a yak," Allan said.

They went into the lab. Its scarred benches were cluttered with microscopes, syringes, cotton swabs, slides, and bottles of supplements, and it smelled of rubbing alcohol and dung.

"You should be nicer to people," Isabel said. "Crotchety isn't as charming as you think."

"Guess what?" Allan said. "Jesse's fertile again. We're going to try semen from that tiger in Seattle this time." Animals were often bred with animals from other zoos to promote genetic diversity. Sometimes the breeding was done in person, but increasingly, artificial insemination was used. A technique that Isabel herself had experienced, it failed as often as it succeeded, especially in the megavertebrates like tigers.

They went into the next room and looked at the small, brown, toadlike frogs. Orange lesions were scattered among their normal blackish markings.

"What's wrong with them?" Isabel asked.

"Some kind of intradermal mites. We can't get rid of them. I thought you might have some ideas."

"Now that I'm gone, you find you can't manage without me," she said.

Allan smiled his leathery, thin-lipped smile. "Actually, Isabel, I'm sure you heard that Mulcahy left. The job is available. Tom and I were wondering if you might still be interested in it." Tom was Tom Henderson, the head of the zoo.

Isabel stared at him. "You're joking," she said.

"We need someone who can start immediately," Allan said.

Isabel didn't know what to think. On the one hand, he was throwing her a lifeline. On the other, why should she come running back the moment they asked her to? Her pride resisted. "You're not going to do another search?" she said.

"Not if you'll say yes," Allan said. "You're a great vet, Isabel. If it had been up to me, we would have hired you instead of Mulcahy in the first place."

Isabel laughed. She didn't know whether to believe him or not. She didn't know, pride aside, whether she wanted to come back. All around her were animals—a juvenile red panda, a Bornean earless lizard, a marmoset—that should have been elsewhere, leading different lives. In forests, in rivers. How had they ended up here, looking out through cages in a climate-controlled building? Was the fact of their presence here acceptable? Were their lives acceptable lives? Safe, dull, predictable, unnatural. She shut her eyes against this train of thought, which she knew to be sentimental and unprofessional. Next thing I know, she thought, I'll become a vegetarian. Like Soren.

"Another thing you should know," Allan said, "is that my job will be available soon. I'm pretty sure Tom will hire an internal candidate."

"Your job?" Isabel said. "Are they finally firing you?"

Allan looked serious. "I'm almost seventy years old. Most people my age have already retired."

Isabel was astonished. She knew that Allan was getting older, but he had seemed like the last person in the world to consider retirement. He loved the work too much. He was the work, as far as she was concerned. "Are you all right?" she asked him. "Are you sick?"

"I'm perfectly fine! But that's part of the reason for leaving now. My mind is all right, my body has a few little aches and pains, nothing serious. But I look ahead to eighty. Eighty looks old. People don't walk so well, they don't think so well. I figure I have ten good years. I've thought about what I want to do with them."

"I would have thought you would have wanted to work."

"I have worked. Gertrude wants to travel. She wants to spend a year in Greece. We always meant to go. God knows how long we've been talking about it. How much more time do we have?" Allan's wife, Gertrude, was a plump, white-haired woman who smiled a lot but never had much to say. She had never held a job, had never gone to college. Isabel didn't understand the marriage. Allan was one of the few truly brilliant people she had ever met. He knew an extraordinary amount about animals. He was also sharp and judgmental, but he always spoke with affection of his sweet, rather dim wife, using the tone of voice he otherwise reserved for his favorite zoological specimens.

"Listen to me," he told Isabel. "You need to get back to work. What have you been doing with yourself all year? Sitting around, watching soap operas? Waiting for something to happen to you?

That's not how it works. An alligator doesn't sit on the riverbank and hope something will swim into its jaws."

"You're the alligator, not me," Isabel said. "Anyway, they'd never choose me for the director's job. I wasn't even first choice for the team."

"So you weren't first choice! So what?" Allan said. "A hundred and fifty people applied for that job. Is second choice really so bad?"

"Let's take a look at those mites," Isabel said.

The first year she worked at the zoo, Isabel had been part of a team of vets operating on Liza, the young Indian elephant, who had a tumor on her leg. She had never seen anything so huge operated on before, and it had been a difficult and exhausting procedure. But Liza had recovered and gone on to give birth to Zorro, the baby elephant beloved by the public. Zorro had raised zoo attendance figures by nearly a thousand per month. Today, on her way out, Isabel stopped by the elephant enclosure to take a look at him. Liza wasn't outside, but there was Zorro curling his tongue around the eggplants that lay on the ground, tossing them in the air and catching them while the spectators ahhed. She felt a flash of pride, remembering his mother limping around with the tumor on her leg and the moment in surgery when her huge heart had almost stopped beating.

"Look, Bill," someone said. "Betcha didn't know elephants ate eggplant."

"They have to eat something besides peanuts, I guess."

"I want peanuts! Dad, can we get peanuts?"

"In a minute, Ethan. Do you know why elephants eat eggplant, boys?"

Silence.

"Because *eggplant* starts with the letter *e*. Elephants only eat foods that begin with the letter *e*. Eggplant, escarole, and empanadas. Do you know what the botanical name for peanuts is? *Empeanutus crunchola*."

"Dad!"

"In fact, if I were you, I'd watch out. What letter does *Ethan* begin with?"

Isabel turned. Simon Goldenstern stood with a deadpan expression by the rail while a small boy punched him in the legs. An older boy stood beside him, skinny and shaggy haired, with big eyes fringed by dark lashes. Simon picked up the smaller child. "Stop that—get off of me, boy!" he said, holding Ethan close to him.

The child screeched with laughter, flailing his arms and legs.

"Dad," the older boy said, "let's go. I want to see the condors." He bit the corner of a cuticle as he spoke, and Isabel could see that his nails were chewed raw.

"Hello," she said.

Simon looked at her. "We do keep running into each other," he said, and then, to the boy he was holding, "Hey—didn't anyone teach you not to hit your father?" He set the child on the ground. "This is Ethan, and that big one there is Bill. Boys, this is Isabel. Is it okay if they just call you Isabel? We can do Mrs., but it seems so . . . I don't know. Smarmy."

Isabel laughed. "I can hardly say I'd prefer it now, can I?"

"Why should you care what I think?" he said. "The boys don't, do you, boys?" The children rolled their eyes. "You here by yourself?" Simon asked, looking around as though to see what children she was escorting.

"Yes," Isabel said.

"You like zoos, do you?"

She could feel him thinking she must really have nothing better to do. "I used to work here."

"Ahh. Were you a docent?" he asked, giving extra stress to the word as though he liked the feel of it in his mouth. "Do zoos have docents? We are here to visit the bird house for the twentieth time. Bill is interested in birds. He has all the accessories. Binoculars. A life list."

"Ornithology's interesting," Isabel said to Bill, who was nine or ten. "They have all kinds of programs here."

"We do all the ornithology programs, up and down the state," Simon said. "Bill particularly likes raptors."

"I'd like to have my own falcon," Bill said, looking up at Isabel with his father's golden brown gaze. "Like in medieval times."

"Dad!" Ethan tugged at Simon's pants. "Peanuts!"

"He's such a wholesome kid, isn't he," Simon said. "Other kids want candy, but Ethan wants peanuts. Peanuts you shall have, my boy! Onward." As they moved away across the asphalt, Simon called back over his shoulder, "See you at the wedding!"

Isabel waved, but he had leaned over to say something to the children and didn't see her.

CHAPTER TWENTY-FOUR

*I*sabel had been going to have dinner with her friend Claire, but in the afternoon Claire called to cancel. Her daughter was sick. "Where's Thomas?" Isabel said.

"Husbands," Claire said. "You think they should be able to handle things, but when push comes to shove."

Isabel wasn't going to argue with her.

There was nothing in the house to eat, so she made a quick shopping list and found her keys, wondering if she would trust Theo with the children as little as Claire trusted her husband, if she and Theo had children. She thought about Alice and Tina, the way the family would stretch outward now. There would be new patterns, new tensions and points of view. What kinds of fathers would Soren and Anthony be? Pretty lousy ones, probably, if their pasts were any guide. Would Alice and Tina always be the ones to stay home with sick children? Or would they, like Doc, hire Cicilys to do it for them? Sunk in the gloomy reflection that this would perhaps be one of the functions of a childless aunt, Isabel did her grocery shopping quickly, then drove home and let herself in through the kitchen door.

Music was playing in the living room. Isabel put down her bags. She hadn't expected Theo to be home. As she stood in the kitchen, someone said over the music, "We couldn't have kept this up forever. It would have ended sooner or later. So it's ending sooner."

"That's not the point. You cheated on me."

"Listen to yourself. *I* cheated!"

"With that full-of-crap, bleeding-heart, save-the-whales moron!"

"He's not a moron," Tina said. "And neither am I."

"You can't blame me for being angry, Tina. I'm angry!"

"I never promised never to have sex with anyone else."

"But you're marrying him!" Theo said.

"Yes!" Tina said. "I'm marrying him! You were never going to marry me, no matter how unhappy you and Isabel were!"

Isabel couldn't imagine what else they might possibly say, but she knew she couldn't bear to hear it. She forced her dead feet across the kitchen floor.

Her sister saw her first as she sagged in the doorway. "Oh," Tina said, taken aback. "We thought you were out."

Isabel looked at Theo. He was wearing a pin-striped suit and a red tie. He had had his hair cut and he was freshly shaved, and although he should have looked haggard—angry or desperate or guilty—he looked only smooth and clean, as though he were made of plastic. It was as though he had gotten so good at looking a part that even now, when everything was ripped open and lying bloody on the floor, he couldn't help himself.

Isabel smeared her tears into her cheeks with her fingers. Some part of her refused to accept that Tina was here even as she looked at her sister's angry face, her brown arms ending in tangerine-nailed fists. It seemed to her that all her life Tina had been there, worming in where she had no business, refusing to go away. Standing outside the door, pounding her fists to get in.

"It's not like you love him!" Tina said. Her china doll eyes were streaked with mascara and swollen with tears, as though she were the one whose life had been sacked and plundered and set aflame.

"How can you possibly know how I feel?" Isabel cried.

"You as much as said so! You never appreciate anything you have!"

"And you always think you deserve anything you want!" Isabel had never felt so wild. Fury seared her. She shouted, "Did you know Soren asked *me* to sleep with him? We had coffee at Xando, and he offered to make me pregnant! Is it true that it only takes him once?"

Tina's face blazed. "You're lying," she said.

"Ask him!" Isabel yelled. She sat on the sofa. It felt hot and prickly and stiff, a sofa chosen for how it would look in the room. "And you, you're such a—" Isabel cried, turning to Theo, trying and failing to think of a word to describe him. She hated him. She was furious with Tina, but she hated him.

He looked at her wearily, turning his palms up in a hopeless shrug, his thick wedding band catching the light. "Oh, Izzy," he said. "Oh, God. What did we do to end up here?"

Isabel's mind fizzled and sparked. "I didn't do anything!" she yelled, and began to weep so fiercely that she surprised herself. Because Tina was right. It wasn't as though she were losing anyone she still loved.

CHAPTER TWENTY-FIVE

*I*sabel went out through the front door and walked to Alice's apartment. No one tried to stop her. She thought she might regret having left the car, but she needed the time walking gave her. Not to think, for she was incapable of thinking, but for her mind to churn and roil down the sidewalk as she tried to comprehend what had happened. She was trembling so badly that halfway there she had to sit on a bench and wait for the strength to continue. It was evening and people were coming home from work, in dresses or coveralls, one in a nurse's uniform, another in khaki pants and a checked shirt. They carried purses and plastic grocery bags and looked eager to get where they were going. How did she look? Like an ordinary person tired after a long day or like the ghost she was? How many people walking down 12th Street on a sunny July evening were choked with betrayal or rejection, loss or despair?

As she approached Alice's, she tried to prepare herself for the possibility that Anthony might be there, too, but nobody was home at all. Isabel had a key, but she hadn't brought it. She began to cry again, there in the vestibule beside the steel mail slots. She sobbed in painful gasps, burying her face in her hands. She couldn't go home. The thought of taking a taxi to Devon, to her parents' house, came to her, and it seemed such an appropriate and terrible idea that she began to cry even harder. Then the street door opened and Alice came in, carrying her battered briefcase. Isabel fell, weeping, into her arms.

Alice helped Isabel up to the apartment and sat with her on the sofa. Isabel looked up at her sister's white, frightened face. "I've left Theo," she said.

Alice's look of terror eased slightly, and Isabel could tell she was already thinking it could be patched up somehow.

"He's having an affair," she said.

"Are you sure?" Alice asked.

"I went into the house and he and Tina were there together."

"No," Alice said. "No. You misunderstood."

"Yes, they are. Yes." The word was like a knife she was pressing into her own hand. "She was breaking up with him. Because of Soren. She's choosing Soren over him." Isabel lay down on the couch and sobbed.

Alice's heart skipped horribly in her chest. She found she could imagine that Tina would do it. Tina would borrow your favorite jeans and never give them back. She would take food from your plate, even if she were eating the same thing. And Theo had grown more opaque as the years passed, saying less, his green eyes glinting as if he wanted something but wasn't willing to say what. She eased Isabel's head into her lap and held her, smoothing the hair back from her forehead the way Cicily used to do when they were children. She remembered one time when Isabel had barreled in from the school bus weeping, flinging the front door open so that it banged against the wall and the cold, damp air swept in. Her face was red and her clothes were muddy, and she threw herself onto the floor. In a moment Cicily was beside her on the polished wood and had gathered her in her arms. There they sat for half an hour or more, Cicily stroking Isabel's

hair and speaking to her softly, as though she were a wild animal
she was trying to tame. Alice had never learned what caused it,
but she remembered Cicily saying to her later, "Your sister feels
things worse than other people. She tries to pretend she doesn't,
but she does."

Now, at last, Isabel stopped crying. She sat up and blew her
nose. "Is Anthony coming over?" she asked, both wanting to
know the answer and needing to feel she could have a normal
conversation, that normal life was not entirely blasted away.

"No. I just took him to the airport."

"The airport?" Isabel said blankly.

"He had to go to California. His friend Simon is going out
there for some reason, and he needed Anthony to go with him."

In all the turmoil, Isabel had forgotten the fragment of conversation she had overheard at the medical group. "Why?" she
asked.

"I don't exactly understand why," Alice said honestly.

"I saw Simon Goldenstern this morning," Isabel said.

"That's strange," Alice said. "What did he say?"

Isabel tried to remember. She thought if she could concentrate on Simon, she could be calm for a minute or two. But the
memory drifted out of reach. She saw Theo: cool, handsome,
weary, as though the weight of their life together were too much
for him. She saw Tina's teary, puffy face, the face Theo had
kissed. Tina, with her shallow thoughts and her selfishness and
her painted nails. Was that what Theo wanted? Tina, who took
whatever caught her eye. Who got pregnant without even trying.
Rage blazed through Isabel's skin, lit her up like a wronged god-
dess. She was shaking uncontrollably, and she held on to the
dusty cushions of the couch with both hands as though they
might save her, looking up into Alice's face as though there might
be something there for her, some calm or comfort. Alice put her

arms around her and held her tightly again, but it didn't help. They weren't children anymore, and Alice's embrace had lost whatever potency it had once possessed, back in those long-ago days when the worst thing one of them could say to the other was, "I wish I didn't have a sister!" Oh how Isabel wished that now.

CHAPTER TWENTY-SIX

*T*hat night Isabel slept on the foldout sofa in Alice's living room. Or rather, she didn't sleep but lay awake staring at the shadows on the walls and listening to the traffic on the street below. Eventually the sun lit up the cluttered, dusty, brightly colored room. Buses roared past and cars honked. People called to one another. It was Saturday morning. Isabel got out of bed and went into the kitchen alcove to make coffee. A minute later Alice came out of her bedroom in her robe, looking as though she hadn't slept, either.

They had agreed the night before that Isabel would stay with Alice for a few days at least, while she thought about what to do. The first thing was to get some clothes from the Quince Street house. The second was to tell their parents something. Both sisters agreed the elder Rubins would have to know Isabel had left Theo, but apart from that, it was hard to know what to tell them. Whatever it was, Isabel wanted to get it over with as quickly as possible. She wanted to do everything she had to do and then crawl into a corner and stay there.

On Quince Street, Alice went to ring the bell and Isabel waited in Alice's Civic. The front door opened and Alice stood talking to Theo on the stoop. Then she came back to the car and said, "He's going to go wait in the back."

Isabel didn't want Theo in her garden, but she nodded. She

was trembling again, and the facade of the house seemed to ripple as she went up the steps, as though she were looking up at it
from under water. She opened the door and went into the dark
hall. Theo's hand closed on her wrist. "Isabel," he said.

She jumped, but he held her tight.

"I told you to wait outside," Alice said. She used her lawyer's
voice, but it didn't work on him.

"I need to talk to you," Theo said.

Isabel tried to shake him off. "I don't want to talk!" Once a
large tree boa had wrapped itself around her arm so tightly, it had
taken two men to get it off.

"I'm sorry," Theo said. "I want to tell you I'm sorry. I did a
terrible thing, but I love you."

She stared at him, at his tired eyes and his taut face. He
looked as though he meant what he said, but he had lied to her
for so long that she thought she probably didn't know how to
tell. "How long was it going on?" she asked.

"Not long, Isabel. God, I wish it had never happened at all.
It was a mistake. I was so unhappy about the way things were
with us."

She wished he would stop using her full name. What did it
mean? It made him seem as if he were reading lines. "Let go of
me!" she said.

Theo let go. "Things have not been good the last couple of
years," he said. "I admit that. But it hasn't all been my fault."

"We were trying to have a family," Isabel said. "Or I thought
that was what we were trying to do."

"You were obsessed with a person who didn't exist!" Theo
said. "You never used to be like that. When you were working, at
least you had something real to focus on!"

"When I was *working*?" Isabel cried. "What does that have to
do with anything? Why are we even *talking* about me? You lied!

You let me take terrible, awful drugs and all the time you were going out and screwing my own sister!"

"I'm sorry," Theo said. "I said I was sorry."

"So you're sorry," Isabel said. "So what?"

"So," Theo said, "I want us to have another chance."

Isabel looked at him in disbelief. She felt she must be missing something, something he could see that she couldn't that made his words somehow reasonable. "I think you just can't bear the idea that anyone would leave you," she said, and walked past him up the stairs.

All the way to Devon, Isabel sat with her knees pulled to her chest. Theo had said that she had changed. He said he loved her. *Had* she changed? Could he possibly still love her? She burned with hate for him. She could see, etched in the blackness inside her eyes, what his head would look like as it exploded: the smug look on his face blasted away.

The car stopped. Isabel looked up and found herself at her parents' house. The roses were blooming. The flower beds were neatly edged and mulched. The air-conditioner compressor buzzed above the sounds of the birds.

Alice looked at Isabel.

"Let's get it over with," Isabel said.

They rang the bell. Prince barked on the other side of the door, and their mother's voice called, "Just a minute! I have to get control of the dog!" This was her way of making robbers think she had a Doberman.

"It's Alice and Isabel," Alice said.

Dr. Rubin opened the door. "My goodness," she said. "Come in. If you'd called first, I would have had something in the house for lunch. Down, Prince, don't jump. Are you all right, Isabel? What's wrong?" She put her strong, ringed hand to Isabel's face. "Are you sick?"

Isabel pulled away. "I'm okay."

For a moment Dr. Rubin looked hurt. She picked up Prince and stroked him. The little dog panted, watching the sisters with his bright black eyes. "All right," Doc said, and led the way into the living room. "I was just talking to Tina on the phone. Which caterers were you thinking of using, Alice? Tina says Clifton's has gone downhill, but Market Square is so expensive. Of course, Soren says the sky's the limit, but there's such a thing as virtue in moderation."

They had reached the living room, in which the faded couches and battered coffee table of their childhood had long since been replaced by low, uncomfortable, elegant furniture from an Italian design store. Only the rug was the same, linking the people they were now to the people they had been. Judge Rubin sat in an armchair, reading the paper, wearing khakis and an old shirt with the sleeves rolled up. He smiled when he saw his daughters and got to his feet.

Isabel let him embrace her. Her only idea was to put one foot in front of the other, to get through the next half hour however she could.

He looked at her with his sharp eyes. "You look tired."

"I'm all right."

"Your mother hasn't slept a wink. You'd think she'd never had a daughter get married before." He smiled at her with a thin warmth like winter sunlight, all the more precious for its scarcity.

"I don't know what to do about Tina," Doc said. "She wants to have an entirely vegetarian menu. But people will be coming from all over the country! They'll expect something substantial. I'm not saying it has to be steak, but we can't just serve them carrot sticks."

"It's her wedding," Judge Rubin said in the tone in which he might have said, "It's her funeral."

Dr. Rubin, who had clearly run up against this dead end before, changed the subject. "Where's Theo?" she asked Isabel.
"Don't tell me he's at the office on a beautiful Saturday morning."

Isabel looked up into her mother's broad, irritating, familiar
face. She tried to imagine what would happen to it when she
spoke, but she couldn't. "Theo and I are separating," she said,
and stopped. Surely there was more to say than this, but she
couldn't think what it was.

"You're what?" Dr. Rubin said. She looked frightened, as
though a part of the roof had just fallen in.

Isabel didn't say anything. It seemed foolish to repeat it.

"What did she say?" Dr. Rubin asked, turning to Alice. Her
expressive face had gone strangely blank, as though she hoped
she was mistaken in what she'd heard and was waiting for confir-
mation.

"She said that she and Theo are separating," Alice said, and
Dr. Rubin's face went from red to white. She had worried for a
long time about what Isabel's failure to get pregnant would mean
for her marriage, and although she usually had trouble keeping
her thoughts to herself, she had been careful not to say anything
about this. Indeed, only occasionally did she even permit the
thought to ascend to her conscious mind. Most of the time it rat-
tled around in the darkness like a mouse in the walls that you
hope will go away.

"Oh, honey," she said, crossing the room and embracing her
middle child, the stubborn, unreachable one who shut herself up
inside her head and peered out suspiciously through her sharp
brown eyes. "Oh, Isabel, I'm so sorry! You must be so unhappy!" She held her daughter tight and rocked her the way she
used to during the long, gray, colicky nights when Isabel was an
infant—so long ago. Before she herself had ever delivered a baby.

Before she had gone to medical school, when the familiar, hectic, fulfilling life she led now lay entirely in the future.

Isabel's face wore the closed look she always had when she was trying not to cry. "I'm all right!" she said, pulling herself out of her mother's arms.

"What happened?" Judge Rubin said sternly, seeking refuge in the facts. "These things don't just come out of nowhere!"

"All marriages go through trouble spots," Dr. Rubin said. "You just have to get through them. Even the best ones aren't wine and roses every minute."

Still, Isabel said nothing. She looked down at the rug with its pattern of fruit and flowers. A garden design, it was called. She remembered suddenly the store on Lancaster Avenue where her parents had chosen it while she and Alice played among the piles of rugs. A dusty store with high, dirty windows and a smell of far-away places.

Dr. Rubin, increasingly agitated, looked from one sister to the other.

"Theo had an affair," Alice said at last.

Isabel flinched.

Dr. Rubin looked startled, as though she had just managed to shore up one section of the roof and now another had caved in. "Not Theo," she cried. "He's never been the warmest person in the world, but he's solid! I've always said he was solid."

"Isabel," Judge Rubin said, "have you tried talking things through with him? Is he determined to keep seeing this woman?"

Isabel looked up unwillingly from the entwined flowers of the rug. "He's not seeing her anymore," she said.

"Well," her father said, "then there's hope!"

"No," Isabel said. "No, there isn't."

"Oh, but sweetheart, you have to try to patch things up!" Dr. Rubin said. "After twelve years, you can't just walk away!"

Isabel made her voice as forceful and steady as she could manage. "There's no hope of patching things up. I didn't come here to discuss my options. I came to tell you what happened."

"You're upset," Dr. Rubin said. "Of course you are, after what you've been through. We're on your side, honey, one hundred percent. Only you don't want to be making important decisions when you're so worked up!"

How many times in her life had Isabel had to listen to speeches like this, as though she and not her mother were the impulsive, emotional one? "I know what I'm doing," she said. She turned to her father, who, at least, could generally be counted on to insert some rationality into any situation.

But Judge Rubin frowned. His gray eyes were stern and stony, and he looked as though, for once in his life, he was in complete agreement with his wife.

Isabel thought about Tina. She only had to say a few words and the family would be destroyed. Wasn't it already a terminal animal limping toward slaughter? Wouldn't it be better to put it out of its misery?

But no. Families were never destroyed. They just went on and on, and the more a fuss you made, the more miserable things were for you. It was better to say as little as possible.

CHAPTER TWENTY-SEVEN

*I*t wasn't very comfortable staying with Alice. The sofa bed made Isabel's back ache, and the whole apartment was so small and crowded that it was difficult for the two of them to maneuver around each other. Still, Isabel was grateful to be there. She felt she had been living in comfort too long, that comfort had dulled her. It was as though she had been sleepwalking and had awakened now to a sharp ocean wind in her face. But when she tried to think about where she would go from here, she found herself lying on the sofa bed again, exhausted by the existence of the future.

Theo called. "Where are the three-way lightbulbs?" he wanted to know. It was ten o'clock on Monday morning.

"Are you at work?" Isabel asked him.

"No. I can't find the bulbs. Don't you keep them in the linen closet?"

"Why are you calling me?" Isabel said.

"I love you," he said. "I want you to come back."

"If you love me," she said, "why did you sleep with Tina?"

"That's behind us," Theo said. "It's over."

Isabel hung up the phone. Her heart was pounding. For years Theo had barely paid attention to her, but now that she was gone he wanted her back.

The next day he called again. "The oil company wants to know if we want a price cap on our bill. Do we do that?"

"Why did you lie to me?" she asked. "Why did you say you wanted a family when you were actually destroying the little we had?"

"It was always little to you, wasn't it?" Theo said. "Without a baby."

"You know what I mean!" Isabel said.

"I know that your whole life had become reduced to a single obsession," Theo said.

"Then why do you want me back?" she cried. She had prided herself on the way she had kept on going through all the shots and the syringe inseminations, the hormone-induced sleepless nights. "To deal with the oil company?"

"I can't believe you can even think that!" Theo said. "I love you!"

"You haven't been acting like someone who loves someone," Isabel said.

"Goddamn it, Izzy, what do you want from me?" he said, sounding more like himself.

Isabel hung up and turned off the ringer. She lay on Alice's couch and thought about her garden, wilting in the summer heat. Theo would never think to water it, and why should he? She hadn't even liked him to be out there.

She tried to stop thinking about Theo. She wanted to save her strength to put on a decent face for Alice when she got home from work. At least Anthony was in California. She wasn't disrupting Alice's life as badly as she might have.

That night at dinner, Isabel told her sister, "When Anthony comes back you can go out and do stuff. You can spend the nights at his apartment. I'll be fine, as long as I can stay here a little longer."

"Don't worry," Alice said. "I won't leave you alone." She looked tired. She had new vertical lines over the bridge of her nose.

"Are you listening to me? I'm worried you won't leave me alone! I don't want to mess things up for you."

"You're not going to mess anything up!" Alice said.

Anthony was supposed to be back on Wednesday, but twice he postponed his flight, and by the middle of the following week, with the wedding getting ever closer, it wasn't at all clear what his plans were. Isabel, seeing how hard Alice was working not to be concerned, didn't ask too many questions, so it was hard to know if Anthony was telling her as little as he seemed to be. Things were "going slowly," Alice said. Complications "had arisen." Anthony expected them to be cleared up soon, and he'd call her the very minute he got his ticket. Isabel wondered who was taking care of his patients. Doc hadn't said anything about his absence, but then again Isabel had managed almost not to speak to her mother for nearly two weeks.

Gradually, Isabel began to feel stronger. Her attempts to think beyond the next half hour were still hopeless, but she had more physical energy. She often found herself on her feet, looking for an outlet for it. She turned on Alice's computer and caught up on her e-mail, accepting comfort electronically from Sarah and Claire and other friends, declining invitations for a cup of coffee or a meal. E-mail was fine—remote, quiet, controllable—but meeting people face-to-face was still beyond her. She didn't want to see the pity in their eyes. She didn't want Sarah—short and spiky-haired and sarcastic, who had never gotten along with Theo—to say or imply that Isabel should have known. Should she have known? Had he always had the potential for what he had done? Was it lurking in him like a bad gene, or like a nettle seed in rocky ground, waiting for rain? To drown out these thoughts, Isabel cleaned Alice's apartment. She emptied drawers and scrubbed their back corners. She took the dusty curtains to the Laundromat. The next afternoon, more restless than ever, she was out on the streets, walking.

She had not thought about which way to go, but her legs took her north on 12th Street, past the church with its redbrick spire and the restaurant where she and Alice sometimes used to meet for breakfast. In another ten minutes she was at the edge of her own neighborhood. She passed the grocery store where she shopped and the local florist, and still she kept going—past Pine Street, past Panama, and here was Spruce now, and she turned up it, walking along under the canopies of the familiar trees.

On Quince, Isabel stood on the brick sidewalk. Her house looked the same as it always had, tall and handsome. The only sign of her absence was the grass that had grown long in the tiny square of front yard. She took out her key and let herself in.

It was a warm, breezy day, but inside everything was shut and stifling. Isabel went around pulling back curtains and opening windows. If she had expected to find a mess, she was disappointed. The couch cushions looked as if they had not been sat on at all. There were no dishes lying on the counters, only a plate and an empty cup in the sink. The house felt listless, lifeless, like a depressed person who didn't want to be disturbed.

She pushed open the French doors and went out into the garden. The coreopsis, the hollyhocks, and the nasturtiums all looked more or less as she had left them. The grass, as in the front, had grown, but the biggest change was against the east wall, where the cleome had burst into bloom. The five-foot plants sprawled out along the brick, pale pink petals drooping from the spidery fingers of the leaves. The sight of it was a shock, and it came to Isabel as she looked at them that life could not be suspended just because you were unhappy. Marriages dissolved, people fell sick or succumbed to depression, families drifted apart—and still life continued on, gorgeous and inexorable. She sat down, feeling on the verge of some great decision. She was still sitting there half an hour later when Theo came in in his gray suit and polished shoes.

"Oh, Izzy!" he said, and came across the bricks to put his arms around her.

She leaned into him and let him take her weight, putting her hands up against the fine material of his suit jacket. He kissed her, and she found herself waiting for something. For her heart to leap, perhaps. For forgiveness to fill her up, or joy, or at least a settled resignation.

"I'm so glad to see you." Theo tilted her chin up with his finger and looked down at her. He wore a serious expression, behind which Isabel thought she could see the glint of victory. He kissed her again, but she drew away and sat down. He sat beside her and covered her hand gently with his. It was the way she used to treat animals at the zoo, wooing them in order to (for instance) ram a needle into their haunches. Gloom enveloped her like a kind of gauze. It was so familiar, sitting in silence here in the garden with him.

"Hey, guess what." Theo said after a while. "We got the permits to go ahead with the building in Pennsauken! Remember the one? The EPA guys had a million questions, but in the end we worked it out. We got our variances, and the neighbors are going to get a little park, and there are clauses spelling out every procedure for every contingency if soil contamination turns out to be above levels once they start digging. But I don't foresee any liability. I wrote those clauses myself, and they're watertight."

He paused, and Isabel knew she was supposed to say something, but what was there to say? So there was going to be another office park on contaminated ground in New Jersey. In another minute she would go into the kitchen and start dinner.

Life would resume as though it were a stopped clock that could be wound up and reset for the correct time.

But still she sat where she was as the light in the garden shifted and faded and the shadows lengthened across the bricks of the patio. The streetlights came on.

"Isabel?" Theo said. "Izzy? What are you looking at?"

"Oh, the cleome."

"They look great," Theo said. "You've always had such a touch with the flowers."

Isabel looked at him. "What?" she said, a worm of anger startling to life. "I what?"

Theo blinked at her. "What did I say?" he said.

"The flowers. I have such a *touch* with the flowers!" It seemed to sum up everything—how small her life had become. The way he patronized her.

"I don't know what you're talking about," Theo said.

"You come home and tell me about your triumphs, and admire my flowers!" She was starting to feel wild again, angry and desperate.

"Izzy," Theo said, "what am I supposed to talk to you about? What else are you doing in life right now?"

"I *was* trying to have a baby!" Isabel said.

"Why couldn't you just have found a normal job?" Theo asked. "Why did you always have to be so exceptional? Why was there only one job in the whole world for you?"

"Not the whole world," Isabel said. "Just Philadelphia." She could hear how ridiculous it sounded.

"If you like to garden, be a gardener! Something. A horticulturist!"

"Why do you keep talking about this?" Isabel demanded. To her mortification, she began to cry. "Are you saying you slept with Tina because she had a *job*?"

"Isabel," Theo said patiently, "I can't make you forgive me. You're going to have to do that yourself."

"I don't forgive you," Isabel said. She got up and looked at him, at the angry, turned-down corners of his mouth and his soft, short hair and his green eyes. Why did people say green eyes were serpent's eyes? She couldn't think of a single species of snake with eyes that color. Snakes were always being maligned, but it was people you couldn't trust. "I don't forgive you," she said again, and went out through the gate, hurrying up the alleyway before she could change her mind.

It was a beautiful night. A handful of stars were visible in the orange-tinted sky above the rooftops and the gray shapes of the trees. The air was warm on her face, but she felt like a shadow moving along the dark streets. No job, no child, no husband: she was all failure. She was air moving through air.

And yet, as she crossed streets with long strides, as she ducked past slow-moving old women pushing carts of laundry and couples walking side by side, not speaking—as she smelled honeysuckle blooming in someone's yard and the sharp scent of a lit match—she began slowly to come back to herself. She inched back into her own body, filled up the space. Because she was free after all, wasn't she? Free of a marriage in which she had been unhappy for years. Theo had cut a door for her and she had escaped through it, had tugged it open and fled. Her will was still intact. It flexed itself stiffly like a disused muscle, wondering how much it could lift. She was healthy, she was educated; she was relatively young. She could get a job tomorrow—some kind of job. Maybe it was true that not working had been a mistake: a mistake born of arrogance. She didn't have to be a herpetologist or a zoo veterinarian, there were lots of things she could do. Weren't there? The brighter stars in Cassiopeia twinkled down at her from the sky, and she began to walk more slowly. Music seeped out onto the street from an open window, and it struck her as though a string inside her had been plucked that she had been given a gift. Life lay all around her. It was the air she moved through.

She walked east through Old City, where Philadelphia had begun. Here and there you could still stumble across a cobblestone street, across eighteenth-century houses with painted cornices and street mirrors. Beyond Front Street lay the Delaware River, a wide black sleeping snake across the back of which the great bridges arched: the Walt Whitman, the Ben Franklin, the Betsy Ross. She loved the names of them and the way the city, spreading weedlike in three directions (and overrunning even the Schuylkill River as though it were nothing but an irrigation ditch), ended abruptly here in a clean line the way a garden would be edged with a sharp shovel. Amid the smells of car exhaust, and the sulfur of the chemical plants, and the acrid stink of the refineries, she could smell the sea, and her heart lifted.

It was late by the time she made her way back to Alice's and climbed the stairs. She was tired from walking, but her mind still felt clear and her spirits were high with edgy euphoria. She had stopped and bought a bottle of wine, but she put down the bag as soon as she came through the door and saw her sister sitting in the corner of the sofa in the dark, staring blankly out the window into the glare of the streetlight.

"What happened?" Isabel asked.

Alice turned and looked at her. She tried to smile, but the effort only brought tears to her eyes. "He's not coming back," she said.

"What do you mean?" Isabel asked severely. "Did you talk to him?"

Alice shook her head.

"Alice," Isabel said, "I know it's hard. But he'll be back! Just give him time!"

Alice held out a sheet of paper crushed in her white hand. It was a printout of an e-mail message. Isabel took the paper and, with growing anxiety, smoothed it out as well as she could.

"Dearest Alice," it began. Isabel looked up at her sister.

"Read it," Alice said.

Dearest Alice,

I am no doubt even a greater idiot than I imagine myself to be to give up the loveliest angel that ever presented herself to man. Being in your presence is like a drug, and I would willingly subject myself to your sweet anesthesia forever. Going cold turkey from you these last weeks has been the most painful experience of my life. But it has also brought back to me feelings of consciousness and—don't laugh—duty that I can no longer blind myself to, no matter how much I might prefer to remain happily senseless.

I told you that I was coming to California to help a friend. That was a lie. I hid from you what I should have been open about—that I had promised my son I would visit him, and that I knew I had to keep this promise. Why I couldn't tell you the truth and trust to your goodness to understand, God only knows. I felt that it would hurt you even to mention my children—my obligations apart from you—despite what you have often said about wanting to know them and be a mother to them. I guess I felt this was too much to ask even from someone as loving and generous as you. Besides which, I admit I selfishly wanted all your love and attention for myself. I wanted to *will* myself back to the young man you made me feel I was again! I wanted to start my life over again with you.

But as I now see clearly, starting over is only a kind of a pipe dream. I've tried it before and failed, and I don't dare try it again. It wouldn't be fair either to you or to the children I already have, two innocents who I have put through some terrible times. I know there is no one on earth more likely than you to understand that, having reclaimed them, I cannot leave them again now. My responsibilities are here, wherever my heart might prefer to reside.

I suspect, too, knowing you, that you are likely to offer to throw everything up—your life, your work, your family—and join me here. But this I cannot even consider. You have your whole life in front of you.

I will think of you always with tenderness.

—Anthony

Isabel put her arms around her sister and held her tight. The thin shoulders shook. Alice's tears seeped into Isabel's hair. Isabel had thought she would never again have to ask herself why these things happened to Alice—bad luck, or bad judgment, or something invisible about her sister: some blemish or crookedness only men could see.

"Look at us," Alice cried. "Two old, spinstery sisters. Are we going to live together forever? Get old? Two old crones, doing needlepoint!"

"Oh, Alice," Isabel said. "I don't think anyone does needlepoint anymore."

"Yes, they do. I see old women doing it on the bus."

Isabel tried to recall the thoughts that had sustained her during the evening; to feel again the sense of freedom and possibility. But even as she sat here, the confidence she had felt on the riverbank began, under the influence of the cluttered room and the glare of the streetlight and the false, terrible words sprayed grayly on the crumpled paper, to drain away.

"You have a great life, Alice," she said a little desperately, trying to convey hope and strength but feeling instead that her words were matches snuffed out as soon as they were lit. "You love your work. You have good friends. You're financially independent. It's not the nineteenth century anymore. So what if you don't get married? Men are rats! Just look at Theo."

Alice sat up and blew her nose again. "You're right," she said. "Of course you're right."

But they didn't meet each other's eyes. They both knew that while they were not impoverished ladies of an earlier era for whom marriage "must be their pleasantest preservation from want," it was equally true that married life formed the core of their expectations and desires. Whatever they claimed to believe to the contrary, neither of them was likely to be very happy without it.

CHAPTER TWENTY-EIGHT

*S*ome days, getting divorced seemed like a full-time job. With Alice's help Isabel found a lawyer, but still there were a hundred decisions to be made, issues to be negotiated and renegotiated, mostly involving money. Eventually Theo offered to move out of the house and let Isabel live there, but she didn't want to. She wanted a place of her own. It occurred to her that the only year of her life she had lived by herself had been when she was twenty-two years old.

For the moment, however, she didn't have enough cash for an apartment. She had started looking through the classified section of the newspaper. The rents shocked her, as did her own ignorance about them. She saw now, sitting at Alice's cluttered, rickety eating table in the corner, that she had not been masquerading—as she had sometimes liked to think—as an affluent, sheltered housewife. She had really been one. And now she would have to become something else. What, she didn't know. She didn't want to go back to the zoo. She felt that her only hope was to move forward, to carve out a new place for herself.

In the meantime she took care of Alice, who, after the first night, refused to talk about Anthony. "I've closed that chapter," she said shortly when Isabel asked her how she was. "I'm moving on."

"All right," Isabel said. "But you need to be sad before you can move on."

"Don't tell me what I have to do," Alice said.

Isabel didn't want to argue with her. In the mornings, Alice got up and got dressed and went to work. In the evenings, she came home and pretended to eat the food Isabel cooked for her, and Isabel chattered about whatever she could think of—her errands, whom she had seen on the street, what she had heard on the news. Sometimes her own loquacity reminded her of her mother, which made her wonder about the origins of Doc's supercharged cheerfulness.

Poor Dr. Rubin hardly knew how to think about the current situation. Only a few days before, all three of her daughters had seemed on the verge of being well settled, and now two of them were cast back to the limbo of singleness. She couldn't help feeling partly responsible for what had happened to Alice. She had seen it coming, hadn't she? She had failed Alice, she felt, in giving up her opposition to the marriage. She should have stuck to her guns. But at least the whole thing was over now. At least the blow had come before the wedding. It could have been much worse.

As for Isabel, Dr. Rubin had sympathy for her unhappiness, but she believed that Isabel was wrong not to take Theo back if he was willing to come back. She felt that Isabel was not taking seriously enough the damage she was permitting to happen to her life and that she was likely to regret it later. Dr. Rubin took to phoning in the evenings, partly to check on Alice and partly to see if she couldn't nudge Isabel back in the direction of safety, stability, and reason.

"Have you talked to Theo?" she asked.

"What is there to say?" Isabel replied, impatient to get back to the TV show she was watching about vampire bats in Argentina. "'How many of our marriage vows have you broken, Theo? Just the one?'"

Dr. Rubin changed tacks. "At least tell him you want to think it over. Buy yourself some time."

"I have thought it over," Isabel said.

"Isabel. The hurt is so fresh right now you can't see past it! But who's to say you won't feel different in a month or two?"

Isabel shut her eyes. "I won't feel different," she said. "I don't want to be married to Theo anymore. What he did was unforgivable." Tina's name rang in her head like an alarm bell, and it took all her self-restraint not to say it out loud.

"But everyone makes mistakes! I would have thought you were a more forgiving person!"

"Well, I'm not," Isabel said. She opened her eyes. On the screen, the vampire bat hung on the neck of a cow, feeding. The cow fidgeted, a dark shape in a gray, flat, nocturnal landscape. It shook its horned head and stamped, but the bat clung on.

"Was there something else?" Dr. Rubin suggested. "Was there another problem you haven't told me about?"

Isabel guessed this was her mother's way of asking about sex. Rather than answer she said, "I wish you would try to see things from my point of view!"

"I do see them from your point of view, sweetheart! What I'm asking is that you listen—just for a moment—to the voice of experience."

This was too much for Isabel. "What do you mean, the 'voice of experience'? Are you telling me that Dad—"

"Of course not!" Dr. Rubin said.

On the television, the bat flew away, sated, into the purple night. It wasn't its fault that it fed on blood, that was what nature had made it to do. The bat didn't have a choice, but what about

Theo? What about Tina? Was she made to sleep with her sister's husband? And if so, what had made her that way?

As for Tina's situation, Dr. Rubin's attitude was clear. The uncomfortable circumstances of the engagement were forgotten as quickly as possible and only the happy fact itself dwelt upon. The wedding was scheduled for mid-September. The couple would go to City Hall in the morning, and in the evening there would be a spectacular ceremony presided over by a friend of Soren's, a Buddhist of German-Jewish extraction with a mail-order officiating certificate valid only in California. Isabel didn't see how she was going to bear it, but there was no way to get out of it. She hadn't had to see Tina at all in the past few weeks, at least, and she tried as much as possible to forget she existed. Still, Tina had a way of worming herself into conversations.

"Maid of honor sounds better than matron of honor, at least," Alice said one evening while she and Isabel were watching the local news.

"At the rate things are happening," Isabel said, "you could be engaged to a whole new person by then."

Alice smiled, but it was such a sad smile that Isabel regretted saying anything.

"What a horrible wedding it's going to be," Isabel said. "It hardly seems worth the effort. I bet their marriage doesn't last five years!" She could feel the anger rising inside her even as she tried to keep her tone light.

"Maybe it will," Alice said. "Soren's an openhearted person. And generous."

"Rich, you mean. And free with his affections."

"I think they can make each other happy," Alice said.

"They wouldn't be getting married at all if Tina weren't pregnant," Isabel said, pushing away, as she always did when confronted with Tina's pregnancy, the thought that Tina had been sleeping with Theo not very long ago. Tina had sworn to Alice that the baby was Soren's, and what else was there to do but try to believe her? "Can you believe Tina's going to be the first one of us to have a baby? It's flabbergasting! Tell me you're flabbergasted, Alice."

Alice didn't answer. She was staring at the television. "Isabel," she said, and pointed at a face that, as Isabel looked to see who it was, seemed at first only vaguely familiar. But as it turned toward the camera, the well-known features seemed to leap off the screen at the same moment the reporter said:

"Cicily Lamont, known locally as the 'Bird Lady,' lives alone in this modest house in Alapocas, Delaware—unless you count her dozens of feathered housemates."

"My God," Isabel said, and leaned toward Alice. Cicily was older, certainly, and her face was thinner. The bones showed through the finely wrinkled skin, but it was her: the same thin nose, the same sharp eyes softened by affection, trained now not on little girls, but on the bright feathered creatures that fluttered and called all around her.

"I started with one little canary," Cicily said, her voice releasing in Isabel's chest a rush of memory and emotion. Here before her eyes was the woman who had spent more waking hours with her than her own mother; who had said good-bye one day and hopped on a bus never to be seen again. She couldn't speak. "My husband had died and a friend gave me Pete as a gift, for company," Cicily said from the flickering screen. "That was fifteen years ago."

"Her husband died!" Alice cried. "I wonder if Doc knew?" Nineteen years earlier, Cicily had left them to get married. It was the year Alice went away to college and Tina was ten.

"After that," Cicily said, "I found a blue jay fledgling on the ground, half-starved, and I just took him on home. I figured I knew about taking care of birds, I could take care of him!" She laughed, her face breaking open with amusement, the sight of it so familiar that it brought tears to Isabel's eyes, although she would have said she didn't remember Cicily laughing.

The reporter's voice-over came on: "But taking care of wild birds was a whole new ball game—as Lamont, who works by day as a file clerk at a local hospital, soon found out. Still, the little blue jay survived. Soon Lamont found herself playing nanny to a whole host of birds, both wild- and captive-born."

"I didn't know then that baby birds imprinted on you," Cicily said. "Well, there was a lot I didn't know! But the word got around, and then the neighbors started bringing me hawks with broken wings. Macaws no one wanted. Even an eagle with a bullet wound someone had pulled out of the river." The camera, pulling back, showed a room filled with birds of all sizes, chirping and squawking, fluttering on the furniture and the windowsills. It cut to an outdoor flight made of chicken wire, twelve feet high, with a red-tailed hawk inside perched on a post.

"Eventually Lamont, who never finished high school, got certified as a wildlife rehabilitator. Now she tends to a flock of up to twenty feathered friends at a time! She loves the company, but when an injured wild bird is ready to be released"—the camera showed Cicily with a kestrel lifting off from her hand—"that's when the Bird Lady of Alapocas is really flying high."

A commercial for dishwashing soap came on. Alice and Isabel stared at each other. "Oh!" Alice said. "Oh, she looked happy, didn't she? I thought she looked great!"

"She always loved birds," Isabel said.

"Only four years with her husband," Alice said. "What was his name?"

"I can't remember." What Isabel remembered was the blue, battered suitcase waiting by the door in the hall, the room under the stairs with the mattress stripped bare, the smell of Cicily's hair oil lingering.

"How old was she when she married him?" Alice asked.

"She would never say how old she was."

"We should call her," Alice said. "How could we have entirely lost touch with her!"

"Imagine her becoming a rehabber," Isabel said. "In a different world she might have been a vet. Or a doctor."

"She looks happy enough being what she is."

"Was she happy when she took care of us?" Isabel said. "Maybe she likes birds better than she liked children."

"Maybe they give her less trouble," Alice said.

Isabel remembered how quiet the house had been in the afternoons, after Cicily left. Alice had gone away to college, and Doc had arranged for Tina to go to the Jacksons after school (Maureen Jackson was Tina's best friend). The houses on their street were far apart. Every now and then you could hear a car pass, but mostly there was only the sound of the wind in the trees and the furnace cycling on. Isabel was fifteen, but the silence spooked her. How could Cicily have gotten married? She had always thought of their family as the center of Cicily's existence, and it was a shock to realize it wasn't true. Of course it wasn't. Once she thought about it, she was ashamed to have ever believed it was. She was still ashamed.

Alice picked up the phone and called directory assistance. There was no listing for any Lamonts in Alapocas, or for anyone named Grenadier, which had been Cicily's maiden name. She got the numbers for a handful of Lamonts and one Grenadier in the surrounding towns and tried them, but none of the people she reached knew Cicily. She called Doc and asked her, but the last number Doc had was years out of date.

"Birds?" Doc said over the phone. "Imagine that. She always

liked birds. She had the patience to watch them that I never had. I remember once she told me she'd seen a pileated woodpecker in the yard. She showed me a picture of it in a book, but I never saw it. Or maybe I did and I didn't recognize it. After all, I can hardly tell a sparrow from a crow.

"Too bad about her husband," Doc went on. "I remember how surprised I was when she told me she was getting married. Somehow Cicily never seemed to me like the marrying kind. But I guess I was just wrong about that."

CHAPTER TWENTY-NINE

*A*lice's colleague Jaime invited Alice and Isabel to a salsa dance party. He was going with his partner, Tom, a high school chemistry teacher. "I told him no," Alice said to Isabel. "I said I couldn't enjoy it."

But Isabel thought it might cheer Alice up. "You love to dance," she said. "It won't be like going on a date."

"Do you want to go?" Alice asked.

"Sure," Isabel said.

Alice's face brightened incrementally.

The dance party was held in a club in Powelton Village, a one-story building set back from the street behind a courtyard. Inside was a big, low-ceilinged room with a bar at one end and a low stage for the band. The walls were painted with murals, one of farmworkers digging, another of people dancing. Colorful wooden masks hung from nails all around the room just below the level of the ceiling.

There were only a few people there when they arrived for the lesson before the dance. The instructor, who was also the singer for the band, sized up the clumsy-looking beginners. "Why don't you come up here," he said to Alice. She was wearing a sleeveless cotton dress embroidered with flowers, and when she began to dance, even without any music, she looked less weary and unhappy than she had in weeks. She and the instructor demonstrated the way to hold your partner, the up and back of the step, the critical hitch of hesitation. Alice's skirt floated around her legs as the instructor spun her. The rest of the line struggled to follow along.

Isabel danced with Tom, a tall, stooping, red-faced man in baggy pants and a blue dress shirt. "I hate dancing," he said, sidestepping the wrong way with his big feet in their worn-out sneakers. "I have trouble with left and right. Did you know even molecules are left- or right-handed? Luckily we don't get into that much in high school. Sorry." He hopped back, pulling Isabel off balance.

"That's all right."

"I'm just here for Jaime. He loves to dance. We've been taking lessons. It's my anniversary present to him, actually." His feet moved up and down like pistons.

"How long have you been together?" Isabel asked politely.

"Five years. And you and Alice?"

"Oh! No—she's my sister."

He looked surprised. "Really?"

Isabel was annoyed. She didn't want to be taken for Alice's date. It was too close to the picture Alice herself had evoked of the two of them spending the rest of their lives together. "Really."

"You don't look alike."

"That's right," Isabel said coolly. "Alice is the beautiful one."

"That would make you the smart one, then," Tom said, trying to make a joke out of it.

No, Isabel thought. Alice was the beautiful one and the smart one and the good one, and Tina had always been the popular one. "I'm the divorced one. Or will be," she said. It sounded hard and bitter. "How about in your family? Which one are you?"

"The gay one," Tom said.

At first there had been just a keyboard player and a trumpeter up on stage, but gradually more members of the band showed up, until, at the end of half an hour, a great wave of sound rolled through the room. By the time the lesson ended, Isabel and Tom could ride it for a few minutes at a time before Tom missed a step and sent them stumbling. Alice was dancing alternately with Jaime and the dance instructor, the two best dancers in the room, and looking as though she had been dancing salsa all her life.

Isabel resigned herself to a long evening. Her hands were damp from being clutched in Tom's, and the gold ring he wore on his left ring finger bit into her skin. She had taken off her own wedding ring and tucked it into a pouch of her suitcase the week before.

There was a break after the lesson. They sat at the bar and had a drink. Tom drank his beer thirstily, his face dripping with sweat. Jaime was a slender man, a head shorter than his partner. He wore a black silk shirt and expensive shoes, and a big gold watch glinted on his hairy wrist. He put his arm around the larger man and said, "Hey, dancing bear. Next we're going to teach you to ride a unicycle."

"Only true love could make me do this," Tom said, wiping his face.

"The price of true love has gone down," Jaime said. "Once you would have had to slay a dragon to prove it, not just take some salsa lessons."

Tom laughed. "Slaying a dragon would be easier, believe me. Ask Isabel."

"You did fine," she said, taking a drink of her margarita. "Anyway, there aren't many dragons around anymore. All the dragon-slaying of past centuries decimated the population."

Tom yawned. "When is this thing going to get started?"

"Tom goes to bed early," Jaime said.

"And Jaime never goes to sleep before midnight. We're mismatched. Still, we make the best of a bad situation." They smiled at each other.

"Of course, we have to stay together for the child."

Isabel took this for a joke, but Alice, who had turned back to the bar, asked, "How is Julieta?"

"She lost three teeth last week," Jaime said proudly. "She looks terrible." His tone had softened, and for a moment Isabel could almost see how anyone could stand him.

Tom said, "She complains that the tooth fairy doesn't leave her enough money."

"Only a dollar!" Jaime said. "The tooth fairy is a cheapskate."

"A dollar is a lot of money when you're six."

"He thinks I spoil her," Jaime said. "When I was a kid, we had nothing. No tooth fairy. No TV. Why shouldn't she have what she wants? We can afford it."

"He walked five miles through the snow to school," Tom said.

"In my bare feet!" Jaime added.

"He doesn't understand about discipline," Tom said. "I spend all day with teenagers. I know what can happen."

"Julieta always gets her own way," Jaime said. "Just like her mother."

"Just like her *father*," Tom said, and Jaime laughed.

"Julieta's mother left Jaime with the baby when Julieta was six months old," Alice explained to Isabel. "She went to Hollywood."

"She plays Marlena on *Living Heaven*," Tom bragged.

"You were married to Lupe Guerrera!" Isabel said, signaling the bartender for another drink. Even she had seen the beautiful Lupe Guerrera.

Jaime smiled. "Julieta looks just like her," he said. "She's going to be a heartbreaker."

"If her teeth ever grow back," Tom said.

By now the room was full, and the band got back up on stage and began to play. The crowd drifted away from the bar and spread out across the floor. This time Alice danced with Tom and Isabel with Jaime. She moved where he guided her, turning and dipping. It was so profoundly different from dancing with Tom that it seemed ridiculous to call the two activities by the same name. Isabel wondered if someone like Jaime, who had been married and later found a male lover, had thought the same thing about sex.

"How's your sister?" Jaime asked, shouting over the music.

"Recovering. She's happy tonight. It was a good idea to bring her."

"I would do anything for Alice," he yelled. "She's an extraordinary person! Half rose, half battle-ax."

Isabel laughed. "Exactly."

"I would kill that *hijo de pendejo* with my bare hands! He deserves to have his balls ripped off."

A vasectomy, at least, would be an improvement, Isabel thought.

They switched partners again. Alice and Jaime moved off across the floor, but Tom suggested that he and Isabel cool off outside. Isabel stopped at the bar on the way to get another margarita.

Sitting on a low wall in the courtyard, Tom stretched his long legs out in front of him and rested his hands on his knees. His shirt cuffs flapped like handkerchiefs of surrender. "I'm just a Methodist boy from Altoona," he said. "We don't dance much. The two-step, sometimes, at weddings."

"Most people over twenty-five only dance at weddings," Isabel said. "That's what weddings are for. They give a boost to the economy, and they get people to dance." She felt light-headed with the heat and the alcohol, and she was glad to be sitting down.

"No, weddings are good for the soul," Tom said seriously. "They remind you what life is about."

"Spending money and wearing fancy clothes?"

He smiled. "You can do those things any day of the week."

"But not on such a grand scale."

"That's true. It took us a year to pay off the credit cards after ours. We had caviar, Nova Scotia oysters. An eight-piece mariachi band. I only wish my parents had come."

"Why didn't they?"

"Oh, they don't talk to me much. They don't acknowledge Julieta as their grandchild." He sounded sad.

"Sometimes," Isabel said, "I think all parents do is torment their children."

"Yes," Tom agreed. "And yet, once you're a parent yourself, you see that they do other things as well."

People kept coming in through the courtyard, opening the heavy door to the club and releasing bursts of music. Suddenly one of them stopped in front of Isabel and smiled. It was Marco, although she almost failed to recognize him in his black gabardine pants and white tuxedo shirt, cuff links winking in the courtyard light.

"Hey," he said. "I didn't expect to see you here."

"Hello, Marco," Isabel said, pleased to see him. "How are you?"

"I'm fine." He turned and offered his hand to Tom, introducing himself. "Your wife has been my guardian angel," he said.

For a long, surreal moment Isabel couldn't respond. "Oh— no," she said at last, for the second time that night. "He's not my—"

Marco covered the awkwardness with a laugh but immediately made things worse. "You trust your husband, then," he teased Isabel. "You don't mind him in there dancing with other women."

"I'm getting divorced," Isabel blurted out to avoid further confusion.

Immediately, Marco sat beside her on the wall and put his arm around her. He smelled sharp, vaguely electric, and she could feel the heat of his arm under the sleeve of his pressed shirt. "I'm sorry," he said. "What a terrible thing."

Tears came to Isabel's eyes. She leaned into him. Her head fit perfectly into the hollow above his pectoral muscle. She could feel the tequila swirling in her head, and when she looked up, the sky seemed to surge with stars.

"You're strong, though," he said, rubbing her arm. "You'll get through it."

"I'm drunk," Isabel said. "I think."

"It's okay," Marco said. "My sister Rina got divorced last year. The guy left her for the secretary at the dealership where he worked. Married six years, three kids! When I was home for Christmas, the first thing I did was take her out to get drunk. You need to let go. You need to stop living in the world where it happened to you for a little while."

Isabel pressed her hands to her face. "I'm all right," she said.

"Of course you are," Marco said. "You'll be fine. You don't need that bastard."

"He is a bastard," Isabel said.

"You're better off without him."

"That's right," Tom said. "Straight men are nothing but trouble."

Marco said, "Because you're a friend of Isabel's, I'll ignore that remark."

Tom said, "Tell me you never broke anyone's heart."

"Only my mother's," Marco said, and the men laughed.

By the time the door opened again, Isabel felt marginally better. Alice and Jaime came out of the club, borne along on the wave of music spilling from the building. Alice, flushed from dancing, smiled when she saw Marco. "I've been calling you," she said. "You're never home."

He released Isabel with a squeeze of her shoulder and stood up. "I'm working all the time," he said.

"Not at nine o'clock at night! It's dark by then."

"I go to sleep early. I have to get up at five, you know."

Alice laughed. "You're young. You don't need sleep." She had twisted her hair into a knot, and tendrils of it curled down her cheeks. "I can't get Rudner on the phone, either. But I'm planning to go out there this week and see what I can do."

"That I would love to see," Marco said. "The bird and the lion."

"Yes," Isabel said. "But most people don't realize that Alice is the lion." She wasn't sure if anybody heard her or not.

Marco's eyes were fixed on Alice. The moon, or else the street lamps, made her skin glow with a milky light. "Would you like to go in and dance?" he asked, and Alice took his hand with a smile. They went up the steps into the club. The door closed behind them. It seemed very quiet in the courtyard.

"Well," Jaime said wryly, "I'm glad she's not so broken up that she can't see the potential in another man."

"Don't be silly!" Isabel said. "Marco is more than ten years younger than she is! He's my parents' gardener!"

Jaime and Tom laughed. "Very D. H. Lawrence," Jaime said, and put his arms around Tom and kissed him.

Isabel thought about it. Alice and *Marco*? The idea was ridiculous. Yet she could see how someone could be attracted to him. Her skin tingled where he had touched her, and the smell of his cologne hung in the air.

CHAPTER THIRTY

*O*n Monday Alice said she was driving out to Rudner's nursery, and she asked Isabel if she wanted to come. Isabel thought it might be interesting, and she didn't have anything better to do.

"Where'd you get the truck?" she asked when Alice picked her up after lunch.

"Borrowed it," Alice replied. "No way that motorcycle would fit in my Civic."

"You're pretty confident, aren't you?" Isabel said.

Alice smiled.

Rudner's was a good nursery, not huge but with a large selection of fruit trees and native plants and some unusual perennials. Isabel liked it. It was pleasant to spend a Saturday wandering among the rows of blooming rhododendron, deciding between the snow bird and the schlippenbachii.

They found Rudner himself by the junipers, advising a customer about a hedge. "Yew is what you want," he was saying. "It grows nice and even. Gives you a nice green wall. Solid. Easy to take care of."

The customer, a woman in her thirties in jeans, muddy gardening clogs, and earrings made of mismatched plastic beads, was unconvinced. "I don't want uniform," she said. "I was thinking more like a mixed hedgerow. A holly, maybe a mountain laurel. A rose of Sharon."

"Could do that." Rudner nodded. He was a broad man, not very tall, with a broad, flat face and bushy hair that enhanced his resemblance to a vigorous shrub. "But you don't want all those different specimens growing into each other. It'll be a mess. Yew is nice, it grows fast but not too fast, if you know what I mean."

"Aren't the berries poisonous?"

Rudner caught sight of Isabel and smiled his shopkeeper's smile. "I haven't seen you in a while," he said. "Be with you in a minute."

"Take your time," Isabel said.

The customer looked at her watch. "I've got to go."

"We have a lot of yew in stock right now, as it happens," Rudner told her. "You said you have what, a thirty-foot area? One plant every three feet is what I'd recommend." But she was walking away across the gravel. Rudner turned back to Isabel and Alice. "Some people don't know what they want," he said.

Isabel introduced her sister. "Nice to meet you." Rudner held out his hand, obviously not recognizing the name.

Alice shook it. "Mr. Rudner," she said, "I'm glad to see you're well. I was afraid you might be ill since you haven't been returning my phone calls."

He looked at her blankly.

"About Marco Peña?" Alice said.

Rudner's face went as red as an autumn leaf. He looked from one sister to the other. "I didn't make the connection," he said.

"No reason you should have," Alice said.

He led them through the rows of plants to an office cluttered with invoices, coffee cups, and forty-pound bags of fertilizer. Behind him, a shut door with a darkened window in it led to another room. "Sorry I didn't have a chance to get back to you yet," he said. "It's been a zoo here. As it happens, I was planning on calling you this afternoon." He had adopted a tone of busy heartiness, smiling and moving papers around on his desk.

"How nice," Alice said.

"I feel bad about Marcos," Rudner said. "I thought he was a nice kid. Kids make mistakes sometimes. I honestly hope that's all this was. He gives me back the money, I'm happy to forgive and forget." He opened his big hands, so encrusted with dirt that the lines of his palms looked like root systems. Through the crosshatched window in the door behind him, Isabel could see the metallic sheen of a rounded, hulking shape.

"Mr. Peña is twenty-five years old, Mr. Rudner," Alice said with the hint of steel in her voice Isabel was so familiar with. "I'd hardly characterize him as a kid."

Rudner shrugged. "From my vantage point, that's a kid. No offense."

"None taken. Mr. Peña worked for you for how long?"

"I don't know. A year? These guys, you know. They're here, they're gone. I don't keep track." He smiled.

Alice waited until he stopped smiling. "What 'guys'?" she said. "You mean your employees? Surely you have records. Pay stubs and so on. Canceled checks."

"Sure. Sure I do. Though at times this is strictly a cash-only business, you understand. These guys, like I said, they come, they go. Carlos, José. Whoever. It's none of my business. As long as they're good workers."

"And Mr. Peña was a good worker?"

"Well," Rudner said cautiously. "So-so." He kept looking at Alice, caught in the gap between the way she looked in her summer dress and the way she was talking to him. "Like I said, he was a nice kid. I didn't have anything against him."

"Except that you say he stole your money."

"Up until that point, I mean."

"And how much money was it, exactly?"

Rudner thought. "Look, I don't want to be a jerk," he said. "Not to put too fine a point on it, I'm just as eager to get this thing settled as you are. Let's call it two hundred bucks, right here, right now, and you can take the piece of junk with you. Otherwise, the price goes up."

"The price, Mr. Rudner? You're not selling anything here, are you?" She paused. "The police report, which I have examined, fails to conclude that any money was missing at all. You were not willing to let the officer look at your books, as I understand it. A cash-only business is one thing. Keeping records for tax purposes is something else. Or for the INS. Now I'm quite sure that before you hired those men you mentioned, you confirmed their immigration status. I'm sure the I-9s are right over there in your filing cabinet. I'm sure you'd show them to me if I asked you to. But I also appreciate that you're a busy man, and it would be a lot of trouble to dig out all that paperwork, especially for an INS agent with a fine-tooth comb." She smiled. "On the other hand, if you give us the motorcycle now, I see no reason to involve anyone else."

Rudner's face had darkened by now almost to the color of a copper beech, but he produced the key to the back room without another word.

"Thank you, Mr. Rudner," Alice said. "And now perhaps you could help us get the motorcycle into my truck?"

A few minutes later they were sitting in the Chevy, pulling out of the parking lot. Alice rolled down her window and waved to Rudner, who stood fuming among the hemlocks like an angry troll. "Good-bye!" she called. Her cheeks were flushed with victory.

Isabel was elated. She felt as though the roof had been knocked off the top of the world. "So right can triumph from time to time," she said. "Oh, Alice, you were amazing! When we were kids, I always thought you could do anything!"

"Child's play," Alice said, looking pleased with herself.

CHAPTER THIRTY-ONE

*A*lice took 30 back toward Devon. "Marco's working at Doc's today," she said. "Do you want me to drop you anywhere?"

"No," Isabel said. "I'll come." It occurred to her that Alice wanted to be alone with Marco. "He's thirteen years younger than you are, you know," she said.

Alice didn't answer.

"Alice," Isabel said, "tell me you're not interested in him."

"Why?" Alice said. "Are you?"

"Don't be ridiculous," Isabel said.

Alice parked in their parents' driveway and they got out of the truck. The air smelled of cut grass and clematis, and the sun beat down on the asphalt. In front of them the long stone facade of the house crouched under the shingled roof. The overgrown dogwood outside the picture window was dying slowly of blight. "I'm never here when Doc or Dad isn't home," Isabel said, feeling the strangeness of it, as though they had stepped back through layers of time.

"It is quiet," Alice said.

"When we were kids we were here mostly without them," Isabel said. "It almost felt like Cicily's house, didn't it?"

"Not really," Alice said. "Cicily would never have had a house like this. Everything in it exudes Rubin." She walked around to

the back of the truck and tugged at the handlebars of the motorcycle.

"Alice," Isabel said, "do you think Cicily was happy when she
got married?"

"Why shouldn't she have been?"

"I don't know," Isabel said. "I always thought of her as so
strong and independent. She didn't seem to need anybody."

"I guess." Alice gripped the motorcycle from another angle.
"But you can love someone without needing them."

"Can you?" Isabel asked.

"Of course you can."

Marco came around the side of the house. He was wearing
jeans and a Georgia Tech T-shirt, and his face shone with sweat
as he pushed a wheelbarrow full of mulch across the lawn. On
top of the mulch, an old coffee can covered in aluminum foil was
balanced. When he caught sight of Alice and Isabel standing by
the truck with his motorcycle in back, he let out a cry of delight
and the handles of the wheelbarrow slipped from his hands. The
coffee can tumbled and hit the asphalt, and the Japanese beetles
he'd picked off Dr. Rubin's roses flew up into the air. Marco
laughed and fell to his knees in the driveway, trying to catch or
crush the escaping bugs. "You're amazing!" he said to Alice.
"You're fantastic! How did you do it?"

Alice smiled, her face glowing with pleasure as she said, "Let
them go, why don't you? They're just poor immigrant bugs trying to make a living."

"Are you crazy?" Marco said. "They'll eat everything in
sight."

Isabel was still thinking about what Alice had said. She remembered how, when she was young, life had seemed like a
choice between the Cicilys of the world and the Docs, between
independence and sentimentality. Now she stood in the bright

summer air, listening to the buzz of the cicadas and the thrum of distant lawn mowers, seeing as if for the first time that life was more complicated than that. Her mother was a doctor, and Cicily had got married. She remembered the toast she had given at her parents' anniversary party. Here they still are after forty years, she'd said, as if the very fact of their endurance meant something. Well, maybe it did.

Marco lifted the motorcycle down from the truck and started it. The engine roared to life. "Come on," he said to Alice. "At least let me give you a ride."

"What about helmets?" Alice said.

"We won't go far. Just for a spin. Once in a while, everyone has to live a little dangerously." Marco smiled.

"It's the living part I'm concerned about, mostly," Alice said. But she got on the motorcycle.

CHAPTER THIRTY-TWO

*O*n Friday, Isabel drove down to Delaware to give her presentation for Soren Zank. The nature center was at the end of a pitted road that wound its way through thin woods and emerged at last at the top of a hill with a view down a mown field to a pond. Isabel was surprised by how quiet and peaceful it was, less than an hour's drive from the city. The sky filled the slope of the hill, and the trees hummed with wind and insects.

It had been a long time since Isabel had gone frog hunting. The best time for it was in the spring after dark, when the mating frogs filled the watery ditches. These vernal ponds, dry all summer, were safe havens, free from fish that would have fed on frogs' eggs. Only the occasional snake might hunt there, or the budding herpetologist with a flashlight. When Isabel was a student they used to take the frogs back to the lab and grind them up. It was the frogs' DNA her adviser was interested in, mostly.

She went down the hill and looked into the green water. Reeds grew at the edge of the pond. A few big bullfrogs lounged in the mud, croaking lazily. A willow trailed its branches into its own reflection, which flickered, making shadows ripple across the surface. She caught a bullfrog and a green frog and put them into jars. She could hear the spring peepers starting up in the woods, but they were too high up and well hidden to catch. She

did find a toad, though—*Bufo americanus*—in the grass, although it was not yet dusk.

At the top of the hill, a car bumped along the road and parked.
Isabel recognized Soren's black Saab and walked up to meet him.

"The naturalist returns from the field!" he said. "You'll let
them out again at the end of the evening, won't you? What's this
big one here? He looks like he's afraid someone's going to turn
him into frogs' legs."

Isabel was surprised that her cousin could not identify a
common bullfrog. "They do use them for frogs' legs," she said.
"But we'll let him go, certainly. They're just for the kids to take a
look at."

"And how are you, Cousin Isabella?" he asked meaningfully.
"I'm fine."

"You're not caught in a glass jar any longer, are you? You're
free as a bird." He took a step closer. "You look wonderful.
Strong and healthy. Your poor sister is really laid low by morning
sickness. Pregnancy makes some women radiant, but others are
like fish gasping on the beach."

She smiled at him, amused by the look in his eyes and gratified by the opportunity he seemed to be offering her. Not that
she would take it. She didn't want Soren, not even for a night or
two. What a life Tina was in for, she thought, but all she said was,
"I'm sure you're very patient with her."

They reached the house. Taped to the door was a large glossy
poster with a picture of an eagle in flight, announcing a nature
talk with Robert Lewes, Ph.D., author of *American Raptors*. The
man's name had been crossed out and someone had written in:
"I. Rubin on Local Frog Populations."

Isabel looked at Soren. "People do know they're coming to
hear about frogs," she said.

"I'm sure the correction went out in our last newsletter," he said.

She had brought a sandwich. Soren showed her a back office where she could eat. When she came out into the nature classroom half an hour later, about twenty people were there, mostly men and boys, looking around at the snakeskins and bird's nests, giant pinecones and mouse skeletons and deer antlers arrayed on the shelves along the walls. One girl, seven or eight years old, sat next to her father. She wore a T-shirt illustrating the footprints of wildlife, and she chewed on a thick strand of her hair. As Isabel carried her jars to the table at the front, one of the boys said, "What are all the frogs for?"

Isabel turned. There in the front row sat Simon Goldenstern and his two sons. It was the older boy who had spoken. He was looking at her suspiciously, his golden eyes blinking coldly.

"I know you," she said. "You're Bill, right? I met you at the zoo. The frogs are to look at. I just caught them down at the pond." She looked at Simon, lounging in a chair with his long legs stretched into the aisle, one arm around his younger child. "I thought you were on urgent business in California," she said.

"I'm back now. Thursday is date night for me and the boys. I couldn't miss date night."

"I thought we were going to hear about raptors," Bill said.

Simon explained, "We didn't realize the topic had been changed until we got here and saw the sign."

"Frogs, birds, what does it matter?" Soren Zank said, overhearing. "They're all just different threads in nature's web."

"Frogs are boring," Bill said. "They don't do anything. I wanted to hear about owls."

"Manners," Simon said. He turned to Isabel. "You're the speaker, are you? 'I. Rubin'?"

"I'm the speaker," she said. "Maybe you won't think they're

so boring by the end of the evening," she told Bill. He wasn't
the most likable child, but he was interested in animals. Besides,
anyone could see how unhappy he was. "One thing I like about
frogs," she said, setting down her jars and addressing the room
generally, "is that you can actually go out in your backyard and
catch them. You can't do that with a hawk. Even a field mouse
will get away from you every time, but you can go out to a pond
and grab a leopard frog. You can find a salamander under a rock.
You can even get your hands on a snake, as long as you're sure it
isn't venomous."

"We had a snake in our basement one time," a boy said. "My
mom called the fire department."

"Snakes are cool," Ethan said. "They can kill you and stuff.
Cobras."

"They don't have cobras around here, stupid," Bill said.

"Some frogs and toads are poisonous," Isabel said. "In South
America they have poison dart frogs—they're beautiful, red and
blue and yellow."

"I bet none of those frogs are," Bill said, looking skeptically at
Isabel's jars. "Poisonous."

Isabel held up the toad. "Actually, this one here secretes a
toxin, bufo toxin, from its parotid glands. These glands here on
the head. Its cousin, *Bufo marinus,* who lives in Texas, has a poison powerful enough to kill a dog or a cat." She was pandering to
the boys' interest in danger, and she knew it.

"Whoa," Ethan said appreciatively. "Cool."

Isabel held up the bullfrog. "Who knows what this is?"

A couple of voices called out the answer. Isabel looked to see
if the girl was one of them. Was she here because she was interested in frogs, or had her father made her come? And why was
she the only one? Had the world really changed so little? Every
year more acres of the earth were covered with houses, and sci-

entists could clone sheep, but still it was almost entirely little boys hiding snakes in boxes under their beds. What were the girls doing?

"This is the largest frog you'll find around here. You can always tell a bullfrog because its eardrums are bigger than its eyes. It eats pretty much anything. It will even eat other frogs if it gets a chance."

She passed around the jar. The real name of her presentation, she thought, was "Sex and Death in Frogs and Toads." Love and death were the great subjects. She told the audience about amplexus and about the different calls frogs made, the mating call to attract a female and the release call if a male found itself mounted by another male by mistake.

A man in the back raised his hand. "What about the females?" he asked. "What kinds of calls do they make?"

"The females don't call," Isabel said. "All that noise you hear on a summer night is strictly for courting purposes, and it's all from the males. The frog's call is like a peacock's tail or a man's flattery. It has one purpose only."

A few people chuckled, but Isabel could hear her own bitterness and was annoyed with herself. She told them about wood frogs, the earliest breeders of the season, which could be frozen solid for weeks in an icy pond with no ill effects. She told them about the dark side and the light side of a frog's egg and that while hawks and snakes and raccoons would all eat frogs, only the hognose snake would eat a toad.

This time, Simon's hand went up. "How do scientists know that?" he asked. "Do they sit around watching toads and writing down what eats them?"

"No," she said. "They cut open the stomachs of all kinds of animals and see what's inside."

"You mean they kill them?" he asked in disbelief, or what sounded like disbelief.

"There are also ways of analyzing droppings," Isabel said. "But in the past, scientists have often just killed them, yes."

She told them how it was believed that the first sound ever uttered by a vertebrate was the trill of a frog. She took the frogs out of the jars and passed them around. They wriggled free and hopped around the room, and the children dove under the tables to retrieve them. The little girl in the footprint T-shirt caught one and brought it back up to Isabel.

"Do you like frogs?" Isabel asked her.

"They're okay," she said. "They're not very smart, though. Not like my cat." Isabel wondered if she had looked disappointed, because the girl added, "Metamorphosis is cool."

Out the window, the sky was already growing dark. "Okay," Isabel said. "Let's grab these flashlights and go see what we can catch."

It was a beautiful night, clear and warm and full of the sounds of frogs. "Hear that?" Isabel said. "That sound like someone thrumming a banjo? That's a pickerel frog."

"Get three or four of them together, they can start a band," Simon said, and whistled the opening bars of "Way Down South in the Yankety Yank." He stuck close by her as she searched the bank with her flashlight beam. "That was very interesting," he said. "I must admit I was surprised. You never mentioned that you were a herpetologist."

"I'm not a herpetologist," Isabel said. "I'm a vet. Or I used to be. That's what I did at the zoo when I worked there." I wasn't a *docent,* she thought, and moved away to look at a frog someone had found.

Simon followed her. "How's Alice?"

Isabel looked at him in amazement. "You mean since you encouraged your friend Anthony to break her heart?" she said.

"Is that what you think happened?" he asked. "Is her heart broken?"

"All I know is, until somebody took my sister's fiancé to California with him, everything was fine!"

Simon looked surprised and didn't have an immediate answer. Before he could say anything they were joined by Soren Zank, who came over to Isabel and put his arm around her. "What a wonderful presentation! A fascinating glimpse into the private lives of frogs. Amplexus, eh? Very educational. I'll never look at a frog the same way again."

Someone tapped Isabel's leg and she looked down to see the girl, a long strand of hair still caught in her mouth, her hands clasped tightly around a bullfrog the size of a softball.

"He's a beauty," Isabel said. "You must be fast."

"I'm faster than my brother," the girl said. "Of course, he's only six."

Isabel thought she would have liked to have a daughter like this, sharp-eyed and serious, with a wood nymph's hair.

Gradually people said good-bye and straggled back up the hill to their cars. Simon and his children were among the last to go.

"Look," Simon said. "I don't know what you think I did, but I certainly didn't do anything I thought would hurt Alice."

Isabel wished she hadn't mentioned the California trip. She didn't want to talk about what Simon had or hadn't done out here in the dark with his sons listening and Soren somewhere nearby. "Forget about it," she said.

"Well," Simon said uncomfortably. "Thanks for the talk. The boys liked it. Even Bill liked it, didn't you, Bill? He wants to ask you something, actually."

Bill scowled up at his father.

"He wants to know if you know anything about owls," Ethan said. "We found one!"

"*Dad* found it," Bill said, scowling harder. "He gave it to me. Well, okay, here goes. My dad says you, like, used to be a vet or something? And he found this baby owl. I think it's a saw-whet owl. It was on the ground under a tree, and he took it home to give to me. We've been feeding it meat and stuff, just like for a week. We got a book out of the library. My dad said you could maybe come over and look at it? We took it to our vet, the one we use for our dog. I mean, my mom's dog. It used to be all of ours, but anyway, he said he didn't know anything about owls. He was eating okay till a couple of days ago, but now he's stopped and he just kind of sits there. I was going to bring him up and train him to sit on my shoulder like Merlin and Archimedes in *The Sword in the Stone,* but now I'm afraid he's going to, like. Die."

It was too dark to see the boy's face clearly, but his voice was clear enough. Back in the room he had been angry and hard, but now, talking about the owl, he just sounded miserable.

"Of course I'll look at it," Isabel said.

CHAPTER THIRTY-THREE

*S*imon lived in West Philadelphia, farther south than she and Theo had lived. On his street the houses were shabby without being dilapidated, brightened by pots of geraniums on the stoops. The address he had given her was for a faded duplex with sunflowers growing in the yard. Steps led to a sagging wooden porch that held cartons, bundled newspapers, potted plants, a rocking chair, and various balls, nets, mitts, hockey sticks, Roller-blades. The front door was scarred and streaked, but the glass in the fanlight was red and blue, and the house number tiles were lovely blue-and-white majolica. She rang the bell. Simon came to the door in jeans and a rumpled, untucked shirt, his big hairy white feet bare on the bare wood floor. He smiled and held out his hand with a jokey formality. "Ah, Dr. Rubin," he said. "Come in."

"Isabel," she said, stepping into the house. "When someone says 'Dr. Rubin' I think they're talking about my mother. Besides, you said you thought using last names was smarmy."

"Let me tell you, if I were a doctor, I'd make everyone use the title. 'How are you, Dr. Goldenstern?' 'You're an asshole, Dr. Goldenstern.' It makes everything sound delightful."

She followed him into the house, taking in the worn blue sofa, the table and chairs, the cracked moldings, and the dusty, golden light. It was quiet. "Nice house," she said, because it was, and also because she was determined to be polite.

"Thank you. Any trouble finding us?" He had e-mailed her directions.

"None at all. Where are the boys?"

"Still at their mother's. She brings them over Saturday mornings, but she's usually late."

"Oh." Isabel was taken aback.

He shrugged. "I'm at her mercy. Worse, the boys are. She's late getting them everywhere. To school, to their friends' houses. It drives Bill crazy. Ethan doesn't get bothered much by anything. He has sea legs."

"Why don't you go pick them up yourself?"

Simon smiled. "She doesn't like me going over there. I don't know why she cares, really. Maybe she thinks I'll kill her new boyfriend in a jealous rage."

The situation, both in itself and in the way it reminded her of her own life, depressed Isabel so much that she sat down, uninvited, on the sofa.

"Want some coffee?"

"Okay." She didn't really, but she suddenly needed a few minutes to herself. Sometimes the image of Theo and Tina ambushed her, and she couldn't catch her breath. How could he have slept with her? How could he have unleashed on Isabel's life not only jealousy and misery, but the endless, deadening, sordid negotiations about retirement accounts and jointly held mutual funds, not to mention pictures and furniture and towels? How much worse it must have been for Simon, having to bargain for his role in his children's lives. When he came back in with cups on a tray, she asked, "How did you decide that your wife got to keep the house?"

"Well, I left her. I moved out. There she was, still in it." Simon sat down and stretched his long legs, crossed one over the other. Despite the topic of conversation, he looked more comfortable and relaxed than Isabel had ever seen him.

Isabel said, "I've left Theo. We're getting a divorce." She hadn't meant to tell him, but the words kept swimming around and around inside her, looking for a crack to escape through. She half expected he would smirk or even make a joke, but he didn't.

"Why?" he asked.

"Because he did something unforgivable." Tears came into her eyes.

"Pretty much everything's forgivable, if you want to forgive someone."

"I don't want to forgive him," Isabel said. "I don't love him." She found a tissue in her purse and blew her nose.

Simon nodded. "You can't be married to someone you don't love. That would be unheard of."

Isabel wished she hadn't said anything. "My sister Tina is getting married," she said hurriedly, bitterly, hardly caring what she said as long as she got the subject changed. "I wonder if she loves the guy! I think she likes his money so much she hasn't thought much about the rest of him."

"He's wealthy?"

"Yes. You met him. He was the big man with the beard at the nature center. It's his nature center, he founded it."

"Soren Zank!" Simon sounded delighted. "So Soren Zank is going to be your brother-in-law! He's made quite a flurry around here with his money and his zany ideas. The paper did a feature on him when he bought Foster's Marsh. That land just missed qualifying as a Superfund site, and he thinks a couple of million dollars will clean it up."

"A couple of million dollars sounds like a lot of money."

"It does. But these things take tens of millions. Unfortunately, the best thing to do would probably be to pave the whole place over and build an office park or something."

Startled, Isabel stood up. "Let me take a look at that owl," she said.

He led her out to the back porch, a long, narrow, screened room with a table and a couple of chairs, a cardboard carton with some rags in it, a dish of water, and a carpet of green Astroturf scattered with owl droppings. The owl was huddled by the wall. It was a small, bedraggled thing with a tawny breast and a white spot between its eyes. Isabel put on the heavy gloves she had brought to protect her hands from the talons and picked it up. The owl rustled its wings feebly and blinked its big, round, golden-rimmed eyes. For a moment she let herself feel the thrill of holding it. She understood why Bill wanted to tame it, but she knew that a human could not really commune with a wild animal. A dog or a cat, certainly, they had been bred for it—but not a lion, not a frog with its tiny brain (she had dissected dozens of them and knew the precise size and shape of that organ, like a damp, shriveled pea), and not an owl. "What have you been feeding it?" she asked.

"Different things. Hamburger. Little baby mice—pinkies. At the beginning it ate just fine, but now nothing tempts it."

The little bird trembled and dug its talons weakly into her gloved hands. It was nothing but bone and feather.

"Get me a couple of towels," Isabel said. He brought them to her. She covered the table with one and laid the bird down, holding it by the feet and examining its head for cuts or bruises. The eyes looked all right, bright yellow and clear. She turned its head to make sure the rotation was normal, looked into its ears, and then covered the head with the second towel to reduce the poor creature's stress. She slid her hand slowly along the body, probing the strength of the pectoral muscles, the bones, and joints of the wing.

Simon watched with interest as she worked. "What are you doing, exactly?" he asked.

There was no obvious swelling or bruising, no broken bones. The owl was healthy except for the dehydration caused probably by the shock of captivity. "Just seeing how much damage you've done."

"We took very good care of it," Simon said. "Bill has a book."

"A boy with a book can't raise an owl," Isabel said.

"He's a very smart and capable boy."

"You should have left it where it was."

"It had fallen out of the nest."

"How do you know?" Isabel asked irritably.

"Because it was on the ground. It was lucky I found it. I knew Bill would take good care of it. He fell in love with it the moment he laid eyes on it."

Love at first sight, Isabel thought. She said, "I need to take it with me."

"No," Simon said. "You can't do that."

Isabel said nothing. She could feel her whole face frown with stubborn judgment—like her father's face.

"Imagine how Bill will feel if he gets here and it's gone," Simon said.

"Imagine how he'll feel if he gets here and it's dead!" Isabel said.

"It's not that bad, is it?"

Isabel spoke as calmly as she could. "Listen to me for a minute. Lots of birds leave the nest before they can fly. Usually the par-

ents know exactly where the fledgling is. They keep it fed until
it's ready to hunt. Just because you found this owl on the ground
doesn't mean it was in any danger. And what's worse, now that it
has accepted food from your son, it's probably imprinted on him.
That means that even if it is revived enough to be released back
into the wild, it won't mate. Ever. It won't recognize another owl
as its own species. It will think it's a person now."

"You're kidding," Simon said, shocked.

"No, I'm not." She busied herself settling the owl, wrapped
loosely in the towel, into the cardboard box, trying to calm both
it and herself.

"You mean the parents were really taking care of it? Even
though it was on the ground?"

"I said probably," Isabel said. "Obviously, I don't know for
an absolute fact."

"But you know for a fact that it won't ever mate?" he pursued. "Or you just think it's a possibility?"

"It's my professional opinion, okay? Isn't that what you
wanted?"

Simon sighed and stroked his beard. Isabel wondered if that
was why he had grown it, because he liked the gesture. "All
right," he said. "Take him."

"Thank you," Isabel said. She picked up the box.

"Thank *you*."

Out on the street, she put the owl in the backseat of Alice's car.

"Listen," Simon said, following her, "I appreciate what
you're doing."

"I'm doing it for the owl." She went around the car and got
into the driver's seat.

Simon followed and held the door. "How would you like to
have dinner sometime?" he said.

Isabel looked up at him in amazement. "With you?"

"We might have fun. I can't say I've ever dated a herpetologist before."

The color rose in Isabel's cheeks. She could hear how much he liked the word—herpetologist—rolling it around on his tongue as he had rolled *docent.* "No thanks."

Simon's smile did not so much fade as freeze on his face. "Can I ask why not?"

"Because you go around meddling where you have no business!" Isabel cried. "First my sister, then the owl! And I'm not a herpetologist. You were more accurate with what you called me before."

"What did I call you before?" he asked.

She looked at him. A pulse beat in her jaw. "The little missus."

He cleared his throat uncomfortably. "That was before I knew you," he said. "And it was in a private conversation."

"Before you knew I'd had an unusual career and might therefore be worthy of your interest," Isabel said.

"I'm not just interested in your career," Simon said.

In the backseat, the owl rustled feebly against the cardboard box. "I have to go," Isabel said.

CHAPTER THIRTY-FOUR

She brought the owl to her vet friend Beth Kaplan, who was pleased, if somewhat surprised, to see her. She was a plump, dark-haired woman in a white coat and sneakers who had worked with raptors in the summers in college.

"Why didn't you bring it to the zoo?" Beth wanted to know.

"I didn't want to give Allan a chance to harangue me."

Beth gently lifted the owl from its box. "What happened to it?"

"It's suffering from misplaced love," Isabel said. She told Beth the story.

"People," Beth said, examining the owl as Isabel had done, "are stupid."

"I don't know that I'd say this guy is stupid, exactly," Isabel said slowly. "Thoughtless, certainly."

"Not to mention unscrupulous. Thinking you could keep an owl around the house as though it were a canary! Stealing it out of the woods." She readied a syringe of rehydration fluids.

"Well, I wouldn't call it stealing," Isabel said. "He thought it was hurt."

"He thought it would make a nice pet for his kid." She injected the owl under its wing. "I'll keep an eye on it for a few days. We'll see what happens."

Isabel thanked her. Beth was right, of course. She didn't know why she was defending Simon.

* * *

That evening when she checked her e-mail she was surprised to find a message from S. L. Goldenstern. Apprehensively, she double-clicked on the subject line ("Saw-whet, etc.") and watched the long paragraphs of text materialize on the screen. This was the letter:

Isabel—

Having already nailed me as a meddler, perhaps you won't be surprised to get this e-mail from me. You're right to this extent: I never could leave well enough alone, or let sleeping dogs lie, or whatever the appropriate cliché is. I know you may be sufficiently fed up with me to want to delete this without reading it, but I hope that, having accused me of at least (by my count) two misdeeds, you will be willing to hear me out.

Believe it or not, I feel terrible about your sister. But believe, too, that what she's going through now is nothing compared to what it would have been like when, once they were married, Tony began to sleep with other women. You may say that I can't know for sure that this would happen, but I do. I've known Tony for almost thirty years. It's his nature to cheat, and he likes women. He likes your sister, certainly—maybe he even loves her, but he is not capable of being faithful to her. Within months of each of his two marriages he was having affairs. Discoveries, tears, recriminations, broken promises—better your sister never marry anyone than that she endure what Laura and Selena endured! I went through it myself with Marla, and I know. I confess that I have done what I could to keep Tony away from Alice. I did bully him into going to California, partly because he had made a promise to his kid that I wanted to see him keep, and partly because I hoped that he would get distracted once he was out there and break things off with your sister. I was pretty sure some other woman would catch his eye, which is exactly what happened. On the plane from Philadelphia to Oakland.

And who is going to protect the new woman? you may ask. Who indeed. Still, I can't feel I did wrong with regard to Alice. I can't say I'm sorry about it, because I'm not. I'm sure Alice is better off, and I have to say that that knowledge makes me sleep better at night.

As for the owl, I still can't shake the picture of it, trembling and blinking in that box. I can only say it looked nearly as miserable to me when I came upon it in the woods, half-invisible in the dead leaves under a tree. I've never seen a bird just sitting on the ground like that. It didn't occur to me to leave it there any more than it would have occurred to me to leave a lost child crying on a street corner. I know you think I should have known better. I may, I admit, have avoided thinking it through more carefully because I was thinking instead about my son. To understand this, you have to know a little about Bill. Even as a baby he was exceedingly sensitive. He didn't like loud noises. If the people around him were angry or upset, he was distraught and couldn't be comforted. Imagine how it must have been for him growing up in a household in which his parents were often upset and angry. He taught himself to read when he was four, and his fantasy life has been his escape and, I truly believe, his salvation. Still, the last two years as my marriage to his mother fell apart have been hell for him, and he has withdrawn even further into himself. Sometimes I think he wants to take scissors and snip himself out of the fabric of life altogether.

And so, if I seized a chance to give him a gift I thought would help reconnect him—to bring one of his fantasies to life—and if I was willing not to think very hard about any harm that might come to an animal because of the benefit to him, well, so be it. No doubt if I had thought it would have done him any good, I would have killed the poor little owl with my bare hands. There's no point pretending otherwise.

As for not considering you worthy, as you say, of my interest before I knew what you did (or at least, as you keep reminding me, used to do) for a living, I am in no way comfortable about it. Certainly a person should be judged by who she is, not by what she does. But at the same time I can't help feeling that any person, man or woman, who has no in-

tellectual or professional attachment to the world cannot be very interesting, at least to me. No doubt this is a personal failing. This e-mail
seems to have turned into a veritable catalog of my failings. There are
more, of course, that I haven't mentioned, but probably you've guessed
most of them anyway.

If, in spite of all this, you at any time reconsider your decision not to
have dinner with me, I would be very pleased. I'm egotistical enough to
believe you might enjoy yourself. And besides, I owe you something for
rescuing the little saw-whet.

S.G.

Isabel read the e-mail through with growing amazement and
outrage. First she was simply appalled by the effrontery of his trying to justify himself to her. She could not accept his excuses
about Alice. Nothing he could say could convince her that anyone had a right to scheme to come between two people the way
he had. If he had reasons he thought Alice should stay away from
Anthony, he should have said so and let her make up her own
mind. Who was he to impose his own judgment?

She began the paragraphs about the owl with the same attitude, so angry that she refused to accept his rather extreme description of his son. The sentence about killing the owl said it all.
He was selfish as well as arrogant. He as much as admitted that
he was interested in dating her only because of her job. The reit-
erated invitation for dinner was beneath regard. She moved the
mouse into position to delete the message—but she was not
ready to click the button just yet.

She scrolled back up to the top of the e-mail and began again,
reading with more attention this time, not skimming over the
sentences to see what came next. On second reading, it occurred
to her that she herself had tried exactly what, a few moments before, she had thought Simon should have done about Alice and

that it had done absolutely no good. In her heart Isabel knew there was nothing anyone could have said about Anthony that would have made Alice change her mind. The more people pointed out his flaws, the more tenaciously she would have clung to him. Furthermore, what Simon wrote about how hurt Alice would have been if Anthony cheated on her was not dismissed so easily the second time. On first reading, she had more or less skipped over this part, as it was so painful to read. But this time she had to acknowledge that she would have done almost anything to preserve her sister from what she had gone through with Theo.

And, she had to admit, it was hard to reread the description of Bill without her heart softening. She had seen him, after all, at the zoo, his fingernails bitten bloody. He was only a boy, ten years old. Who could blame a father for wanting to help his child? What struck Isabel this time about the reference to killing the owl was not the horror of it, but the honesty.

She was touched, too, and could not help being flattered by the way he had bared himself to her in print. For the letter, as she reconsidered it, was a confession as much as a self-justification. He had to trust her judgment, and her discernment, not to mention her powers of sympathy. It occurred to her, as she read the e-mail through for the third time, that she had very little experience with men who were willing to open themselves up the way Simon had. Theo had never done anything like it. He had smiled and swathed himself in layers of impenetrable charm.

CHAPTER THIRTY-FIVE

*T*he next day was Sunday, and the family was due in Devon. It had been only two months since they had last had brunch
together, but the Rubin constellation had altered dramatically.
Theo and Anthony were gone. Only Soren represented the males
of any generation younger than Judge Rubin—unless, of course,
the fetus swimming in Tina's belly turned out to be a boy.

A grandchild on its way at last! Dr. Rubin could not contain
herself. She fussed over Tina, who slumped on the couch, her
face pale and faintly green even under her heavy makeup. "Not
eating is worse than eating," Dr. Rubin said. "I know you don't
want to, but just nibble on a cracker, sweetie. Have you tried
those acupressure bands? Some of my patients swear by them."

"I'm all right," Tina said irritably.

"I didn't suffer from morning sickness myself, thank God,"
Dr. Rubin said.

"That was with the second two," Judge Rubin said. "With Alice you lay in bed for weeks with an enamel pot on the floor."

"I did not," Dr. Rubin said. "I loved every minute of being
pregnant! I had that wonderful OB with Alice—Dr. Vernon."

"He was sued for malpractice a year or two later," Judge Rubin said.

"Doctors get sued all the time, William, as you well know! I
never believed a word of it. His patients were devoted to him. He

told me he would take Alice back within thirty days if I wasn't completely satisfied."

Soren laughed. He poked Tina and said to her mother, "You must have had a close call with this one. Lucky for me you decided to keep her."

"Lucky for you they didn't ask me or Alice our opinion," Isabel said brightly. She was getting through the morning better than she had expected, not possessed by her rage, but more or less in control of it, as though anger were a powerful horse she had saddled.

"Is anybody hungry?" Dr. Rubin said, and they moved into the dining room.

It was an awkward brunch, there were so many subjects to be avoided. Isabel could feel the care Dr. Rubin was taking as she dragged the conversation from topic to topic like a child trying to step only on the white squares of a checkerboard tile floor. Isabel herself didn't feel much like talking. Alice was quiet and seemed distracted, and Tina was too nauseated to participate. She put a bagel on her plate and then did her best not to look at it. Judge Rubin read the newspaper. Soren and Dr. Rubin discussed wedding plans, house hunting, possible names for the baby.

"For a boy we can't decide," Soren said. He had loaded his plate with bagels, cream cheese, deviled eggs, and fruit salad. "I like Olaf, but Tina likes Sebastian. For a girl, though, we've agreed on Tyne."

"Tyne?" Dr. Rubin said. "Olaf?" She looked at Tina. "The old-fashioned names have come back into style, you know, honey. Sam and Max. Sophie."

"Doc," Tina said warningly, rotating her plate with the tips of her fingers so that the bagel was as far away from her as possible.

"We hope everyone will like the name," Soren said. "I have an idea! Tina and I will generate a list, and everyone can vote."

"Soren," Tina said sharply, pushing the plate away.

"I guess after you've named half a dozen children, the novelty wears off," Isabel said. Her mother shot her a look.

Alice, who was sitting by the window, suddenly said, "Isn't that Marco? What's he doing here on a Sunday?"

"It was the only day he could come," Dr. Rubin explained. "He's gotten very busy."

Isabel turned and saw Marco out in the yard staking the foxgloves. "Oh—look at that pale orange!" she said. "It's exactly the color of Alice's hair!"

"Excuse me," Alice said, and got up from the table.

"Alice," Dr. Rubin said, "we're in the middle of a meal."

"I'm finished." Alice left the room. They could hear her going out the front door.

"She hardly ate anything," Dr. Rubin said. "I think Soren is the only one who's appreciating the food! I don't know why you won't try the salmon, Soren. I always think of fish as a kind of vegetable that you pull up out of the sea."

Soren eyed the thin, translucent slices. "I've been doing some reading about physiological responses of wild animals to pain. Animals, you know, don't have the luxury of dying in their sleep or of a heart attack, but instead they often get torn limb from limb. Apparently they're able to put themselves into shock—like self-administering an anesthetic—so they don't feel it so much at the end." He picked up his fork and lifted a slice of smoked salmon onto a bagel. "I don't know if they've done those studies on fish. When you see them flapping around in the net, they don't look anesthetized."

"Maybe," Isabel said, "you don't get the same response with suffocation as you do with dismemberment."

"Yes," Soren said. "Maybe that's it." He took a bite and chewed.

Out the window, Alice stood among the foxgloves, deep in conversation with Marco. "What is she talking to him about?" Dr. Rubin said. "Do you think she's all right, Isabel? She's very quiet lately. I don't want to ask her about—you know. I don't want to pour salt in the wound."

Tina pushed her chair back from the table. "I'm done, too," she announced. "Come on, Soren. I could use some fresh air."

"I'm eating," he said. "The salmon is wonderful, actually."

Isabel folded her napkin. "I'll go with you," she said.

Caught by surprise, Tina said nothing. Isabel pushed back her chair and led the way out of the room.

As they walked through the hall and out the front door, Tina glanced sideways at her sister, who was wearing a blue skirt and white blouse Tina recognized as belonging to Alice. Alice was thinner than Isabel, and the clothes fit more snugly than what Isabel usually wore. She looked good, Tina had to admit. Even her face, bare of makeup as always, seemed to glow with a stern animation that surprised Tina and made her uneasy.

All during brunch she had been uneasy, in fact. Whom had Isabel told what Tina had done? Whom would she tell? She could pick any moment for her revelation. All through the meal Tina had found herself wondering, Now? Now? If she hadn't already felt sick, the tension would have made her so. Amazed and frightened by Isabel's self-restraint, she had wondered at first if Isabel knew how much power she had. Now, looking up into her sister's blazing eyes and seeing the way her skin shone with contained rage, Tina saw that she did know.

On the front steps, with the door shut behind them and Alice and Marco out of sight around the side of the house, Isabel turned to her. "How could you do it?" she hissed. "Tell me how!"

Tina felt exhausted. Nothing had prepared her for pregnancy being like this—like an illness that went on and on—tiredness like a hammer on your head. She knew it had been wrong to sleep with Theo. She had known it was wrong from the beginning, but she had been willing to live with that. With her own disapproval. When she had felt Theo's eyes on her—the same eyes that had dismissed her for so many years, had seen her only as the kid sister, not smart or successful enough to be interesting—she had felt not merely aglow but alive. Theo was different from the men she dated. It wasn't that he was better-looking or more sure of himself or even smarter, but he was someone who had always been in a category that excluded her, and one day, quite suddenly, he had welcomed her in. He had had Isabel—the creative, critical sister, the one who did things her own way and didn't care what people thought—and then, instead, he wanted her. "You didn't love him," Tina said.

"You don't know that!" Isabel cried.

Tina made an effort. She had to speak carefully—to find the words, not to make her sister understand, which was of course impossible, but to maintain the status quo. She had to keep herself from making things worse. If things got worse, Isabel might tell.

Of course, she might tell anyway. Tina found herself thinking that what was done was done. She wanted Isabel to see how things were. Whatever else happened—whatever else was or wasn't true—Theo had wanted her. "You never appreciated Theo," Tina said. "He's a great guy! And you were always putting him down."

"Oh," Isabel said. "A great guy! A great guy who would sleep with his wife's sister!"

"You were always snide about everything he did," Tina said. "You thought he sold out!"

"He did sell out."

"You never supported him! You never made him feel really good about himself!"

"You always wanted everything Alice and I had!" Isabel cried. "Even if it was junk, you wanted it!"

"And you, you always shut me out!"

So this was what it came down to, Isabel thought. You put him down. You never appreciated what you had. You shut me out, so I found a way to get in. It was almost funny. Surely other grown-up siblings felt these things, but they didn't actually destroy one another's lives. "You're my sister," she said.

For a moment, Tina seemed to sag. Her flesh looked heavy on her bones. Already her face was thicker than it had ever been, and Isabel could see what she would look like when she was old. Like Doc, but without Doc's energy or drive. Or her kindness, either.

"Oh, Isabel," Tina said irritably. "It really didn't have anything to do with you."

Isabel shut her eyes. It couldn't be resolved, she thought. It couldn't ever be resolved. One day the wound would scar over, the hole covered with thick, hard, white, ugly flesh. That was the best that could be hoped for, under the circumstances.

"You won't tell Doc. Will you?" Tina said.

Isabel opened her eyes. "Do you think I would?" she said.

Tina shrugged uneasily.

"You should have thought of that before," Isabel said. They looked at each other, each sizing up the situation.

The door opened and Soren came out, spreading his arms expansively. "Two beautiful women," he said. "What a happy sight!"

"You certainly got the prize, though," Isabel said to Tina, and she slipped past Soren into the house.

Her parents had left the dining table and were sitting in the living room on opposite couches. "You're handling Tina's pregnancy very well, I must say," Dr. Rubin said to Isabel as she came in. "I'm proud of you, sweetheart. Well, people are having children so much later in life these days. There's still lots of time."

"What a relief," Isabel said.

Her mother looked hurt. "You've been using that tone of voice all morning," she said. "I know it's a hard time for you, Isabel. But I don't know why you should be angry with us."

"It just seems ridiculous even to talk about me and babies!" Isabel said, despite her determination to control herself. "Not right now. My life is like something after an earthquake."

"And what are you doing to rebuild it?" her father said. He sounded as though he'd been waiting to ask for some time.

Isabel flushed. "Thinking," she said. "Sorting through the rubble."

The telephone rang and Dr. Rubin got up to answer it.

"If you ask me," Judge Rubin said, "you should make a decision and stand by it. All this reconsideration isn't getting you anywhere. Your life was nicely on track when you were twenty-five, and what happened? You reconsidered." He didn't have to say, And look at you now. They were both looking.

At first Isabel couldn't speak, but after a minute she said, "I know you're concerned for me. I know my life is a mess right now, but the problem isn't that I changed my mind about graduate school when I was twenty-five. Or that I've changed my mind about Theo. I met Theo when I was just out of college. We got married barely a year later. I didn't know anything about anything."

"Your mother and I got married when we were even younger than that, Isabel. We had known each other an even shorter period of time."

Isabel laughed. "As if anyone in this family could forget that!"

Dr. Rubin appeared in the doorway, blinking back tears of utter consternation. "That was a woman on the phone," she said. "She says she's Soren's wife."

"Ex-wife, you mean," Judge Rubin said impatiently. "Oh, what now!"

"No," Dr. Rubin said. "You don't understand! She says she's *still* his wife!"

The room went very quiet. Isabel looked out the window. At the bottom of the garden, Alice was laughing, her hair sparkling in the sunlight, and Marco was smiling, his hand almost touching hers on the split-rail fence where Isabel used to sit while Cicily pointed out where the cardinals were nesting. Closer to the house, Soren and Tina sat on a bench in the shade of a crab-apple tree. Soren slid his arm around Tina's waist. She leaned away.

"What are we going to do, William!" Dr. Rubin cried. "It's too much to bear! Oh, poor Tina. And the invitations have gone out! Oh—what have we done to deserve this?" She was gasping now, barely able to catch her breath.

Judge Rubin got up and stood over his wife. "Evelyn," he said, "stop it!"

She grabbed on to his shirt and swayed from side to side. "We did our best for them! Why are their lives all in pieces? Why can't any of the three of them find any happiness?"

"Pull yourself together!" Judge Rubin said.

"I can't bear it, William! I'd do anything for them—you would, too—but there's nothing—nothing that can help—nothing we can do!" She began to moan. Her face grew blotchy and she gasped for breath.

He raised his hand and slapped her. A red shadow rose in her cheek, and she fell silent.

"Dad!" Isabel cried.

Dr. Rubin gaped at him.

Judge Rubin straightened his shirt and stepped away from his wife. "You were hysterical," he said.

CHAPTER THIRTY-SIX

*T*he next day, Dr. Rubin stayed in bed. Isabel and Alice had spent the night, and in the morning Alice went to work. Isabel tried to tempt Dr. Rubin with her mother's favorite foods, prepared in the kitchen where Cicily had once clattered pots and pans. But Dr. Rubin wouldn't eat.

"I can't," she said when Isabel brought up a tray. Her hair lay disheveled on the pillow. "You're so good to me, fussing like this, as though things weren't hard enough for you already. Oh—you were such happy little girls!"

"Doc," Isabel said, "we're doing fine."

It was true. They *were* doing fine—even Tina, who had frowned when she heard about Soren's situation and then said, "Nothing is going to interfere with this wedding!" It was Doc who was suffering.

Alice came back to Devon for dinner. Isabel made their favorite childhood meal: fried chicken and whipped potatoes and green beans with almonds. Judge Rubin blinked at the food through his glasses and pushed it around on his plate.

Alice asked him, "Did you find anything out?"

He raised his eyes to her and sighed. "I confirmed the facts," he said.

"Which are?"

"That Soren initiated divorce proceedings against this woman, Frieda Somers Zank, with whom he has two children, eighteen months ago. That they hit a roadblock when it came to the financial settlement. That the division of property was apparently insurmountable. There's a house in Palo Alto and a cottage in Napa, as well as millions in stock options. The divorce was never finalized. Nevertheless, Soren applied for a marriage license in the city of Philadelphia, describing himself as divorced."

"How could he do that?" Isabel said. "It's beyond comprehension!"

"In the course of my life," her father said, "I have seen people attempt all sorts of things that defied what I would have called ordinary comprehension. This has led me to the conclusion that the way you and I see the world is not at all as ordinary as we might have thought. Look at all the people who believe they have been abducted by aliens. Look at the check forgers, tax cheaters, wife beaters, retirement fund embezzlers! Do they think of themselves as deviant? Not at all. They have their way of looking at the world that enables them to consider themselves to be reasonable human beings."

"I hope you don't put Soren in the same category with the embezzlers and UFO abductees," Alice said.

"Where else to put him?" their father said sharply. "When I spoke to him today, he kept saying, 'It's just a matter of technicalities'! Those were his words! He's adamant that he won't give in to what he calls 'that woman's extortion.'"

Alice sighed. "He's a good-hearted man. If the circumstances had been different, he might have made her happy."

"If a man like that could make her happy under any circumstances," Judge Rubin said, "she must have a greater natural capacity for happiness than we have so far seen evidence of. Thank you for dinner, Isabel. It was good of you girls to come out here

and take care of your mother and me. Don't think we don't appreciate it." He got up from the table and left the room.

"I went to see Tina today," Alice said, watching Isabel to see
how much of a discussion of their sister she could tolerate.

Isabel put down her fork. "And?"

"She and Soren have checked into the Four Seasons. They're
sitting up there with the curtains closed ordering room service,
and Tina keeps saying how they're going to go ahead with the
wedding. She told me she's been waiting all her life to wear a
dress like that, and nobody is going to tell her she can't do it
now."

"She's lost her mind!" Isabel said.

"Maybe," Alice said. "I don't know. Maybe she's in shock. I
can understand wanting so badly not to believe something that
you find a way of convincing yourself it doesn't matter."

"Alice," Isabel said, "your situation and Tina's are not the
same. It's one thing to hope a person's nature may have changed,
and another to pretend the laws of the country simply do not exist!" When her sister didn't say anything, Isabel went on, "Even
when she was little, Tina liked to change the rules of a game if she
thought she was going to lose."

"Every child does that," Alice said. "You used to do it yourself."

That night the sisters slept again in their old beds in the Devon house. Isabel could hear Alice turning over restlessly in the
next room. She couldn't sleep, either. She listened to the wind
moving in the trees outside the window, the same wind in the
same trees as when they were children. A few crickets chirped in
the bushes, but otherwise the night was silent. She lay awake a
long time, wondering if her mother was managing to get any rest.
She thought of all the things she had criticized her mother for
over the years. For working too much, for being too emotional,

for not understanding who Isabel was or what she needed. For interfering in her grown daughters' lives and feeling responsible for everything that happened to them. For purveying the myth of love at first sight, which Isabel had rejected and then bought into and now rejected again.

Why had she married Theo? Why hadn't she waited, like all her friends—lived with him for a couple of years first? Was it stubbornness? A determination to be different from everyone else? It was so hard to remember now. Had she chosen Theo for the ways he was like her father—or for the ways he wasn't like her father—or because he was in the right place at the right time? The questions roiled in her mind like water in a clothes washer. Turbulent, dirty. Going around and around without getting anywhere.

Well, she thought. Was it so strange that Doc felt responsible for her daughters when Isabel herself, at thirty-five, was still blaming her for things? What had she done, after all, that was so terrible? Become a doctor? Chosen to do what she loved, to treat the sick, to share the financial burden of the household? Was this what Isabel was holding against her? Isabel, who had all the freedoms of her generation. It was true that Doc was irritating, tactless, interfering, sentimental. But wasn't Doc just trying to live her life, as her daughters were trying to live theirs? Wasn't she doing her best?

Isabel turned the pillow over and tried to get comfortable. The crickets sang and the smell of honeysuckle drifted into the room. Around three she heard the ghostly hooting of a great horned owl, and she sat up in the dark and looked out the window.

The moon had risen above the tops of the trees, faintly illuminating their feathery shapes. The owl hooted again: one hoot, and then two, and then another two. Once the owl had been considered an omen of evil, but it was just what it was. A wild creature—gorgeous, swift, and hungry. A great bird soaring over the August woods on silent wings.

In the morning their father made phone calls, and Alice visited Tina and Soren at their hotel, but nothing changed. Soren refused to take steps to finalize his divorce, and Tina made calls to the caterers and florists and musicians from the bedside telephone, determined that every detail of her "wedding" be as she had imagined it since she was six years old.

Isabel took care of their mother, who seemed to have literally made herself ill with worry. Whatever her faults, Dr. Rubin had never been a hypochondriac or a malingerer, but now she lay between the monogrammed sheets, her forehead hot and the tips of her fingers cold, tears occasionally leaking down the sides of her face. "Oh, Isabel," she said whenever Isabel came into the room.

"What?" Isabel would ask. But Dr. Rubin shook her head and wouldn't say.

On the third afternoon, when Isabel came in to bring her a cup of tea, Dr. Rubin put a hand on her daughter's wrist. "Thank you," she said.

Startled, Isabel spilled some of the tea. "You're welcome."

"I've been thinking. Lying here. Thinking about the three of you. At your age, I was a resident and had three children. I lived here, in this house. My life was all sorted out."

Isabel found a towel and mopped up the spill. She sat on the edge of the bed. "It was a different time," she said. "People lived differently."

"Not so differently," Dr. Rubin said.

"I don't know," Isabel said. She waited for her mother to

bring up her friends and their children, most of them settled now, with children of their own.

Instead Doc said, "I always worried about what it would mean for you, me having the kind of job I did. Everyone told me I couldn't do it. My parents, my friends. My medical school class- mates. You can't answer to two masters, they said!" She took a drink of the sweet tea, her hand trembling, then set the cup down clumsily on the bedside table. "I tried to make sure you girls knew that the family came first. And I was so happy when I found Cicily! I thought you were in such good hands with her. She was patient, and you could see how much she enjoyed being with you. I remember when she came for an interview. I must have interviewed a dozen women before her, and they were all terrible. Alice was three and you were seven months old and screaming, and Cicily just took you and held you on her knee and smiled at you, and I was so impressed that she could do that. Just be calm with you, when you were crying.

"I was such a mess when Alice was a baby. I loved her to death, but at the same time I thought I would die of boredom! The endless days. The weeks stretching out like years. My God! It was partly postpartum depression, I suppose, though we didn't have that term then. The baby blues. She was hungry all the time, but the doctors told us babies had to be on a schedule. Don't feed them more than every four hours, they said. She would cry, and I would cry, and your father would come home and want dinner."

Dr. Rubin stopped. Isabel held her breath. She had never heard her mother talk like this before. After a long silence, she prompted, "He should have helped you out. It shouldn't all have been your responsibility."

Dr. Rubin shook her head. "No," she said in a tired voice. Her hands lay on top of the sheets, and she twisted the thick wedding band around and around her finger. "That was how things were." Her lined face looked gray and her hair was gray and her large, expressive eyes looked faded and shadowed. "I was never the right kind of mother," she said.

Isabel watched the gold ring twisting and glinting. She wanted to reach out and touch her mother's hand, but it was so unlike the kind of thing she did that she couldn't bring herself to do it. "You were a good mother," she said. "And you did do both, didn't you? Had your work and your family, too. Despite what anybody said."

Dr. Rubin's eyes swam. "Yes," she said dully. "I suppose."

CHAPTER THIRTY-SEVEN

*O*n Saturday Isabel called Beth Kaplan. "Your owl's better," Beth said. "Why don't you come and get it?"

"It's not mine," Isabel said. But she borrowed Alice's car and headed out.

It was early and there wasn't much traffic on the roads. Isabel sped down Route 30, feeling free and happy. It was good to be out of the Devon house, to be alone and on her way into the city. The sun beat down through the windshield, and the car was hot even with the air-conditioning on high, but Isabel didn't care. She remembered how she had felt at seventeen, driving down this road to college in her parents' car, boxes piled high in the backseat—so eager to be on her own in the world that she thought she might explode with anticipation.

Who would have guessed how little ways away she'd get? Here she was, almost twenty years later, still spinning in her family's orbit. All three of them were: she and Alice and Tina. Why was that? Was there something backward, stunted, unfinished, about their family life? Overgrown children, unable to separate, a therapist might say. Or was there a better light in which to look at it? Was it love that held them? Did maturity mean, of necessity, moving away—or not? Once the answer had seemed obvious, but nothing seemed obvious anymore.

It was a beautiful morning. The sun sparkled, reflecting silver

off the towers of Liberty Place. Cars honked and radios blared.
The air was rich with the smells of hot tar and car exhaust and
the river. Isabel found a parking spot only a couple of blocks
from the animal hospital, dug out quarters for the meter. On the
corner, a vendor was doing a brisk business in snow cones.
Across the street, a woman walked three greyhounds on leashes.
The dogs wagged their tails, sniffing and straining in Isabel's direction. Each familiar intersection, the sight of each store she'd
shopped in—Vera's Shoes, Park Lunch, the L&M Carpet Empo-
rium—made her heart lift.

The little saw-whet owl was transformed. It tilted its head to
get a better look at Isabel and flapped its wings energetically, its
feathers sleek and glossy.

"It's eating fine," Beth said. "It made a great recovery."

"You did a great job," Isabel said. "It looks ready to go get a
mouse."

Beth smiled. "We'll give it a week or two with a rehabber first.
I know a good place up in Buck's County you could take it to."

"Actually," Isabel said, "I have someone in mind."

Alapocas, Delaware, lay in the flatlands of Kent County, not far
from the Maryland line. A small town in a landscape of chicken
farms and truck farms, the suburban sprawl of Philadelphia,
Wilmington, and even of Dover had barely touched it. A couple
of fast-food chains and convenience stores had sprung up on the
edge of town, but along Oak Street the diner, the junk shop, the
hardware store, the hairdresser, and the Alapocas Bar and Grill
looked as though they had been unchanged for thirty years.

Isabel took the box with the owl out of the backseat and
tucked it under her arm. It was too hot to leave it in the car. Heat
shimmered off the sidewalk. A man in a baseball cap hurried by
with a package under his arm. A teenager in thick mascara jiggled

her bracelets, and a young mother, not much older than the teenager, dragged a toddler along by the arm. Each one glanced at Isabel as they went by, and she tried to work up the courage to ask them if they knew the Bird Lady of Alapocas. They had to, didn't they? In a town this size. But something held her back. Cicily must have been a chameleon to fit in so well in Devon and Philadelphia and then to come home every weekend to a town like this. Again she wondered whether Cicily had really loved them or whether she had just been doing her job. How would she feel to see Isabel at her door now, wanting something, so many years after she had stopped being paid to give anything at all?

Isabel went into the diner, sat at the counter with the box beside her, and ordered a grilled cheese sandwich.

"How about this heat?" the waitress said, bringing over the plate. "Every day that guy on the radio says it's going to break. Been saying it nine days now by my count."

"It's not so bad in here with the fans going," Isabel said.

"I brought those fans in myself," the waitress said. "The owner, he don't do nothing. Sits in his air-cooled office all day with his feet up. Want some ice cream? We've got pie, but ice cream will cool you off but good."

She was a black woman, about twenty-five, in a turquoise uniform with her hair done in braids that swung when she walked and two-inch frosted white fingernails. In her voice Isabel could hear a trace of the accent she associated with Cicily, a soft, twangy way of speaking, as though Delaware were in the foothills of Appalachia. Was a job like this what Cicily had escaped by taking the Greyhound bus to Philadelphia every week and sleeping more than half her nights in someone else's house? Was taking care of other people's children better than pouring coffee and making change, or not?

"Ice cream sounds good," Isabel said.

"Vanilla or peach?" the waitress asked, wiping the counter.

Isabel asked for peach. She listened to the chatter of the other customers—about a daughter starting community college, a sick dog, and the best place to buy children's clothes. It was soothing, sitting on the stool with the fans whirring in the open windows, eating ice cream with a long-handled spoon, and listening to other people talk.

"What you got in that box?" the waitress asked when she brought Isabel her check.

"An owl," Isabel said.

The waitress laughed. "You looking for Cicily Lamont? Why didn't you say so? You see her on that TV program? Who'd have thought being a, what you call, eccentric, could make you famous!"

Ten minutes later, Isabel was standing in front of a small white house at the end of a rutted driveway. In the back, behind some bushes, she could make out the long, board-and-chicken-wire flight she had seen on the television news. There was an old car in the driveway and red curtains in the windows. She rang the bell, and the next moment Cicily opened the door.

"Yes?" she said.

A handsome woman in a sleeveless yellow dress, she looked younger than Isabel had expected—younger, certainly, than Dr. Rubin. Her hair was not wrapped in a scarf as Isabel remembered it, but shaped close to her head. Instead of wrinkles, a few deep grooves ran along her face, from nose to mouth and across her forehead, as though they were symbols rather than consequences of age. She looked at Isabel's box. "Is there someone in there for me?" she said, and her voice went straight to Isabel's heart, opening it like a key.

Isabel said, "Cicily, do you remember me?"

The older woman looked at her and clapped her hand over

her mouth. "Isabel Rubin! My Lord!" she said, and then she took Isabel's face in her hands and kissed her on both cheeks.

The house was filled with birds. Canaries, budgies, lovebirds, and chickadees looked out from cages or perched on the furniture. They spread their wings and darted from room to room. There was a macaw as well, and a large gray African parrot that turned up its beak and looked down at them haughtily as they passed. "I had to pull up the carpets," Cicily said, leading Isabel through the house into the kitchen at the back. "It's all linoleum now. Sit down and let me look at you. So big! Well, you were almost all grown-up the last time I saw you. Too big for a babysitter, according to you! And it was true, too. You could practically take care of yourself when you were eight years old, and your sister Alice the same way. Only that little one was a handful of trouble. Lord, how she could scream when she didn't get her way! Pretty little Tina. How is she? How is everyone?"

Isabel felt so odd, she could hardly answer. She felt as though she were dreaming, or as though she had stepped into an old photograph that had come to life. It had been twenty years since she had seen Cicily, yet here she was, her back straight and her head held high on her elegant neck, only somewhat thinner and older, and her voice more gravelly than it had been. Here she was, living all these years in this house as Isabel went about her life in Philadelphia as though it were the only place in the world, as though towns like Alapocas did not really exist. She sat at the kitchen table and accepted a glass of iced tea. "We're all right. Alice is a lawyer now."

"That's no surprise, with that mind of hers! She always took after your father. Looks, everything. The way you and Tina took after your mother."

"I never took after Doc," Isabel said in surprise.

"My God, what a likeness! And so emotional, both of you. I always thought you had the most open face in the world, with those big brown eyes. So full of whatever you were feeling. Of course, when you got to be eleven or so you learned to hide it pretty good. And both of you stubborn as bulls when you wanted something." Cicily shooed a pigeon off a chair and sat down.

"And how are you, Cicily?" asked Isabel, who had come precisely to hear about herself and her family but suddenly wanted only to change the subject.

"Well, my Paul passed fifteen years ago. It doesn't seem so long. I still miss him. But my feathered friends are good company. I've got a place here, and something I like to do that's useful in its way. I've even earned myself a little fame." She laughed. "I bet you saw me on that TV show. Everyone did!"

Isabel laughed, too. "Alice and I were watching the news, and there you were. Alice tried to get your number from information, but they didn't have it."

"What do I need a phone for?" Cicily said, and Isabel could hear a trace of the old scornfulness, the old way Cicily might once have said, "What do you need a new bike for?"

"In case people want to get in touch with you."

"They just have to come to my door, like you did."

Isabel looked around the little kitchen with its yellow Formica counters, its crooked cabinets, its worn dishcloths and pot holders, its newspaper clippings and pictures of birds stuck to the walls with bits of tape, its water dishes and hanging perches and saucers of seed, and its birds. The pauses in conversation were filled with twittering and squawking. "I remember when you used to take us to the zoo," Isabel said. "You loved the bird house. Who would have thought you would have ended up with one of your own!"

"There's no telling how any of us will end up, is there?" Cicily said. "You used to like the reptile house, if I remember. Did you end up in a house full of snakes?"

Isabel told Cicily about studying zoology, and being a vet, and about her work at the zoo. "I think I took after you," Isabel said, leaning across the table. "Not Doc. Not Dad. You're the one who brought us up, after all."

"I did not!" Cicily was indignant. "Your mother and your dad raised you. I just took care of the details."

"Oh yes, the details! Like feeding us, bathing us, looking after us when we were sick. Advising us when we had problems. Teaching us how to look at the world. If I had children, I would take care of them myself!"

"That's the Isabel I remember," Cicily said. "Always sure you could do things better than everybody else."

"We were lucky they found you," Isabel said. "Suppose they had hired somebody stupid?"

"I wasn't so smart," Cicily said. "Not like your dad, or your mother, either. It wasn't so easy in those days for a woman to become a doctor and all. Even to get into that medical school! I think she got the highest scores on those tests they'd ever seen. And she'd already had a couple of babies. She was a tough lady, Dr. Rubin. I always admired her for that."

Isabel sat with her hands around the sweating glass of tea, thinking about all the people over the years who had told her how much they admired her mother. Women whose babies she had delivered, nurses who had worked with her, old friends. Your mother made me feel like I could push that baby out, they said. Or, The only reason I got a job when Tommy went to school was because your mother made me see I could. Isabel had always let these remarks sweep through her, confident that she knew better. Now she said, "I never thought of her that way."

Cicily laughed. "No," she said. "You never did."

A loud yowling started up in the yard, and the birds all went still on their perches. "Must be that darned cat," Cicily said. She got up and went to the back door. "It's been coming around all week. I don't want to feed it, that will just encourage it. On the other hand, it's half-starved. I can only think it's been catching a sparrow or two to keep body and soul together."

Isabel got up and stood beside Cicily. A small gray cat with a white paw sat by the door. Behind it, in the flight, a red-tailed hawk stood on a post, watching it. Cicily filled a bowl with milk and slipped it out onto the stoop, careful not to let a budgie hopping near the mat escape. The cat arched its back and stalked toward the bowl on cautious feet, as though worried that the milk, like a mouse, might get away.

When Cicily came back in, she looked tired. "Now I'll have to take it to the SPCA and hope for the best," she said, and sighed.

"I see the red-tail back there," Isabel said. "What else do you have?"

"That one's got a wing that never healed right. There's a blue jay that was shot with a BB gun, and a crow on the mend."

"Do you have room for another? I have a little owl that needs to be looked after for a week or two and then released."

"Let's take a look." Cicily opened the box. "Lord, if he isn't a prepossessing little fellow. Somebody didn't want him for a pet, did they? It wouldn't be the first time."

"How selfish and terrible people are," Isabel said. She looked at the bright yellow eyes of the little owl and out the window in the direction of the blue jay that had been shot, and she thought of Theo, and Soren, and of Anthony, too. "No wonder you live alone."

"I hardly call this alone," Cicily said.

"You know what I mean."

"The reason that I live without another person is that I haven't found anyone yet to match Paul. Not even close. I'd rather be alone than settle for second best."

"You used to tell us not to pin our hopes on a man," Isabel said. "You used to say we should rely on ourselves."

"Certainly. Rely on yourself. But I never told you not to recognize a good man if and when he came along!"

"I don't know that I've ever met one of those," Isabel said. "I only seem to meet the other kind."

"I thought you got yourself married," Cicily said.

"I did. I've been married for almost twelve years." Twelve years, she thought.

"You hitched up young, then."

"Like my parents," Isabel said.

Cicily nodded.

"Now I'm getting divorced." Isabel's words felt cold and heavy in her mouth.

"Why don't you tell me what happened," Cicily said. Just like that—as though Isabel had come home from school crying or run in from the backyard with a scrape on her leg. Isabel's chest felt tight, the past and the present collapsing.

"My husband, Theo. He had an affair with Tina."

Cicily's eyes narrowed. "Your sister Tina?"

"Yes."

"Oh, she was always grabbing, wasn't she? That girl! Taking this, wanting that."

"She says I shut her out," Isabel said, beginning to cry now, at Cicily's kitchen table covered with its clean, vinyl checked tablecloth. She pressed her hands to her eyes, remembering how Cicily used to hold her when she cried, and she half expected the strong arms to go around her now.

"You didn't really shut her out too much," Cicily said gently.

"Not more than any older sister would have. Not as much as Alice did, that's for sure."

"Alice and Tina get along fine now."

"Oldest and youngest," Cicily said philosophically.

"Oh," Isabel cried, feeling how much she had missed. "Oh, I wish we had stayed in touch!"

"We wrote a few letters back and forth, as I recall," Cicily said. "And cards on your birthdays."

"I missed you," Isabel said. "I felt like you dropped off the face of the earth." She hadn't meant to say it, hadn't wanted to accuse Cicily. But she waited tensely to hear how Cicily would respond.

Cicily nodded. "It was sudden," she said. "With me and Paul. I was—distracted."

"Love at first sight?" Isabel said dryly.

Cicily shook her head. "No," she said, and an uncomfortable look settled over her face. "Well, this is how it was. I might as well tell you. I had known Paul for a long time before that. Only he was married." She paused. "Well, we would see each other every now and again. He was a deacon at the church. That was where we got to know each other. He was tall and thin and strong! Worked in the lumberyard. The gentlest man, with a smile like an April morning. And her . . . well. I won't talk about his wife, except to say she used to go and visit her sister for a week at a time down in Virginia, and we would see each other then.

"We both knew it was wrong. So we would stop, for a while. A month, half a year. Then, after a time, find ourselves starting back up again." Her face looked different than Isabel ever remembered seeing it. Her sharp, evaluative certainty was gone, and in its place was an openness. Doubt. "And then one day his wife went to visit her sister, and she was killed in a car accident on the road. A van full of drunken teenagers hit her." Cicily raised her brown, bright eyes to meet Isabel's. "It was a terrible thing. But for me, it was a blessing. Paul and I hadn't seen each other hardly at all for about a year at that time. I thought it was over. Dead. But suddenly, my whole life opened up before me."

"Yes," Isabel said.

"I was so happy," Cicily said. "And I felt so sick about it, too! Sick about being happy about something like that. I think I did just disappear. I was so absorbed in my own life."

"Of course you were," Isabel said.

"I wasn't thinking about you girls too much."

"I'm glad you were happy." Isabel reached across the table and took Cicily's hands. They were thin and hard and rough, like a bird's feet.

"You didn't hardly seem to need me all that much," Cicily said. "But I know sometimes children need you most when it seems they don't. I knew that then, only I chose not to think about it."

"I wish I could have met him," Isabel said. "Paul."

"I wish I could have had you all to the wedding. I thought of it, but it was just the two of us and our witnesses. Under the circumstances."

"Of course," Isabel said.

"Still, you would have liked him," Cicily said. She leaned back in her chair. A parakeet that had been hopping along the rim of the table flitted onto her wrist and sat there, its head cocked, warbling. "Pretty little Mabel," Cicily crooned softly, and ran her finger across its feathers.

Isabel thought Cicily might ask her more about her life, or her marriage, or what had happened with Tina. But she didn't, and Isabel didn't feel she could bring it up again. They chatted about the birds and the heat, and Cicily showed her the new bedroom set she had saved for, a cherrywood bed and a matching dresser and a nightstand that was empty except for a lamp and the remote control for the television.

When Isabel left, Cicily walked her to the car. The gray cat leapt out from behind a tree and threw itself at Isabel's ankles.

"Why don't you go ahead and take him, honey," Cicily said. "You'd be doing me a favor. Not to mention probably saving a life."

Isabel knelt and ran her hand along the cat's thin, bony, silken back. The word *honey* on Cicily's lips melted her. "I don't even have a place to live. What would I do with the poor thing?" she said.

"Or maybe you know somebody who would want him," Cicily said.

CHAPTER THIRTY-EIGHT

*I*sabel got off 95 and took the Schuylkill back into town, which brought her near Simon's place. As she cruised down his block, half looking for a parking space and half deciding whether to stop, she saw him out in the yard playing football with his children. Simon tossed the ball high in the air. The boys watched it with a competitive intensity, then threw themselves on it as it bounced in the weeds. They were like small wild animals, cute from a distance but not, Isabel knew, to be underestimated. She parked the car and picked up the cat. She could feel the ribs under its fur as it pawed her shirt.

If Simon was surprised to see her, he didn't show it. His cheeks were flushed from the game, his hair askew. "Boys, say hello to Isabel," he told them.

"Hello!" Ethan yelled, more to the football than to her, as he threw it hard against the fence and flung himself after it.

Bill walked up to her and glared. "Where's my owl? When are you bringing him back?"

Isabel looked at him, scowling and dirty, holding himself awkwardly as though his limbs were growing faster than he could get used to them. He was going to be tall, like his father. "Owls weren't bred to be pets," she said.

She thought he might yell, but he said nothing. His pale face got a little paler, and he went and stood next to his father. Simon put his arm around him.

"I took him to someone who can get him ready to be released," she said. "Someone trained to do that. She'll teach him how to hunt so he can survive in the wild."

"A rehabber," Bill said.

"That's right."

"What's a rehabber?" Simon asked.

Isabel waited for Bill to explain, but he didn't. He slipped out from under his father's arm and walked stiffly into the house.

"Hey, where you going?" Ethan yelled after him.

"Bill!" Simon called. But Bill ignored them both and let the screen door slam.

Ethan hurried after his brother. "Hey, Bill!" he yelled again.

"Ethan, leave him alone!" Simon said, but Ethan was gone. The screen door slammed a second time. "Never mind," Simon called to the silent face of the house. "Do whatever you want!" He turned back to Isabel and shrugged.

"I'm sorry," she said.

"He'll get over it." He picked up the football and tossed it disconsolately in the air.

"I don't know if there's any chance that you would be interested in this cat? It's looking for a home. I know it's not exactly the same."

Simon looked at the gray sack of bones in Isabel's arms. "Does it catch mice?" he said. "The house is infested with them."

"Probably."

He stepped toward her and scratched the cat behind the ears. Close up she could smell his hair, and the cotton of his Flyers T-shirt, and the grassy scent of his Saturday afternoon sweat. The top of her head just reached his chin. The cat purred and turned its head to bring Simon's fingers to the perfect spot. "Thank you," he said. "That was thoughtful."

"Only you have to take him to a vet and get him looked over. He might have worms, or feline leukemia."

"Can't you examine him?" Simon said.

"They need to do a blood test," Isabel said. "Take him." She leaned forward to transfer the cat into his arms. For a moment they made a cave together over the animal, their arms touching, Simon's shoulder against her hair. Then Isabel stepped back. "I got your e-mail," she said.

Simon rubbed his cheek against the top of the cat's head, cradling it like a baby. "Oh, God," he said. "I hoped maybe it had disappeared into cyberspace. The moment I clicked the button I wished I hadn't sent it. I know I said some terrible things, but I've been trying hard not to remember what they were."

"It was fine," Isabel said. "I was more defensive than I needed to be. Or more offensive. I understand that you had good intentions."

"I'm hopelessly interfering." He laughed unhappily. "Marla used to say I was like one of those dogs. You know, Newfoundlands. They use them to rescue injured swimmers, but they don't know when to stop. They're always coming up to you in the water and dragging you back to shore, whether you need rescuing or not."

"You care about people," Isabel said. "That's very nice."

"I was stupid about the owl. I appreciate your finding someone to take care of it."

"Anyone might have done what you did. I don't have children. I don't know what it's like to see them unhappy. I had no right to say what I did."

"Hey," Simon said, "I'm a news guy. I can handle the truth."

They stood awkwardly in the yard, each embarrassed by the

other's apology, neither one of them able to move the conversation back to more neutral ground. Isabel felt that her words
sounded false and insufficient, but she didn't know what else to
say. They were both grateful when Ethan came banging back out
of the house, yelling, "Dad! Bill locked himself in his room
again! I told him you said he couldn't do that, but he's ignoring
me!" Then, catching sight of what his father was holding, he said,
"Hey, what's that?"

"It's our new dog," Simon deadpanned. "Like it?"

CHAPTER THIRTY-NINE

*I*t was after six when Isabel got back to Devon. She parked the car and let herself in as quietly as she could, but instead of the mournful, hushed atmosphere she had expected, voices and laughter drifted down the hall from the living room. She went in and found her parents and Alice drinking champagne out of the glasses Dr. Rubin's mother had brought with her from Germany. Isabel couldn't remember ever seeing them used before.

"Isabel!" her mother exclaimed. "Sweetheart! Come in, where have you been? Have you heard the news?" She wore a pink robe over her nightgown, and her feet were bone white in fuzzy pink slippers. Prince lay on the rug at her feet, panting alertly.

"What news?" Isabel said.

"He's getting a divorce! An official, legal, legitimate divorce! Isn't it wonderful? William, pour Isabel some champagne."

"But what happened?" Isabel asked, sitting down and taking the glass from her father.

"I always knew he was a reasonable man. His great-grandfather was my grandmother's uncle. They had a margarine factory outside of Heidelberg, and a house by the river."

Seeing that she was unlikely to get any useful information out of her mother, Isabel turned to Alice.

"He just seems to have seen the light," Alice said. "Tina called about an hour ago to tell us."

Why was anyone surprised? Isabel thought. Didn't Tina always get what she wanted, in the end? If Soren Zank was what she wanted, Isabel wished her luck.

"Didn't she sound happy?" Dr. Rubin said. "You could hear it in her voice. I must say it's gratifying to see things work out so well. What's more important than finding someone to love and starting a family? Surely you and I, William, for all our professional achievements, are proudest of our girls!" She picked up Prince and stroked him, and he licked her face affectionately with his small pink tongue.

Judge Rubin looked pleased as well, but he couldn't let go of his skepticism entirely. "What really persuaded him, that's what I'd like to know," he said.

"What do you mean, 'really'?" Dr. Rubin said.

"I mean that a sudden conversion for no apparent reason is suspicious. I asked Tina if the wife had agreed to take less, but she said not."

"What happened to innocent until proven guilty?" Dr. Rubin said.

"Dad," Alice said, "is it so hard to believe that after a few days to think it over, Soren wanted to do the right thing?"

"Marriage," Judge Rubin said, "is a serious business that requires as much patience, perseverance, and application as any career. Whether either your sister or her Romeo is capable of such sustained effort remains to be seen."

"Really, William," Dr. Rubin said impatiently. "You make marriage sound like digging the Panama Canal!"

Alice stood up and reached for her handbag. "Good night, everyone."

"Where are you going?" Dr. Rubin said. "We haven't eaten yet."

"I have a date."

"A date! With whom? Oh, Alice, I knew you'd bounce back!"

Alice smiled. "I'm going salsa dancing with Marco."

Dr. Rubin was caught off guard. "Marco?" she said. "Marco the *gardener*?" The dog, sensing her change of mood, jumped down and growled, dilating its black nose to catch a scent of the intruder he couldn't see.

"Oh, Evelyn," Judge Rubin said. "Let the girl be happy if she can."

$\mathscr{A}$fter dinner, since Alice had taken the Civic, Judge Rubin gave Isabel a ride back into the city. "You're going to need to get a car," he said as they crossed the river.

"Eventually."

"I know someone who has a dealership. He has some good secondhand things available." Isabel didn't answer. They drove for a while in silence, and then Judge Rubin said, "And you can't live with your sister forever, either. If you don't want the Quince Street house, you'll have to find an apartment. If Theo is giving you a hard time about money, I hope you'll let me know."

Isabel looked at her father, but in the dark his expression was hard to read. He spoke in his usual dry, neutral voice, but the acceptance of her situation his words implied made it difficult for her to speak. When she felt ready to match his steady tone, she said, "I'll be all right."

"Your mother and I only want what's best for you, Isabel. For all three of you girls."

"I know," she said, but he went on as though she hadn't spoken.

"Sometimes it's hard, as a parent, to believe that your children are all grown up, even if they are legally adults. You worry they're not seeing things as clearly as they might. You want to keep them from making the same mistakes you made. Or different mistakes."

"I think I'm seeing things clearly," Isabel said. "Or at least, more clearly than I used to."

"A colleague of mine has an apartment to sublet in Old City. The price would be reasonable for the right tenant. I just thought I'd mention it."

"Thank you," Isabel said.

"The last few days, with you at the house, I've been thinking. I reacted badly when you first told us about you and Theo. I guess I thought you could have hung on if you wanted to, that there would have been integrity in that. But what you did had its own kind of integrity. Anyway, it was your decision to make. I should have behaved more impartially. I can't change that, but I would be happy if I could help you now." They had reached Alice's building. There was nowhere to park, so Judge Rubin pulled into a loading zone and put on his flashers.

Isabel kissed his cheek, feeling the sharp bone beneath the skin. She put her arms around him and he hugged her back, smelling of clean cotton and shaving cream. The smells that, all her life, had meant righteousness.

She got out and watched the car drive slowly away down the dark street. She didn't envy him, on his way back to the woman who had worn, one summer afternoon, a yellow bathing suit, and to whom he had bound himself for life on what might have seemed, in hindsight, rather flimsy evidence.

On the other hand, she thought, reaching into her pocket for Alice's spare key, maybe he was happy to be going home to her, looking forward to making coffee and telling her about his conversation with Isabel. To climbing into bed beside her: the bed they had shared all Isabel's life. How did you know what went on in other people's lives? In other marriages. Isabel unlocked the

door and ran up the narrow steps. Who knew? Maybe they did
love each other after all.

It was nearly two in the morning when Isabel, asleep on the sofa
bed in the living room, was awakened by the apartment door
opening and the hall light coming on.

"Oh!" Alice exclaimed. "I'm sorry!"

Marco, whose arm had been around Alice's waist, let go and
took a step back.

Isabel sat up. "Oh, hello!" she said in confusion. "Come in—
I didn't realize—"

"It's my fault," Alice said. "I didn't think—"

Neither of them could finish their sentences.

"It's okay," Marco said. "I'm going! It's late. Alicia, *buenas
noches.*"

"Don't let him go," Isabel begged Alice. "Make him come in.
I'll put my robe on."

"We were just going to have coffee," Alice said tentatively.

"Marco," Isabel said, "please come in and have coffee! I'm
getting up. I'm up. Come in and help me fold this thing."

"No, no," he said. "I just wanted to make sure Alice got home
safely."

"You have to help me," Isabel said. "It's stuck. I can't do it
myself." She pretended to be unable to fold the foot of the bed
back onto itself.

"You don't want to fold it up," Marco said. "Go back to sleep."

"No, I want a cup of coffee. Alice, hurry up and make the coffee, will you!"

At last Isabel prevailed, and they were all seated in the tiny
living room, each holding one of Alice's bright, Aztec-patterned
mugs. Isabel was quite sure this was not what the other two had
had in mind. "Was it a good dance?" she asked.

"Wonderful," Alice said.

"So-so," Marco said. "It wasn't the usual band. Alice is going to come back next week for the real experience."

"I should be gone by next week," Isabel said quickly. "The first of the month and all."

"That's not necessary," Alice said. "I like having you here."

"But I need my own place."

Isabel expected her sister to put up a little more resistance, but Alice just sighed and said, "Everyone's moving! Tina and Soren have found some palatial house near the art museum."

An awkward silence fell. No one could think of anything to say, there in the cluttered room under the lights in the middle of the night.

Isabel turned to Marco, handsome in his black tuxedo pants and white shirt and his silk tie. "Work going well?" she asked brightly.

"Yes. I have lots of jobs. All over Devon, and Tredyffrin. Newtown Square. Your mother recommended me to some people, and then they recommended me."

"Good for Doc," Isabel said. "Lawns, mostly?"

"Lawns, mulching, pruning. Flowers. A few landscape designs. I've never done that kind of work before, but I like it. There are so many plants people never think of using."

"Not just roses, then?"

"I think that should be my slogan when I get business cards," Marco said. "'Beyond roses and rhododendrons!' I know this supplier who has the most beautiful hellebores. Fothergilla. Cherry dogwoods."

"You can't do all that work yourself, can you?" Isabel said.

"I hired someone last week, but I'll need somebody else pretty soon, too."

"And a truck," Alice said. "He needs a truck. After all that work I did to get him his motorcycle back."

A few hours after going to sleep, Isabel and Alice were awakened by the door buzzer. Isabel stumbled out of bed and pressed the button for the intercom. "Hello?"

There was a silence, and then Tina's voice said, "Isabel?"

Alice's bedroom door opened as Isabel said, "Come on up if you want to," and buzzed her in.

Isabel folded up the bed and opened the curtains so that the sun streamed in onto the rug. Alice dumped out the dregs of last night's coffee and put on a new pot. Even half-asleep in her old cotton nightgown, her hair rumpled, some of the glow of the night before clung to her. What a contrast to Tina, whose face when she came in was pale and hollow-eyed, and who flinched at the smell of coffee brewing. She was, however, beautifully dressed in cream linen trousers and a plum-colored linen sleeveless blouse. At her neck, heavy gold links glistened, and two thick bangles clanked on her wrists. She looked around at the fusty room, and at her yawning sisters, and she said, "I never thought I'd be waking you up."

"I know you think we go to bed at eight o'clock. Like nuns," Isabel said.

"I've been up for hours," Tina said. "I don't sleep well. I don't understand how people can get pregnant more than once on purpose! I can tell you right now, this baby is going to be an only child."

"You'd better get your tubes tied, then," Isabel said. "And with Soren, even that might not be enough."

"Where is Soren?" Alice asked quickly. "You should have brought him with you. We could have all gone out for breakfast."

"He's with his lawyer. So many papers! What's the point of it all?"

"The baby needs legal protection," Alice said patiently. "It's a good thing in the long run."

"You sound like Dad," Tina said irritably. "He can't keep his nose out. This is supposed to be the happiest time of my life, and all anyone can do is harass me! But that guy yesterday really takes the cake."

"What are you talking about?" Alice asked. "What guy?"

"The one from the anniversary party! I should have known he was bad news, seeing how he's a friend of Anthony's."

"Simon went to see you?" Isabel said. "Why?"

"To make trouble! Did you know he was a journalist?"

"What kind of trouble?" Alice asked.

"First of all, he got in on false pretenses," Tina said. "He said he had met me at the anniversary party and could he come in, and then the minute he was inside he started badgering Soren about the whole marriage license thing! He said he was going to write a story for the *Inquirer* about Soren trying to commit bigamy. He said people would be interested because of the Zank Foundation, and all the money Soren's giving to environmental causes. All the good he's been doing, and this jerk wants to turn it against him!"

"I don't understand," Alice said. "How did he even find out about it?"

"Because of Anthony!" Tina said. "Anthony and Soren have the same lawyer, right? And now that Anthony's back in California, he went to see this lawyer about something and he mentioned that he had met another client of his, Soren Zank, and that the lawyer had done two divorces for each of them. And the lawyer said yes, but that Soren's second divorce never went through, and Anthony mentioned this to this Simon person.

How he knew Soren was planning to get married again I have no idea! He must have picked it up around town somewhere. Soren is quite well-known, you know."

Isabel looked out the window at the opposite apartment building. Alice asked, "What did Soren say?"

"That he would finalize the divorce! Not that it was that simple. That newspaper guy was in our suite all morning until finally Soren pulled the rug out from under him by calling his lawyer and saying he was accepting the settlement terms after all."

Isabel couldn't help smiling at the picture of Simon, sitting in a replica Louis XV chair in the suite at the Four Seasons, his face a mask of dogged sincerity, hounding Soren until the poor man picked up the telephone. She thought how angry she had been just a few days before at Simon's meddling in her family's business, but now all she felt was an embarrassed gratitude.

"I'm so afraid I'm going to have to get the wedding dress let out," Tina said, running her hands up and down her waist. "I'm already swelling up like a balloon."

CHAPTER FORTY-ONE

On Monday morning Alice went to work, and Isabel sat down with a piece of paper to try to organize her life. She made a list of items from the Quince Street house that she wanted: books and pictures, some pots and plants, clothes and dishes. She was in a good enough mood that she could smile over the question of the Royal Copenhagen china, whether she had lost her claim to it now and should return it to her mother, or perhaps even give it to Tina. Certainly there would be no place for it in the small apartment she pictured herself occupying, which she hoped would be less cluttered and crowded than the one she sat in now.

Alice had left the Sunday paper spread on the table, and Isabel brushed off the crumbs and read through the classifieds. One or two ads caught her eye, but in the end she called her father instead. Why not let him help her? She might never go back and finish her doctorate, but she could at least look at his colleague's apartment, maybe even go see his friend at the dealership.

"Do you think they allow dogs?" Isabel asked him on the phone as they arranged to meet and look over the apartment together.

"We can ask," Judge Rubin said. "I'll take you to lunch afterward. Remember how we used to have lunch when you were at Penn?"

"I remember how you used to tell me all the courses I should take."

Judge Rubin laughed. "All the courses I wished I had taken," he said.

Isabel thought about that now, folding the newspaper and stacking it with the others on a chair. Maybe it wasn't possible to reach her father's age without wishing you'd done some things differently—taken different classes in college, chosen a different career or a different town in which to raise your children. A car that got better gas mileage. Maybe she was lucky to have recognized her mistakes early, while there was still time to rectify them. But who knew what new blunders she was making even now? She felt clearheaded, clear-eyed, as though the dark clouds inside her had been chased away by a strong wind, but maybe that was just a new kind of delusion.

Still, she couldn't worry about it too much. She could only move forward and hope for the best. Hope she found an apartment she liked, to start with. Someplace with a lot of windows and a deep bathtub. She had never liked the bathtub in the Quince Street house.

And after that—who knew? The big decisions still lay ahead of her, waiting just over the horizon. What kind of work would she do, for one thing: veterinary medicine or zoo consulting? Landscaping? Garden design? Maybe Marco would take her on, she thought—lightly at first, but then more seriously. They could go into business together. He had the expertise, but she knew some things, too, and she had capital. She could afford a truck— or would be able to once the house was sold.

Or perhaps it wasn't a good idea. Maybe what she needed

was to strike out on her own in some new direction entirely. Was it too late to go to medical school? The idea made her sit up suddenly, either because it rang a chord inside her or because it was appalling, she couldn't tell which.

But if she became a doctor (*say it,* she thought: *like my mother*), she knew she wouldn't be able to have children, too. She was too old to be able to crowd into the rest of her life two such inflexible, exhausting callings. No, better to choose something else, something that wouldn't preclude having a family later.

Or maybe not. Maybe that was the worst choice she could make, she thought, as cars honked outside the window and a man's voice sang in Spanish and the pigeons fluttered onto the fire escape in a shimmer of green and gray. She felt tired and discouraged and put her head down on the table, then sat up again immediately and rubbed the jam off her forehead. Maybe she wouldn't ever have children. How terrible, then, to have held herself back in other ways. To have left space for what she most wanted and to end up with nothing at all.

She shut her eyes, opened them again, got up from the table and went to wash her hands, wash the breakfast dishes, put out the recycling. The smell of burnt toast and scented candles hung in the air. She couldn't understand why Alice liked scented candles. I have to get out of here, she thought, suddenly breathless, as though the candles had sucked all the oxygen out of the room.

Later in the day, Alice called. "Would it be a big problem if I didn't make it home for dinner tonight?"

"Tonight? But I was going to make beef Wellington and pot de crème. No, of course it wouldn't be a problem."

"Marco wants to take me out. But, I mean, it's nothing important."

"Go, by all means! I won't wait up for you."

"I won't be late," Alice said.

Isabel laughed. "Be late," she said. "In fact, I'm going to bolt the door from the inside, and I won't let you in until at least two A.M."

"No, really," Alice said. "I have to work tomorrow. And Marco gets up at five."

"Who needs sleep when you have love to sustain you?" Isabel teased.

"You're as bad as Doc," Alice said. "We don't even really know each other very well yet."

"Poor Doc," Isabel said. "After all these years, events have finally come up to the level of her emotions."

When she got off the phone, Isabel found that she was thinking about Simon Goldenstern and the amount of her family's current good fortune that was owed to him. Not only had he run interference between Alice and Anthony, but he was responsible for Tina's good luck as well—if marriage to Soren could be considered good luck. Somebody should say something to him, she thought. Since Alice wasn't coming home for dinner anyway, Isabel took the Civic and nosed her way through the afternoon rush hour.

She found Simon drinking beer on his front porch, sitting in a kitchen chair among the piles of sports equipment and stacks of old newspapers. He looked tired and gloomy, but when he saw her he stood up immediately and assumed something of his usual aura of restless energy.

"Bad day?" she asked.

"No, no. It's just Mondays. The shock of transition and all. The boys go back to Marla's. She lives out in the suburbs where the schools are better."

It was hard to know how to respond to his mixture of irony

and honesty, and Isabel's own embarrassment didn't make it easier. "Which suburb?" she asked.

"Wynwood."

"That's not too far."

"If they're not actually in the house, they might as well be in Kuala Lumpur as far as I'm concerned." There was a pause. "Want a beer?" he asked her.

She followed him into the house. The gray cat looked up from the sofa.

"Remember Isabel, Merlin?" Simon said. "She saved you from the jaws of death."

"Merlin's a good name."

"Bill named him. Of course. Ethan wanted 'Whiskers.'"

"The boys like him, then?"

"Bill's pretending not to, but yeah. Merlin was in his bed this morning when I got him up for school. Thanks for rounding him up. He's just the ticket."

Isabel said quickly, "I should be thanking you. I found out yesterday what you did. About my sister Tina, I mean. I'm very grateful. You can't imagine how upset my family was about the whole thing." She felt awkward and ridiculous, but she thought the best thing was to be as straightforward as possible.

"Interfering again. Poking my nose into your family's business. You must think I'm quite obsessed with you Rubins."

"No, really. Thank you."

Simon smiled, the playful, ironic smile she had come to recognize and to like. "Actually, I enjoyed it. They say information is power, but in general I find that power is power. If information has its day once in a while, it gives me a kind of thrill."

"That's the journalist in you," Isabel said.

"No, the journalist in me would have written the story. It's the ten-year-old boy in me. Honestly, I thought you would be furious if you found out."

"No. Not furious at all," Isabel said. She paused, and then, gathering her courage, she said, "You'll think I'm totally capricious, especially since it's only been about two days. But you said if I changed my mind about, you know. Dinner. That I should let you know." She made herself look at him and saw him regarding her thoughtfully with his golden eyes.

"To thank me, you mean? Because of your sister?"

She blinked. "Yes."

His expression didn't change exactly, but his face seemed to tighten. "Great," he said glumly. "What did you have in mind?"

"Not just to thank you," Isabel went on, blushing. "I thought it would be fun. I could tell you about reptiles. You could tell me about, I don't know. Manipulation. It could be a good exchange."

"All right."

Isabel was looking at the warped porch floor, so she missed the expression of pleasure that suffused his face.

"Actually," Simon said. "I have these fish the boys and I caught yesterday. I could cook them for you, if you want. If you're not busy."

"I didn't know men over thirty cooked," Isabel said.

He held up his hand. "No bitter generalizations, please! I have an ex-wife, as you know, but you don't hear me attributing her faults to you."

"That's funny," Isabel said. "I seem to recall something or other."

Simon's face reddened, and he laughed out loud. "Oh, yes. You mean how I assumed you were a hypercritical, parasitic harpy? Well, no wonder you thought I was a jerk!"

"Just the first few times we met."

"But you've gotten over it now? I like a woman who's willing to change her opinion."

"I don't have much choice," Isabel said. "My initial instincts about people seem to be so completely off base."

"In that case," Simon said, smiling, "I hope you really hated my guts."

"Oh," Isabel said. "I did."

CHAPTER FORTY-TWO

*O*ne Sunday in late October, Isabel woke up feeling too sick to drive out to Devon. Usually she wouldn't have minded missing brunch, but today Alice was bringing Marco, and Isabel felt she should be there. Besides, she had arranged to take Simon and his boys on a behind-the-scenes tour of the zoo in the afternoon. She knew bribery was not the most virtuous road to the hearts of your boyfriend's children, but she hoped it would be an effective one.

An hour later, however, she felt better. Not the flu, then, but something she had eaten. It was only in the car (her new used Volkswagen Passat), and almost all the way to her parents' house, that it occurred to her that perhaps the old diaphragm she had been using wasn't up to the job after all. She pulled into the driveway and sat in the parked car, actually trembling. She had waited so long and wished so hard for the first symptom of pregnancy, and now that it seemed to have arrived a mixture of elation, disbelief, skepticism, and horror rolled through her. Did she want to be pregnant now? She was newly enrolled in landscape design courses at Temple, working part-time at the wildlife rehabilitation center up in Buck's County, and not yet even officially divorced from Theo. Her relationship with Simon was still so new that she didn't know what it could withstand. Would Simon be angry? Would he distance himself from her? Would he want her to terminate the pregnancy?

Letting herself into the house, she found everyone in the living room. They were looking at pictures of Tina and Soren's wedding, which had taken place the week before, privately, in Judge Rubin's chambers. "You looked so gorgeous in that dress," Dr. Rubin was saying. "Oh, look at the lace!"

"Hello," Isabel said. "Am I late?"

"Nobody cares here, sweetheart," Dr. Rubin said, putting down the photo album to give Isabel a hug. "But now that you're back in the working world, you'll find you have to be punctual. People will be depending on you."

"Birds and foxes, anyway," Alice said, smiling. She wore a pale yellow dress, and her hair caught the autumn light slanting in through the windows, making it blaze the same color as the trees in the garden below. Marco sat close beside her, one hand on her knee, his feet planted firmly on the rug.

"Animals, people, what's the difference?" Soren said. "Aren't the man and the sparrow just two sides of nature's coin?" It was the kind of thing he always said, but Isabel thought it sounded more perfunctory than usual. He seemed restless, looking around the spacious room as though he wished he were out in the open air.

"I don't know about the sparrow, but the president and the eagle are certainly two sides of the quarter," Judge Rubin said, chuckling. He had been in an unusually good mood lately. In response to his wife's anxiety about this brunch, Isabel had heard him say cheerfully, "Think about it this way, Evelyn. If he and Alice do get married, he'll have to do the garden for nothing."

They moved into the dining room. Dr. Rubin offered the food to Marco, explaining, "This is smoked salmon from Nova Scotia. This is belly lox. Our cuisine is traditionally salty, you know." She was having a hard time adjusting to the idea that Alice was dating someone like Marco—who could, Dr. Rubin worried, offer her so little security, but she was doing her best to get used to it. She could see that Alice was happy. And in any case, the whole thing might just blow over.

Isabel passed the fish platter to Tina, but her sister held up her hand. "I can't tolerate anything that tastes strong at all," she said. "And I'm in the second trimester! I know you used to want to be pregnant, Isabel, but really, you're not missing out on anything."

"No," Isabel agreed. "I'm almost sure I'm not." She helped herself to salmon and a large chunk of smoked whitefish as well. She had suddenly developed an enormous appetite.

That afternoon, after she had shown Bill and Ethan around the off-limits section of the bird house (Bill's choice), the primate reserve (Ethan's choice), and the reptile house (her own bit of propaganda), the four of them wandered down to Bird Lake. She and Simon sat on a bench while the boys took a rented paddle swan out on the water. Her earlier apprehensiveness had ebbed away. The boys' enthusiasm for the animals had pleased her (Bill's in particular), as had the gradual tide of warmth she felt from them—or from Ethan, at least. Maybe she was pregnant, and maybe she wasn't, but either way life seemed to be opening up all around her. And if she wasn't pregnant today, why shouldn't she be in a year or two, if that was what she wanted? And if she was, how could Simon, who sat beside her on the bench, slitting blades of grass with his thumbnail and seeing how loud he could make them whistle, be anything but happy about it?

Still, she did not actually broach the subject with him but asked instead, "So, when did you first become interested in me?"

He frowned at her, amused. "You want to play this game? All right. The moment I laid eyes on you, I knew you must be mine.

Or at least, however much mine you are. I hear men can't possess women anymore, more's the pity."

"I'm serious. I know you didn't like me at that party. You thought I was a boring housewife."

"I don't know, Isabel," Simon said. "You grew on me. I can't pick out an exact moment. You were cheeky and obnoxious at Anthony's place when your sister was sick. I have a weakness for obnoxious people. And you took such good care of your sister. That was touching."

Isabel thought how, a couple of months earlier, she would have thought he was being sarcastic.

"But you didn't like me then," Isabel said. "Or at least, you didn't act as though you did." She remembered the note of disdain in his voice that afternoon and how it had roused her to a bright, hard, energetic dislike. Or maybe it hadn't been disdain. "Did I totally misread you?"

"I take pride in being hard to read, so you can hardly blame yourself."

"That's right," Isabel said. "You disguise yourself as a beast and then wait to see who can find the prince hiding inside."

"As beasts are your specialty, you were perfect for that."

"Animals aren't beasts," Isabel said.

"Only people are?" he asked, smiling.

"Only people," Isabel agreed.

"You're not," Simon said. "And you're not a witch or a damsel in distress. What does that leave?"

Isabel laughed. "I don't know," she said. "I guess I'll have to improvise something."

"I can't wait to see," Simon said. He put his arm around her. Isabel laid her head on his sleeve and watched the rays of the sun stretch and flicker across the lake. The boys zigzagged their paddle swan back and forth over the water, and a sea lion roared behind the reptile house, where pythons and corn snakes and burrowing toads dozed silently in their cages. Beyond the gates, Philadelphia spread itself out around her, and beyond the city lay the green primal suburbs of her childhood, old stone houses shaded by ancient trees and new developments where the raw earth dreamed of grass. Beyond that, the whole world waited, including a future in which anything might be possible: work and children, a new married life.

But for now, marriage was still a distant country. Who knew what it might be like there? What the customs and climate might be, or whether she would like the view. For now it was enough to be here, in the distant outskirts, on a bright October afternoon.